ALEX C(

The Pollutant Speaks

First published in Great Britain in 2023 by Bee Orchid Press

First published in paperback in 2023

ISBN 978-1-3999-6792-1 (eBook)
ISBN 978-1-7395781-0-7 (Paperback)
ISBN 978-1-7395781-1-4 (Hardback)
ISBN 978-1-7395781-2-1 (Audiobook)

Bee Orchid Press
www.beeorchidpress.com

1   Poverty or the nearest thing

Daylight burned my eyes as I collected the box from a painfully cheerful NomNomBot. It chirruped other meal suggestions, scanned my sore retinas, then tilted its cherry-red body over the guard rail and whirred off into the void between residential towers to pick up another meal. *And malt does more than Milton can / to justify God's ways to man.*

Why, oh why, had I stayed up with Annie and her friends? I rammed hangover pills into my mouth. After the delivery bill, my remaining cash expired in a dozen hours. I needed a source of income quickly. *Money, money, in a hurry.*

The sun loomed behind a dirty curtain over the Javod tower blocks, and the air smelt of graphene and concrete. I closed my door and sat in front of the lone window of my apartment. Pulling open the box, I ate the eggs and Critishin-style toast from a disposable tray. The pills started to take effect, and the chemical fog began to clear.

My brain wasn't in good shape to tackle this. Why did I tell Green I was ready to leave the hospital? Memories slipped through my head like grease, but I put everything else aside and focused on that one crucial thing: saving myself from life-basic. The DomestiFab printed a new set of clothes, and I threw the remains of my breakfast into the bacterial waste. Without rent, I'd have to return to the Feng bunkhouses, the place I'd escaped from a decade ago with the earnings from *The Pollutant.* That thought didn't fill me with morning cheer.

In life-basic, you always get a bed, some bandwidth to the net and food, but your activity and biometric information are sold to pay for it. You don't die in life-basic, but you don't live much either. Losing my single-room apartment with its one big window was a depressing prospect. I rented my table, two chairs and a sofa bed from *Better Rooms*, all of which would be derented tomorrow if I didn't find a way to get some money. *Derented*, a much nicer term than repossessed.

The pills completed their job as I forced myself out into the daylight to seek credit. My mind cleared. Fragments of the previous evening's proceedings came back to me. The partycast, a load of cheap *Twisted Courage* and the crazy installations by the augmented reality artists Annie invited. That's the problem when a partycast goes viral, you can't keep the crashers out. The boyzoids and the glitterbeasts are fine, but the Cannots got under my skin. *Stealing my lines.*

Crossing the skywalk to the public square, I squeezed past a group of parents with babies and toddlers. They carried on their nattering without paying me any attention.

I fixated on the Cannots, the Cannot Be Grouped. Assholes. It wasn't the first time someone messed with *The Pollutant Speaks*. I had poured all my broken parts and anger into that long, punk epic of discontent. People re-junked it over and over: inserting it into advert ballads and slip-beats. It was recited, broken up, put under music, and borrowed without credit. The Cannots were fascinated with it, but they couldn't divorce me from my work, and I contradicted their worldview. Rage crept up the back of my neck. "Sell-out", they'd called me. I'd show them who was the sell-out.

I punched the worn, brassy call button for the elevator in anger. I didn't have to touch it, the inner eye could summon it, but the resounding clack made me feel better. In a way, the Cannots had what they wanted. I wouldn't be writing anymore. Evans Ezra Evans, writer, deceased—the Crush had seen to that. News of my months in Green's hospital was followed by my online support quickly drying up, and somehow the details of my condition got out too. Another patient, perhaps? When there was no chance of a sequel to shut the Cannots up, what threat was I?

I mulled over forms of revenge I could take in the elevator. Problems: the Cannots were many, and they seemed so genuine. And our way of life *was* broken. You couldn't disagree with them on that. Seven miserable, overpopulated systems and no signs of founding a new one. The Cannots were an upsurge of discontent and the Crush combined. No wonder they didn't present a rational, consistent argument.

I decided to record some objections and post them over the net as soon as I'd sorted out my financial nightmare. That made me feel better, resolving to do something definitive at an undefined time in the future. Classic procrastination.

On Warjeck Avenue, pedestrians were packed shoulder-to-shoulder, the crowd thinned in the retail-lease showrooms on the company level, and MovLoCredit had a pair of booths there, back-to-back, no bigger than the space taken up by a public toilet. This was the only time I'd ever been to one because my financial world existed completely online, but now I was asking for some serious credit they would want to scan me. *Blood leaked out to slake a hussie's thirst.*

An augmented reality advert for *Alone* ran in one of the showroom windows. A beautiful semi-transparent girl crushed shoulder to shoulder with a shadowy, half-dozen sweaty Movey types. The program's inventor, Lucien Crossley, appeared like an archangel in a white suit. As he touched each uncouth person around the girl, they disappeared until he smiled and faded from existence. A look of silent ecstasy spread across the actress's face as the advert offered a free sample of the *Alone* program. With a blink, I swiped the advert out of my reality and headed for the nearest booth.

I took a seat inside the little cubicle, which reminded me more and more of a toilet, the bank proxy linked to my inner eye so that it could project an image of a comforting-looking gentleman behind a small desk. My proxy asked if the booth could have complete access for a few minutes. The kiosk smelt faintly of rubber.

The only person I'd ever given total access to was Green, my doctor, and even then, not all at once. So, though I knew it was necessary, I paused for a moment or two to think it over.

The first thing you lose in life-basic is privacy, and this was just a minute or two for my bank. It still felt like an invasion. My proxy raised its trust in MovLoCredit to the highest level.

'Mr Evans, just a moment while we gather a few details,' said the homely fellow behind the desk. 'Would you like some entertainment while you wait?'

'Will I be waiting long?' I asked.

'A minute, two at most,' he replied.

'You think I need entertaining for a minute?'

'Some clients do,' he rearranged objects on his desk, moving a trusty notepad from one side to another, putting a stylus into his pen pot, and glancing at his monitor. A few moments later, he adjusted his tie, moved the notepad back across the desk and pulled the stylus back out of the pen pot. After a few more cycles of this dance, a soft ping sounded, and the clerk focused his attention back on me.

'Alright, Mr Evans, we've looked at all the factors and at this moment in time, we won't be able to loan you any longer-term cultural capital.'

My stomach clenched as if filled with icy liquid and a tightness gripped my neck.

'You don't think I'll find work?' I asked.

'Correct, at least not work that will allow you to pay back a compound loan. We think it would be better for you to invest in a life-basic Save-Away programme at this time. You need to think about your long term goals and scale your expectations appropriately.'

'Scale my expectations!' I roared. *Evans' gate is open.* 'I have been sixteen years out of life-basic and never missed a payment. I can find work. I've got a Shang Lo diploma and experience!'

'But your latest hospital report says graphomania has left you unfit to write? Correct? So, we're sorry, but that seems like too much education for the kind of work you're looking for,' he said.

'What kind of work am I looking for?'

The clerk paused to consult his monitor. 'Work that requires no previous skills.'

*

The soft-shut mechanism ruined my attempt to slam the door on the agent and his smiling face.

On the mezzanine level of the corporate plaza, I stared through gantries and buttresses at the sky above the leisure blocks. It was like looking through the workings of a giant clock. MovLoCredit was a heartless, capital-eating machine, but its predictions were usually accurate. I gazed at the distant blue for inspiration but found only a cryptic message written by the hundreds of white streaks of passing aircraft. *The ancient heavenly connection is still free.*

'I'm screwed,' I told myself, still looking up. A couple dressed in the latest skin-tight business suits steered clear of me, on their way to the retail-lease mall and taking me for a neverrider or one of Crossley's *Alone* freaks. Just another victim of the Crush. They were right about that. Another attack of graphomania scared me more than a return to life-basic. My eye twitched. The urge to virtually scrawl my misery on every object around me crept in: on the contrails in the sky, the chic backs of the business couple and, most of all, on the brushed metal of the MovLoCredit booth. With the inner eye, you could label and annotate the universe. Another drowning moment. *What is not written is lost.*

"Resist", Green had said at the clinic, "and don't be surprised when the demons find ways out". I trooped back along Warjeck Avenue, hoping the exercise would fend off the mania.

Pumping blood about my body finished the job for the detox pills. Was life-basic such a lousy prospect? I was still young enough to find something else to do, and maybe I'd be back out in a couple of years? Sure, I'd miss my apartment window with its view over Movampton. There comes a time when you hit rock bottom, and you realise it can't get any worse—you have nothing to lose. *One step a day, to hell, we're on our way.*

Warjeck led onto the Fei-Fei Stack with its escalators surrounded by the vertical thoroughfare. Starlings always thrive around it. God knows what they found to eat. On the down escalator to the conurbation circular, I saw them.

Sometimes, you notice people and know that they aren't another group of strangers; you know deep inside that something will happen between you. It's their body language and the way they look at you. Whatever it is, you can tell that something will kick off. Four coachgirls, dressed identically in black and white checked skirts and jackets, were just such a group.

They came up the opposing escalator, staring right at me.

I looked the other way, then turned around in time to see the four harpies get off at the top and switch straight back onto the down escalator behind me. My proxy grabbed my attention. Going half-in, I saw on a burner forum where someone had posted a thread titled "Found!! – Pollutant Speaks **Foul Source**". Two linked inner eye feeds were streaming directly into the forum, and I could literally watch my own back.

When the coachgirls arrived at the next level, they opened their black leather purses and pulled out something that they quickly swallowed. Their faces blanked. I recognised that little gesture: engram mematonin, called *slice* on the streets, for those who just can't get enough of a kick out of biochemical feelings: why not stuff preloaded thoughts into your head at the same time? I wasn't going to wait around and see what the result was supposed to be.

Meanwhile, I saw the thread filling with hundreds of hate-filled comments from the Cannot Be Grouped in my inner eye. I rushed through the crowd on the conurbation route, breaking into a run and making for a cab rank. *His wings are clipped, and his feet are tied.*

The rank was empty.

A Movampton mass transport carrier pulled in, and three badge-carrying, mother killing, neverriders piled out. One of them, head and shoulders taller than the other two, spotted me through the crowd and pointed. They moved to cut me off from the cab rank. I turned to see how far behind the coachgirls were and saw they had spread across the sidewalk to ensure I couldn't double back. The crowd streamed around the hunters and the prey like unthinking water.

Even if I could jump the barrier, crossing the eight-lane highway would be suicide. The only remaining direction was to sprint headlong into the nearest Hotiocha Fast Drink bar. It wasn't the vast warren of hidey-holes that I'd hoped for. In fact, there were just six skinny tables and an automated server.

Time to stop running.

I slouched on a stool and looked casually at a menu. *I was beaten down / long ago / in some alley / in another world.* The massive neverrider came in with two cronies, closely followed by the coachgirls. His legs moved in an unnatural stalking motion, and his forearms exposed flesh-wrapped cylinders of titanium jacks. I hadn't dealt with gang violence since breaking out of life-basic and the Feng dormitories, but there had been plenty to go around. Sometimes you have to fight. Sometimes it's just mouthing off at each other. I hoped for the last but got ready for the first.

'What's good in here? You guys like Hotiocha?'

'Shut your fucking hole, Evans,' said the neverrider while his comrades pushed the chairs and tables into a mangled pile as if clearing a dance floor. I could tell from the way they moved that they were half-in. Playing out the scene to some net group and getting orders in return. That made me wonder who organised these morons and how?

The cybernetic giant reached out to grab me, too quick to be avoided, but I threw two punches at his face as he pulled me in. The coachgirls screamed with excitement, opened their purses and took another dose of the memetic.

The giant threw me into the front doors of the Hotiocha, smashing the plastic on one side, where one of his colleagues and a coachgirl, who couldn't believe her luck, started kicking me with all their might.

'Eloi! Abba! Save us great and stray—fit us with cinema of the head! HEAD! HEAD!' They chanted. As if being kicked wasn't enough, I had to listen to The Pollutant Speaks being misquoted.

Adrenaline overrode the pain for a moment, and I took a blow in the face to grab the foot of one assailant and pull him over into the coachgirl. I got to my feet just before a runaway train struck me. The half-machine thug smashed me back through the doors and onto the street, where I lay flat on my back.

He put his foot in the centre of my chest.

'Be the Cannot!' The ecstatic coachgirls screamed out. 'We lay off the cloaks and speak the truth in sewers, the river whose source is foul!'

'Foul source!' The giant bellowed down at me.

The golden period of adrenaline-powered fighting rapidly passed, and pain spread through my back and ribs. The immovable boot crushed the breath out of me. I thought the red in my vision was blood. Actually, it was my proxy asking me to authorise emergency payment.

Authorised.

Instantly, the weight lessened on my chest, accompanied by an ear-popping decompressive sound. I watched as one of the coachgirls was blasted, mid-chant, in a cart-wheel backwards down the road. Above me, the giant cradled his arms over his head as he appeared to be beaten by massive invisible fists.

As the neverriders and the coachgirls fled, I spotted the approaching Order unit, a metal skeleton with compression cannons on each arm and the face of its remote operator projected across its visor. The operator appeared to be a teenager. *Long live exact demonstration!*

'Duration of engagement: seven seconds. You sure took your time calling for help there, buddy,' the operator received an off-air reprimand. 'But you're the customer, man. You want me to call an ambulance?'

The skeleton leaned over me and gestured a weaponised hand over its shoulder to indicate where medical attention might come from.

'No thanks,' I said, 'just a cab home.'

The truth was that the extortionate charge for seven seconds of rescue had used up the last of my culcap. I couldn't afford an ambulance. People on life-basic get the knockout drones for medical attention, and I just wanted to get home while it was still mine.

If the Cannots were trying to kill me, I'd be safest back in my apartment in Javod, but if I returned to life-basic and the dormitories or worse, the Shang Lo commune, they'd be able to buy my net activity for the cost of a cheap meal. That was the kicker of life-basic, no privacy, and privacy seemed to be all that was keeping me alive.

The remote-controlled skeleton helped me to my feet. Amazingly, I didn't seem to have broken any bones, but an army of bruises erupted over me. *Haematoma hero.* My proxy noted the snowballing excitement online as my friends checked if I was OK and hurled abuse at the Cannots, who in turn were posting all the gory details of the encounter on sites and forums everywhere. I let trusted contacts know that I was on the way home, battered but unbroken.

'You sure you don't want to file a police report?' the concerned teenager on the faceplate screen asked.

'I can't afford the deposit, and I'd rather go home. Maybe I'll make one when the shock wears off.' I stumbled over to a cab rank, where a newly arrived vehicle played its jingle and opened its door.

'*Order* is glad to be of service in this private dispute matter,' the young operator launched into his sign-off script. 'Damage and injury sustained by the plaintive and other involved parties are at the discretion of the engaging client. No liability is assumed for property or emotional wellbeing. *Order* is a profit-making capital lease engagement organisation…'

When the controller finished his spiel, the faceplate went blank, the machine crouched into a tight box and waited to be picked up. It occurred to me that I'd forgotten to thank the gamer for saving my life.

I levered my beaten form into the back seat and asked to be taken home. The cab pulled away. A fog of calls from friends and acquaintances stacked up. *Exclusive: public execution.* I ignored them and leaned my head on the plexiglass window. I was glad to be alive, but the future seemed like a closing trap. I'd blown my savings, and tonight the last of my culcap would expire. I would be evicted, then automatically detected as homeless and enrolled into life-basic, immediately back on the radar for the Cannots and whatever other groups had developed a taste for my blood. *Foul source,* they'd shouted at me. What possessed people to butcher something so entirely? They must have searched the *Pollutant* for hours to find some line that seemed to void the author's opinion. Didn't they see it made no sense? You can't tell the reader they have to believe you and that you're a liar at the same time.

I stumbled onto the pavement and ignored the departing taxi's sales pitch for premium service. Through the pain, my inner demons were still at work. *Vision omens. Precious hallucinations.*

The elevator was a few crouched, painful steps away. The Cannots wanted to stop me denouncing them by calling me a sell-out. That only works if the target has buckets of culcap, but not if they live in life-basic without a stick of furniture to their name. I rested my face against the cold wall as I pushed the floor button with a shaky hand.

A young couple kissed on a bench on the sky plaza and didn't stop to notice as I struggled by. My eyes fixed on the ground, concentrating on getting one foot in front of the other over the last few strides. If a Cannot spotted me, or even a friend of a friend of the CBG, I'd give away the location of my apartment. Maybe they weren't searching, perhaps they were happy to wait just one more day for my financial demise, but they didn't strike me as the patient type.

Inside the apartment, I eased myself onto the couch. No matter how I tried to clear my head, problems welled up around me. The inner eye babbled with so many messages I had to mute it. I was the magician trapped in the water torture cabinet. *The night Houdini died. 'Someone, please fix the trick', he cried.*

As time marched on, applications in my inner eye faded to grey and disappeared, signifying my accounts were suspended.

I reported the attack to the police for no charge as I was utterly bankrupt. A polite reception program took the details of my case and promised me a summary of the investigation within seventy-two hours. When I told the system that I might be beaten to death by then, it sympathetically said it hoped that wouldn't happen, and statistically, it was uncommon.

I put my affairs in some order and dictated a protest at my treatment by these radicals—Green's orders still forbade me from writing so much as a greetings card—then reassured friends that I was alive. I mothballed a character in my favourite drama and enjoyed for one last hour the power that came with a fully-functioning proxy with all my tastes, privacy and best interests at its heart. For the last time, the proxy patrolled the virtual wilderness of humanity, looking out for my concerns. It noted video and images of me used without my consent, watched for things of interest and even safeguarded my opinion. Soon that extension of me was amputated too.

When the proxy blinked out of existence, I knew what it was like to be truly alone, not the willing delusion of an *Alone* addict. I sat and listened to the pipes gurgle.

The hot night of the city stared in at me through my wall-sized window, and when the power to the apartment failed, the sparkling towers and starry highways seemed all the more brilliant. *Press close magnetic nourishing night!* A watery, sapphire moon lingered above. The glow was bright enough to allow me to gather my possessions into a bag. *Grim list, nothing missed.* A glass paperweight and a hand-edited hard copy of the *Pollutant* were the only two personal possessions I had, so it didn't take long.

My clothes, towels and food were delivered or printed as needed, so there were no spares. Everything else in the apartment was a rental: the sofabed, the video screens, the drinkomat, the DomestiFab, the cleaner—everything.

There was a soft knock at the door.

Could the Cannots have found me so quickly? Anger rose up in me. After all, I was destitute. Let them do their worst. I pulled the door open with a self-destructive flourish, ready to face my accusers.

'Do you want some fucking coffee?' asked Annie.

She leaned against the wall with one hand jammed in the pocket of her grimy open bathrobe, absently revealing the sullied t-shirt and underwear beneath. *A symphony in tobacco stains.*

She didn't wait for my reply, just walked straight back into her apartment, leaving the door open. I took a sentimental glance back through my former home. My own face bid me adieu from the mirror on the far wall as I turned and left it behind.

Next door, Bugatti's place was identical to mine, but she embellished it with a thousand gothic trinkets. A giant black wing was pinned across the ceiling, liberated from the props of a failed *Paradise Lost*. Framed vidtures crammed the walls alongside holograms and paintings. Even with all this paraphernalia, it seemed her apartment was more substantial than mine. From the sound system came the drawl of some Titan blues player.

'Flat broke, eh?' she said and handed me a grimy commemorative teacup, probably from one of the system landings, with a brown smear of espresso in the bottom. I suspected that Annie found the whole concept romantic and, if my life weren't in imminent danger, would have congratulated

12

me on being a bankrupt and hunted poet. She considered such things *authentic*.

I nodded and dropped my bag by the door.

'Maybe we can find you some priest hole to hide in?'

'Things don't look good,' I said and sank my aching body into an armchair. 'Maybe you shouldn't get too close to me either. I always knew the Crush was going to kill me. I just never thought it would be because of a few lines of verse.'

Annie came over and kissed me on the forehead.

She gently pulled off my shoes, followed by the rest of my clothes and took me to bed.

We crunched through the black snow, past the Wuhan-Xin dicey bars, our paper coveralls and plastic face masks made us indistinguishable from the other people out on the streets during an air purge. *The maximum lawmen run down Flamingo / chasing the Rat and the barefoot girl.* Any of them could have been the Cannots.

That morning Annie had executed a full intervention. She called in all the favours that an influential art blogger could summon. Annie had a badly-kept secret: her grunge-punk look hid a mile-wide good streak, a trait she concealed with her brass-and-black streaked hair, lockdeath tattoos and grotty dress sense. *I knew a woman, lovely in her bones.*

Still, she was trying to save my life, and I was grateful.

Electrostatic tankers droned along the roads and sucked the dark flakes off the sidewalks into glistening vents. I tried to make myself heard over the machinery. The air stank of ozone.

'Where next?' I asked.

'Get off the street before the purge is over,' Annie said. 'The Marketoria should hold off the Cannots.'

Marketoria: moving, cubic, matrices of offices. Magnifying glass windows inflated tiny details of the executives inside. Giant corporation initials embedded into the superstructure. Every crevice brimming with business superego and product worship. The g-Russ lived and worked in the seventh circle of it all.

I glanced at Annie as we headed for the sparkling main reception. She was barely identifiable under the billowing paper coverall and mask. *We are the straw gods leant together.* How had she come to have influence with the g-Russ? Five power-hungry market makers with their brains cabled together.

The gestalt way of life is rare and dangerous. The g-Russ gained fivefold brainpower and imagination, but if one of them succumbed to the Crush or had a breakdown, it would pass on to the others, who would, in turn, pass it back again. The results were always death.

Sometimes gestalts ask for small favours or suddenly change behaviour when they think it might secure their mental wellbeing. Maybe Annie had been involved in something of that sort.

We passed through the entrance into a gluttonously empty reception area. At the front desk, two attendants blinked into existence. A spark of fear cut through me. What if the g-Russ couldn't help me? I'd be back out on the street after a short, fruitless interlude where I'd be hunted down by the Cannots. *Run down by the drunken taxicabs of Absolute Reality.*

The last time I'd felt that helpless was when I stood in the foyer of Green's hospital pleading to be admitted. Luckily there'd been a real person on the reception there and not a programmed image. She'd listened and watched as I showed her the mess I'd made of my world, every item in the augmented universe annotated with compulsive writing, mostly in fragments of verse. She gave me a chance to see Green himself.

A wall of bored-looking muscle came out of an elevator, striding over in a well-tailored suit.

'Mz. Bugatti, Mr Evans, let's get out of sight, shall we?' he glanced at me and returned to the elevator.

We descended sixty-seven floors then the guard held the doors while motioning for us to exit. We stepped into a reception area with administrative staff, beyond which glass doors led onto a gigantic circular office, brightly lit, opulently furnished and populated by just five people. All five were men with a lean, handsome build and immaculately dressed in haute couture. They moved unnaturally, passing fragments of tasks between them. *Does my sexiness upset you?* It was rumoured that qualifications to be in the g-Russ were greed, vanity and a predatorily bisexual hunger.

Bugatti unhooked her plastic mask and pulled back the hood of the paper coverall.

'Let's see what they've come up with. They may seem like a bunch of jumped up corporates but stick with them; they've got a softer side,' Bugatti thought for a moment while stripping off the last of the coverall. 'At least some of them have.'

'Are they going to market me?' I asked.

'I doubt we'll merit that much of their attention, all you need is for all five of these pinstriped shits to focus for a minute or two. Bam! Like a fucknado. You've got yourself a lifeboat.'

'Listen, Annie, I haven't had a chance to thank you. You put yourself in harm's way for me. I know that. Just wanted to say I appreciate it.'

I touched her arm.

'Sheesh, Evans, when we're done here, you can write daytime soap operas. Don't get all caught up in your skirts. I don't like seeing people get shafted for making art that challenges the system. Fuck the Cannots. Screw life-basic too.'

Two of the g-Russ turned their attention to us as we came through the curved glass doors into their high circular office, the crystal ceiling showing the blinking neon innards of the Marketoria above.

'Welcome, valued associates. I'm Kio and this—' said Kio, hand on heart.

'—is Johan,' finished Johan. 'In a moment, we'll get down to your little problem, Mr Evans, just after we've finished the launch strategy of a new fashion obliquor.'

'Obliquor?' I asked.

'It's a trade term,' said Kio.

'For something that ensures this season's items go out of fashion,' continued Johan.

'At the expected time,' concluded Kio.

Annie tutted in disgust and dumped herself in a leather armchair. She began to raid the drinks cabinet situated next to it. The g-Russ politely ignored her.

'All done! I'm Christopher,' said a blonde g-Russ.

'And Manuel.'

'And Lawrence.'

They crowded around me, shaking my hand and examining my tatty three-day-old disposables.

'You are a fascinating item, aren't you, Mr Evans?' said Lawrence.

'Quite the kingpin of tragedy at the moment,' said Kio.

'If Annie hadn't asked us to help,' said Christopher.

'We might have looked you up ourselves,' said Johan.

'You know, just out of curiosity,' said Manuel.

They were undoubtedly aware of how disconcerting their attentions could be, but I needed their help, so I coped with their split speech and casual touches as calmly as possible. I backed into a seat where I thought I'd be safe.

'I appreciate your help. Maybe all I need is a good job?' I asked hopefully.

'Good job?' laughed Kio. 'That's almost exactly what we were thinking.' He waved the others away. 'Look, my beautiful poetic friend, what you've done with the *Pollutant Speaks* is a work of genius—really—you've managed to set up precisely the right circumstances so that you make no cultural capital at all out of your work. Incredible.'

'I had some bad advice.'

'Of course you did. Let's look at things as they are now, shall we? We've taken a few,' he waved his hand in the air, 'moments to consider your situation. It seems best to us that you'll need to take a little journey.'

This piqued both Bugatti's and my attention.

'Anywhere in Movampton, the Cannots will have him in a flash,' said Bugatti.

'Just what kind of journey are we thinking of? Offworld?' I asked.

'One that someone else pays for, of course,' Kio chuckled, as did his gestalt brothers from where they stood about the office. 'You see, what's especially appealing about your case for us is that there are so very few things you can actually do about it.'

'Glad to provide a minute of entertainment for you,' I said.

'Not quite a minute,' Kio was suddenly distracted.

'Idea!' Johan pointed joyously at the projection table.

'Trachtenbuchs, how quaint,' said Lawrence.

'With just a dash of pricing arbitrage,' added Christopher.

'And a soupcon of indentured subscription,' sighed Manuel with pleasure.

Bugatti lost her patience with the preening executives. She clapped her hands loudly and stood up with a thunderhead expression.

'Hey, brainiacs! How about a little bit of service here?' she said.

Kio returned his attention to us with a wistful smile. I could see their thoughts flit in and out of each other's heads, similar to the lack of awareness when someone is half-in the net. All five oracles frowned at each other and returned to their separate tasks. Kio leaned in close to me while he sat on the arm of my chair.

'She's quite something, isn't she?' he whispered.

'That she is,' I agreed. 'But if you don't stop being quite so pleased with yourselves, I hate to think what she might do to this office of yours.'

Kio puckered his lips as if he found that particular thought overwhelmingly sensuous. He ambled around the table and then took a seat opposite, steepled his fingers and finally began to explain.

'Your situation requires two things: ensured long term survival and a new career. Since having enough capital to defend your privacy and fending off attempts on your life are effectively one and the same thing, we consider getting you appointed to a job our immediate goal. You can't directly return to your previous profession, but we can look at the base properties: the innate skills that led you to it in the first place. Normally the obtuse leanings of a poet are of no use *whatsoever* in the commercial sector. You lack the cut-throat compromise which would make you a success. There is one recruitment scheme currently looking for such strange basic properties. They demand no experience, they're not fundamentally a commercial concern, and their interview process is open to all.'

'Who are they then?' I asked.

'The Border Institute for Languages, they're running the last few days of operations on Shang Lo to screen potential applicants.'

'I'm about to be killed, and you are telling me to buy a lottery ticket to meet the Paraunion?'

'Not at all,' Kio shook his head. 'The aptitude programme for Border is incredibly selective, and a vast amount of effort is spent on overseeing it. We have an intense interest in the commercial applications of the system they use to categorise people. In fact, some of the methodologies are imported from the alien culture that is so stand-offish. Ironic, don't you think? We can't pry anything out of them, but you can't keep a good marketing scheme down.'

'What makes you so sure that Evans here can pass this test?' asked Annie.

'Profiling techniques from an advanced civilisation are of great interest to us. We've acquired all the details we can about it, and although we may be fuzzy on the whys of the tests, we can say with almost ninety per cent confidence that Mr Evans here has that 'right stuff' that they are seeking. He simply needs to turn up, be himself and get signed up to go to Border for the final examination.'

I was stunned. There it was, a life raft. *As I was going down impassive Rivers.* It would involve leaving absolutely everything and everyone I knew, but it would put me beyond the reach of the Cannots.

19

'Why do I need to go to Border? Nobody goes anywhere for an interview. It'll cost a fortune.'

'Oh, exactly, exactly! Why are people being shipped in their droves to a remote facility? Why not set up yet another virtual cathedral to study the mystical language of para? Except, of course, that all those cathedrals have failed to produce a single candidate who can speak it! Perhaps the review system is beyond their control, or the lonely Professor Spindle just wants to look his adepts straight in the eye? Who knows? Wonderful, isn't it?' Kio looked positively ecstatic.

'Although,' remarked Manuel, 'physical confinement of information is a powerful thing.'

'And', mused Christopher, 'it all depends whose time is the most valuable, doesn't it?'

The others nodded in appreciation of their wisdom.

I glanced to Bugatti for help, but I could tell that she appreciated the g-Russ plan for its finer points by the look on her face.

'I'm not getting on an eight-year flight to save myself from religious thugs.'

'Then you'll be beaten to death by those religious thugs,' Kio replied. 'Perhaps you'll become a famous martyr for your art if that kind of thing turns you on.'

'Oh yes,' muttered Lawrence at his projection desk.

I had to buck up. Since I'd stumbled out of Green's hospital, I hadn't made a single good decision. I'd leant heavily on Bugatti, who sat in the leather armchair waiting for me to come to my senses. *The red bill and flyers kill.* What right did I have to grumble about the nature of my salvation? Unlike the Oracle of Delphi, the g-Russ spelt it out clearly. Even the voices in my head were getting impatient with me.

'Alright, can I interview here?'

'No,' Matthew shook his head, turning from a view of the Marketoria.

'We'll make arrangements to get you to the Civic centre unscathed,' Kio said.

'But for now,' said Lawrence.

'We're a bit busy,' finished Manual.

'Please see yourselves out,' said Christopher.

The lift opened, and the heavy-set security guard stepped out. It occurred to me that the g-Russ must have ordered him down at least a minute beforehand. A thought that only annoyed me some weeks later.

*

We rode on the roof of a bulky goods wagon through the vertical farms. Neither Bugatti nor I had ever seen them before. Nano-flies hummed through the hot air tending to the thousands of tiers of crops. Light lensed down and filled every crevice with mid-summer sun. Sweat crept down my back as the wagon lumbered on. There were no public cameras or passers-by to observe us. It was the most idyllic spot I had been to in years.

Annie looked unhappy.

'This should be open to the public. You shouldn't have to get some five-brains to let you in through the side door.' Bugatti; always the questor for social justice.

A bee, a real one, settled on her shoulder—a pink dot marked on its back. I looked at it for a moment before it went on its way.

'Sixteen years I'm going to be away,' I said.

'You going to miss Shang Lo? Movampton? Critishins?'

'I don't know. That's assuming the soothsayers back there are right. I always thought I'd travel, then I lost the hunger for it. I've been too comfortable since I wrote *The Pollutant*. I used to be angry about things. I used to have real opinions. Hell, I used to think that I had important thoughts. I miss that me. I guess the Crush squeezed it out of me. I used to be like you, Annie.'

'Tell you what. Once you've been out, seen the universe and built up a backbone, and I'm taking my first old pills, you can come back and wow me with how real and important you are,' she kissed me on the cheek just as the wagon juddered to a halt.

'You're going that way,' she said and pointed at a sub-door through a path in a wheat field.

I tried to summon up something fitting to say and failed. Bugatti gave me an understanding look. *Not goodbye, not good night.*

I dismounted the wagon by the maintenance ladder and made my way up cement steps to the exit path. The engine hummed harder as it prepared to set off again. By the time I'd got up a dozen steps to a slanted bean field, she was standing on the roof shouting some final advice over the din of the heavy vehicle. *Don't get dead,* I thought she said as she waved, but in retrospect, I'm sure it must have been something else.

3   And fibre your blood

Fear is strange.

It serves an essential purpose, but we live in unnatural times, so it often becomes self-destructive. All I needed to do was follow the plan of the g-Russ, who'd said I should be able to breeze this interview, but my demons hadn't been paying attention during that part of the conversation.

I conjured up impressive things I could say about myself, some even true. I levered answers into the imaginary interview in my head and assumed questions I had no way of predicting. By the time I arrived at the Ai Sung civic buildings, I was a wreck. The thought of being assassinated on sight by the CBG didn't help.

The hall was a typical government building with a large foyer on the ground floor. An atmosphere of purgatory hung in the air, unchanged since the invention of the welfare state. The feeling caused a natural counter-reaction – do I really want to join this queue? Do I deserve what I'm asking for, or is it worth the time? We were still unable to remove the implicit shame from poverty. *Am I [I am] scum / why did I come?*

Trials for Border had been on at the civic hall for weeks and would carry on for days more. The whole operation had stepped up a gear. Everything I'd heard about the previous recruitment drives had targeted academics. Why had it opened up so much now?

While I waited, I scoured the forums about Border. Para enthusiasts commented on and raved over every detail of the super-culture that leaked out. At least you never completely lose access to the net: even life-basic wasn't that cruel. On the other hand, the CBG bought up my activity at a carnivorous rate. They wouldn't assault me in the confines of the civic buildings, but they sure as hell were going to catch me the moment I left.

Impatience hung like smoke in the air. Serving counters protected by tempered glass and entirely unstaffed, relics from a bygone age of human assistance goaded us. Dusty screens looped helpful information above the seats, all dutifully ignored by the people waiting in the plastic chairs. Was it any wonder that an alien super-culture wasn't interested in talking to us?

An inner eye exclamation mark told me that someone was ready to see me. When I gave it my attention, it floated in front of me, morphed into an arrow and guided me to the elevators, where we rose to the eighty-third floor. I plodded behind the virtual pointer, passing others in the corridor doing the same. The arrow changed to an upheld hand at the door to an interview room and displayed an hourglass for a few seconds. A blonde woman in a grey striped three-piece suit opened the door.

'Mr Evans, come in. We're sorry to have kept you waiting,' she said.

Her pronunciation was crisp, almost certainly Earth-accented. It reminded me of a diplomat I once knew. Behind her, the local facilitator sat with a dictatorial look and her arms folded across her chest. Next to the facilitator, a rotund, bearded man smiled at me but had the unmistakable attitude of someone who was half in the net. I guessed he was there as a scorer of some kind.

'I'm Ursula Gleick-State, our facilitator is Rana Cardinal, and this is Jame Moore, who will be helping interpret data for us today.'

Gleick-State: a big-money, virtual family. I wondered why she was stuck with a civil servant job. *Few of the rich are callen.*

'Pleasure to meet you all,' I said and fumbled my way to a seat before realising that everyone I had been introduced to still stood. Just as I made to stand, they took their seats.

'Your resume is quite impressive, Mr Evans. I hope you won't mind a preliminary question? Has it been explained to you that what we are looking for is innate ability?' Ursula, the Earther, asked.

'That's how I understand it,' I lied.

'Good, good. I mention this because any results will in no way be a reflection on your academic history or how you behave or 'click' with any of us. What I am saying, in short, is that at this point, it's best to relax. There's nothing you can do either way to affect the results of this interview.'

She oozed reassurance. Unwind. Even the scowling facilitator ceased to bother me.

Moore, the bearded operator, delivered the test. His voice was flat and controlled, so no candidate had an advantage by receiving a different inflexion, the same policy actors get when doing an audition.

'I'd like you to imagine a ridiculous world,' he said, 'much like a children's story. Take a moment to think and then just give me a few details about that fictional world – anything is acceptable.'

I considered options for a ridiculous world, still feeling the need to show off for the interview. What was ridiculous? Upside-down realms or nonsense comedies like a medieval illumination? I realised that I was using an arbitrary standard to sort the quality of an idea—these people weren't interested in that—I gave them the next thing that came into my head.

'A world where it only rains inside,' I said.

'Can you give me a little more?' the operator asked.

'The clouds all huddle in attics because they enjoy collecting antiques.'

'Was it always that way?'

'No,' I said, 'one cloud found out what was in peoples' roof storage and told all the other clouds. Now they huddle up there, holding auctions and discussing Ming vases.'

The operator scratched his beard and focused on readouts that the rest of us were not privy to. At least I assumed the other two were not. The Gleick-State woman looked amused by the idea of my antique collecting clouds, but the facilitator wore a pained expression. You had to sympathise with her if she'd sat through several hundred deranged babblings in the last few days.

At an unseen prompt, the operator asked me to add more details to my off-the-cuff alternate universe. How did the plants survive? In one particular house, what were the inhabitants? Could I give them names? What were the concerns of that one cloud? What did it sound like when it rained inside? And on and on.

I soon found that trying to be smart got in the way of making a prompt answer, and as one response was as good as any other, I let them flow out of me. *Fictionally true, a frictionless truth.* By the end, I enjoyed the experience as long as I avoided the baleful stare of Rana, the facilitator. Only the AI selection program and perhaps some input from the smart-looking Ursula, who sounded like an expert, would really matter. The facilitator was just a third wheel.

As operator Moore finished his last question, he turned to Ursula with raised eyebrows and gave her a nod.

The g-Russ had been right. Whatever the interview program was encoded to search for, it had found some of it in me. A troubling thought crossed my mind, what else could the g-Russ do? Was I acting as an unwitting pawn? Those paranoid suspicions were interrupted by the realisation that I would not be checking into a life-basic hostel that evening, that I would not be kicked to death in the night.

The facilitator missed the quiet cue from the operator and looked deeply surprised when Ursula cleared her throat and started to address me.

'Mr Evans, I am delighted, possibly more than you can imagine, to inform you that your aptitude for our test is very high. You're probably unaware that we have vetted close to four thousand candidates from this district alone, and not a single one has reached the offer mark.'

By now, the facilitator was attempting to compose herself. She looked at the operator to confirm the result. The bearded technician paid her no attention and instead gave me a delighted grin and a thumbs-up.

Facilitator Rana Cardinal collected herself enough to launch into a befuddled offer speech.

'Ah. Yes! We are pleased to invite you to attend second-round selections on Border. You will, of course, be compensated for this, but—more importantly—you will be a part of the most significant undertaking of our epoch.

'Naturally, you'll need time to go over the details of this proposition and discuss the matter with friends and family. The Border Institute will allocate free-to-travel tickets which can be used at any time within two months of this offer...'

'Anytime?' I interrupted.

'Absolutely anytime,' Gleick-State replied.

'Golden, I'd like to set off this afternoon.'

'That's the spirit!' said the facilitator. 'It's so encouraging to see a young person with real get-up-and-go.'

She couldn't have known that without that ticket, I'd be checking into the lowest form of accommodation available, a life-basic community dormer, if I was lucky enough not to be gutted on the doorstep of the civic hall. The prospect of a sleeper cabin while getting off Shang Lo and out to the heliopause was a dream come true.

The facilitator shared a contract with me as an inner eye document, which I signed, and icons fluttered back to life in the corner of my view. *Vampiric applications.* The vital flow of cultural capital was restored.

I resented those applications. They'd cut me off one moment and then start suckling again as soon as it turned out there was life left in the animal.

All three of the interviewers shook my hand. Their enthusiasm for my success was heightened by their long, tedious search. Moore politely ignored some of the tell-tales about my bankrupt state: explicitly when I didn't need to pick up any belongings before having a car booked to take me to Fletcher reachport, the nearest one on this side of Shang Lo.

I thought I saw the point where the operator had his proxy do a background search on me and turned up the whole story with Green's hospital and the leak that led to my current state of affairs. He leaned in when he shook my hand and said, 'You'll enjoy Border. They say you can walk around and see no one else for hours.'

Only when I was installed in a cab, an hour or two later, did I realise how lucky I'd been. I'd escaped and in some style. Just me and my little bag of belongings. I hadn't even considered for a moment going back to thank Annie and the g-Russ. What a bastard. Concerned only with my own imminent salvation, that's what makes poets a detestable lot. *Best read and left unmet.*

I wanted to write them something while the cab whisked me to the reachport, a few lines of thanks, but Green had explicitly forbidden it. The pressure to break his commandment mounted, and I felt that something was needed to show my appreciation, especially to Annie. Fragments of my suppressed graphomania forced their way to the front of my mind, *all things are ready if our mind be so*, as if unhappy with being unwritten, they could transform themselves into sound in my head.

I called Green via inner eye to ask if I could be excused from my ban. He didn't answer but replied with a message almost immediately.

Under no circumstances are you to resume writing. New job. New life. Learn to make friends with the character within. It seems worse when emotional, so Border may be good for you. May you always be floating, never falling. Your friend, Green.

There it was: I couldn't disobey Green without risking a complete relapse into the Crush. I recorded a short verbal thank you for the g-Russ and promised to keep them updated.

At Fletcher, I went into one of the shops and got a courier to send my battered card-and-twine bound version of *The Pollutant Speaks* to Annie. It took willpower to write only her name on the inside cover and not give in to the graphomanic itch. My near empty bag sat up on the counter and I caught a reflection of myself in my crumpled, dirty disposables. *Homespun collars, homespun hearts, wear to rags in foreign parts.*

Green had said to make friends with my inner demons. I was to be shipped off to a place where I could be alone, but those alien thoughts could still ruin it. I handed my package to the shop clerk, who ritually covered it in tracking stickers.

I still needed to send messages to my mother, father, half-brothers and sisters. To be out of touch for a few years was becoming more the norm. What we earn in longevity we seem to casually give away to travel—and I travelled light—the bag on my shoulder now held only a dandelion paperweight.

The space elevator cabin hummed overhead, a building-sized ring around a graphene needle that periodically disappeared up into the heavens. *He dreamed and behold, a ladder was set up on earth.* The last time I travelled off-planet was when my parents first moved to Shang Lo.

I'd been no more than four at the time. They'd split eighteen years later and decided on different habitations as if to put as much distance between themselves as possible. I stayed on Shang Lo, being generally young and angry.

The boarding gates were a lonely scanning machine, so I gave my credentials and walked through gloriously un-busy corridors and junctions. I avoided the check-in for my non-existent luggage and sat in the same line of chairs as the only other person waiting, a nervy bear of a man in a squaddie Peace Core uniform. He wore white dress gloves and an all in one camo-jumpsuit set to appear a smart navy blue colour.

'Going up?' I asked.

'Yep,' he looked nervously at me. No doubt he wasn't used to being alone: core types are forced to spend every waking and sleeping moment with their units.

'You know much about this TransPop group? Is the food ok?' I asked, reading a snippet of local news out of the corner of my inner eye.

'It's the same as the last lot before they went under. Fuji-khan still runs the tower and the platforms. TransPop just sell tickets and doles out the chow. But the food is OK if you can get served.'

As a Peace Core soldier, he'd probably have been in and out of this reachport hundreds of times. We shook hands, and our proxies automatically established a little trust with each other— in other words—they let down their guards and got chummy. A fraction of a second later, my proxy prompted me with a tiny nugget of information it believed I would find important.

'You're going to Border?'

'Yep. I guess you're Evans, then? Sorry man, I was told to find you and introduce myself in the dovecot. I didn't realise we'd be on the same elevator: Cadet Rolliard Banks.' We shook hands again. 'You know there have only ever been a hundred and ten candidates chosen from all over Shang Lo? Makes you feel pretty special.'

'So you just happened to be catching the same flight out of Shang Lo?'

'No,' he blushed, 'I don't like to travel alone, so I've been waiting for the next selectee for four months. It's a bit of the Peace Core and a bit of the Crush, you know?'

Nearly half of the population had some form of Crush, whether hypertension or full-on schizophrenia. Meeting someone who appeared completely well-adjusted was remarkable. *Poisonous vanilla people.* Rolliard's symptoms were positively dull.

As we swapped points of view on the privilege of being sent to Border, the reachport entered a busier phase in the timetable of large vessels travelling between factories, planets, or moons. A little of that traffic was to the dovecot, the staging area for inter-system ships just outside of the heliopause where the influence of the Taucity star drastically diminished.

I asked Rolliard about his interview, but it was just as cryptic as mine; he couldn't make much sense of it even though he was an avid amateur Para enthusiast. *Daydream believer.*

I was happy to have the company. After a call to Annie to check she got my gift and to say thank you and goodbye for the next sixteen years, my spirits hit a low. Rolliard was a continuous stream of chatter and Para facts. I carried his second kit bag through the gate and let him use my luggage allowance to get it through. I wasn't going to use it after all.

The reachport tower took groups of fifty up to the orbital dock. The rocker seats were arranged in concentric circles facing outward toward the circular window of the ascension platform. Once described as the most over-elaborate lift ever designed, the window was an excuse to keep fifty people orderly and well-behaved for the twenty minutes it took to raise them all four hundred kilometres.

I insisted on us taking outer ring seats so that I could get a good view out of the windows, even though Rolliard swore that people on the outer circle always got served drinks last. Once we settled, he turned to me and asked a question with an earnest look.

'Why do you want to speak Para then?'

'I don't know that I really do.'

The big man's smile dropped like a five-year-old that had been told Christmas was cancelled.

'Why spend years of your life on it then?'

'I'm just trying to stay out of life-basic. You get that, don't you?'

He certainly could have understood that if he'd chosen to, nearly everyone in the Peace Core joins to get out of life-basic, but Rolliard found the idea of someone entering the grand Border scheme for financial gain distasteful. He sulked for over three minutes.

TransPop were offering up some promotional material in my inner eye. It was my first adult trip up the reach tower, and I stared out of the window as the augmented reality guide pointed out nearby visible buildings.

As the carriage accelerated up the needle, the guide changed from pointing out buildings and statistics about the tower to noting geographic features, whole districts of Shang Lo, atmospheric conditions and flight lanes. We ascended through scale and perspective. *Alice: drink me, here comes the ceiling.*

Rolliard lounged in the seat next to me and continued his obsession with in-flight drinks by trying to flag down a steward. Meanwhile, the curvature of the horizon evolved, and the blue to blackening of the sky as our height increased. *The thin skin of life.*

The inner eye displayed the disembarkation procedure of the shuttle, a simplified diagram showing the carriage being popped off the top of the tower and slotted like a coin into one of the two rotating wheels of the orbital. There were a few minutes of zero gravity until the shuttle came under the station's spin. The doors opened, and the stewards thanked us for using TransPop.

Rolliard looked at me as if it was my fault that he hadn't been served a drink.

5   They fly like bats

We spent the following weeks in a habitation unit that passed between three different vessels. I couldn't complain. The conditions were far more spacious and sociable than in my apartment on Shang Lo. I had the occasional dizzy feeling when I thought of my close scrape with the Cannots, especially when I followed their subsequent rage at my disappearance on the net. The g-Russ officially asked me to stop sending notes of thanks. It appeared I was not only embarrassing them but boring them too.

Rolliard was a faithful travelling companion due partly to the withdrawal he felt from his Peace Core platoon. *Sancho Puppy*. We socialised with the other eighteen people in the unit and dabbled in the odd voyage romance, but it soon became apparent that Rolliard was the person I'd keep in touch with once all the Border business was over. You sometimes meet a person who fills a hole in your life that you didn't know you needed: Rolliard was one of those people for me. He talked endlessly about the necessity for humanity to set up an entente cordial with the Paraunion. We got into it all again in the lounge area while queuing to get dinner from the self-serve dispensers.

'We're blind to the big politics of the cultures around us, cultures that dwarf our own. We're a spot in the corner of a spiral arm. There's only one defence when you're as ignorant as us – find a bigger boy to stand up for you,' he waved a disposable fork in the air.

'As you said, we're just a spot – a speck. It's insignificance that all this first contact business fails to consider: we're uninteresting, a glob of seven stars, a grey stone on the beach too ugly to attract the interest of bored children.'

'Not that uninteresting!' Rolliard retorted, feeling he'd caught me out. 'What about Border? It's a test, an invitation.'

'Or a standard response letter from a bureaucrat up in the realm of the gods: "here's something to keep you amused, humans". And look at what's happened! Just building the installation has billions of people shouting that we can't afford it, that it's a total waste. Look at the Cannots. Is the test to see if we can rise above the mob and if we really want to grow up? The results are pretty much in: we're selfish, and the vast majority are victims, more interested in food and lodgings than friends from across the universe.'

That hit Rolliard where it hurt. *Craftsman of pain.* He thought of people as deserving, the silent majority with nothing but good in their hearts. Out there, drifting through the dark in the best quality box our race could summon up, I was unnecessarily rough on him. Like a child hurt in early life for being innocent, I dished it out to other people. And later, I felt ashamed. The notion crept over me that I was seriously wrong, not only about the facts but on deeper grounds of hope and right. To apologise to Rolliard as that feeling spread through me would have been the stand-up thing to do. Instead, I shuffled through a series of face-covering arguments.

I rejected human isolationism, not that Rolliard was putting this argument to me, which made me feel I held a reasonable middle ground. Later, I accepted that some representation of relations with the surrounding super culture was essential. Finally, I moved to discuss the terms of potential membership and special conditions we needed with our new neighbours. *The led horse drinks.*

Eventually, Rolliard and I huddled around the dim, flickering fire of hope for humanity: the Paraunion. He didn't gloat in my weeklong conversion. No intellectual humiliation was used. *No Evans were killed in the making of this movie.* It ended with me in the camp that my heart told me was the right place.

I talked a lot with Annie showing her the thoroughly unremarkable view from my cabin window. *Space is miraculously sparse.* She mentioned that people drop their prejudices and nationalism after surprisingly short periods off-world. I noted I was never entirely sure where I stood politically anyway. I'd just wanted to eat and live without fear. Years ago, around the time I started to write *The Pollutant Speaks*, I could have been a signed-up member of the Cannots. In her recorded reply Annie said that she looked forward to seeing if my opinions changed – then she'd know just how bigoted people from Shang Lo were. I assumed she was joking.

It only took us a few weeks to reach the jump station *Some Prefer Nettles*, a large installation that followed the qubit factory naming convention of book titles. Each factory produced enough entangled material to communicate within the system and re-supply every ship which swooped around the star. As a minor part of its remit, it also housed passengers, cargo, supplies and jump ships: nimble vessels whose only purpose was to catch and dock with the passing starships that never slowed or sacrificed their precious momentum. And to do that, they used kappa units.

That didn't do my peace of mind any good. *Scattered dust of Evans / over clothes of heaven.* A kappa unit transferred momentum stored in tiny higher dimensions back into ordinary space. All parts of the object being 'jump started' must be acted on equally by the unit; otherwise, the result is an incoherent mess of differently speeding particles.

I fidgeted in my aisle seat. The spear-like shape of the jump ship only allowed for rows of two on either side of the aisle, so Rolliard was peering disinterestedly at the drones wandering over the hull of *Some Prefer Nettles*. Our jumper was too mundane and insignificant to deserve a name, only the number: J12.

'Nice. We've cast off,' said Rolliard.

I hadn't felt it. I gripped the arms of the seat and tried to look on the positive side. At least if the kappa malfunctioned, I'd be dead before I knew it. One moment I'd be there, and the next, gone.

6   Clocks drift in the night

Within a week, we had piggy-backed onto the *New Osaka,* a city-sized vessel that weaved its way between the stars at a good fraction of the speed of light. For that reason, it attracted a population of people who wanted to see the future. The common factor among them was not what they hoped for in the coming world but that they all agreed the present was a low point for humanity: they wanted out and used relativity to make it happen. *New Osaka* carried a crew of one hundred and fifty thousand permanent residents.

The *New Osaka* had a messy superstructure, rotating habitats, qubit factories, material warehouses and engines. *Wabi-sabi toy box.* A mass of iron and ice compacted together at its front provided a small planetoid of source materials.

Rolliard and I craned our necks to look at the ship's log in the open promenade, a sculpture in gold and crystal fibres strung from the ceiling, a living artwork, updated as the ship's history played out. The creation of the sculpture coincided with the start of an independent identity for the people of *New Osaka,* who turned out to be far more nationalistic than anyone I had known on Shang Lo. The ultimate insult on board was being told to 'go to sleep', referring to the short-term passengers entering medical hibernation for long periods. Their philosophy mutated from travelling into the future to the idea that *New Osaka* was the future.

It was the first place I encountered a true regional character. Osakans quickly became grim if you mentioned the outside government or the constant pressure to supply planets. An Osakan acknowledged their duties to the rest of humanity but with a mix of contempt that suggested everyone else wasn't pulling their weight.

To a certain extent, I had to agree. It wasn't until much later that I understood how vital the lifeline was that Osakans supplied. Their embattled mentality poured out in the art and music they spawned, severe and passionate; it was full of their wayfarers' cares.

Rolliard and I were lucky enough to have the option of hibernation or wakefulness. Passengers with cheaper fares were shuffled quickly off to the somnatarium, where they passed the eight-year voyage with a medical butler examining their body in cellular detail and excising any defects. In theory, a passenger woke up in perfect health, having only aged a day or two.

I made a late-night pact with Rolliard that we give ourselves a few weeks to get to know *New Osaka* before we settled into our deep sleep booths in the stowage of the vessel. The thought of lying down to drop into a coma for years turned my stomach.

Annie still chatted with me, using a tiny fraction of qubit material we had taken on board with us from *Some Prefer Nettles*. I sent her footage of the theatres, restaurants and music halls— I even sat respectfully in the back of a local government session as they graciously obeyed Robert's rules of order. Annie's replies came uncannily quickly from her longer time frame. She sent some crazy footage of a Cannot rally where every other person seemed to be an *Alone* victim, and of course, they ripped more lines out of *The Pollutant*. Quick, quick, slow.

I couldn't write anything in my usual fashion, so she became my video diary. *Sweet repository*. Like a petulant teenager, I put off my bedtime week after week. Instead, we watched the zero-gravity burlesque dancers kicking, hid in the back of a café to spy on experimental bodyists who spouted ecstatic visions of the future and even took part, in disguise, in an anti-Cannot rally because there were free drinks at the end. The fear of the CBG still haunted me; I thought that perhaps they might be able to reach out to *Osaka* and make another attempt to kill me.

The Osakans had an odd attitude to entertainment and insisted that their amusement be educational or horizon-broadening, pretty much the polar opposite of how I chose my amusement. The spacefarers shunned media you'd find in Shang Lo or even dull old Movampton as unfit for a futurist to waste their time on and watched plays that bordered on light entertainment with unease, searching out the educational or the morally rectifying. An eighth of a million people managed to culturally distinguish themselves from billions in humanity: they were freakishly remarkable to Annie, Rolliard and me.

A dozen other ships hurtled between stars, and I discovered that *Avant Le Mans, Denver, Río de las Estrellas* or *Nay Be'er Sheva* had futurist colonies of their own, but none so profound as the society of *New Osaka*. Annie found them too conservative for her rakish tastes, Rolliard respected them, but I loved them for their otherness.

It was only after the agreed date of our hibernation had passed its second anniversary that Rolliard let slip a critical fact that I should have suspected before.

'How much longer do you think you'll want to keep up this site-seeing?' he asked.

'What can I say? I'm enjoying myself. I know we sketched in a date for it, but I'm not stopping you, Rolly. No need to feel bad on my account.'

I happily sipped espresso while sitting 'outside' on the eight-o-eight-no-michi promenade. Rollaird looked into his g'tashi bowl as if it contained the world's woes.

'Ok. I just want to get there and get started on Border. Maybe you should think a little more about that too? We could be a long time out there.'

It was unlike Rolliard to give advice. *To the selfish, the hearts of the good lie open.* I put my coffee cup back down on the table. I had recently accepted that Rolliard was the conscience I should have been born with.

'I get the feeling you want to tell me something.'

'No, I really don't. It's not my business.'

It was as if the information were suddenly unveiled to me. The answer came to me with a jolt.

'Annie,' I said.

Rolliard's face didn't look up from the cloudy surface of his bowl.

'You should think about her,' he said.

'What do you mean think about her? I spend all my time thinking about her—most of it talking to her.'

'And she has much more time, doesn't she? Even if you spent every waking moment talking to her, she'd still be out living her life for seven days to your one. I don't know her, but I used to be Peace Core, and I've seen this before.'

Though it was painful, I pictured her sitting in that armchair: her spiralling, messy hair, wearing that manky bathrobe. I tried to imagine her just sitting, waiting for me to wake up each day. *Relationship dilation.* But I just couldn't picture it. Fiery, irrepressible Annie Bugatti wouldn't do that. She was under no obligation to be faithful to me, and like the rational, passionate person she was, she took care of her own needs wherever she saw fit. She'd had the odd casual relationship over the last few weeks and made no attempt to cover it up. I hadn't asked for the details. Every time we spoke, my messages were buffered, sped up and played back to her, and every time she replied, it was slowed down for me. I usually waited no more than an hour for something from her—she might wait a week or more to hear from me. *A flower reincarnate in the heavenly clothes of jazz.* She seemed always to be with me, always thinking about me, but she wasn't. At some point, Annie would find someone important. She had all the time in the world to do it. *When you go, my cold house will be / empty of words that made it sweet.*

'There's a pilgrimage along the length of the ship. Have you heard about it? It's like the Camino de Santiago. The first captain laid it out, I guess he was an Earther, who thought it would encourage people to reflect on their purpose aboard the ship and where they were going—I'd like to walk it before I go into hibernation.' Rolliard looked up at me, 'I think you should come too.'

Rolliard had a grave sense of right and wrong because of his deeply old-fashioned Peace Core upbringing. *He's misstra know-it-all.* He acted as a simplifying mirror, reducing events and principles to their bones. I looked at his face and saw a great deal of heartache in my future if I strung out my time with Annie into the strangest of long-distance relationships. She would be strong and sensible. I would be aggressive and jilted.

Within an hour, we had set off along the hundred-kilometre spine of the ship, a flimsy cardboard passport in each of our pockets to collect stamps from stalls, hostels, restaurants and bars along the route. I sent a message to Annie that we'd started the pilgrimage and that I wouldn't be in touch for a while.

A very long while, as it turned out.

7   We shall walk softly there

In three weeks, we hiked the meandering route of the deceased and possibly senile, first captain of the New Osaka.

All that wandering through steel corridors, humid green cropland, night boulevards and ballast canals taught me to travel. On Shang Lo, you were only concerned with getting to your destination or not getting hassled by crazies, with no change in the scenery or people. On the pilgrimage, we had to ask for directions and help. I saw a thousand hand-painted strange matter tanks in technicolour rows, and later that evening, as we stumbled along a street, we were invited to join a passing-out party where a couple's youngest son had become an officer of the ship. Rolliard had a one-night fling with a girl making the pilgrimage from the opposite direction. *Yet the jasmine season warms our blood.* This was travel in its truest sense, the accumulation of experiences and the point of arrival irrelevant.

In the last section, we walked for hours along the exposed observation gantries just because that was the way the old captain had said it should be done. Hours passed, walking side-by-side in silence, our steps causing the gantry to ring with a high metallic note. We saw the bright, motionless starscape above and to our side. Through the grating beneath our feet, more stars glimpsed through the superstructure. *Sparks on black.*

A sensation came over us while we travelled through the night; we were consumed by it, blanketed by it for hours. We became eyewitnesses to a story, a vast and unlikely tale that, though you knew it happened, you couldn't tell someone else and, you suspect, they would never believe you if you could. *Truth as encounter.*

We saw the forward section doors while at least a half hour's walk away from them, and as we neared, I spotted the mosaic of items that surrounded it, mementoes left by thousands of travellers at the end of their pilgrimage. Rolliard sorted through his pack for the Peace Core patch he had brought to the odd shrine, but I had nothing to leave. I'd so little of any personal value—only the paperweight of my Shang Lo possessions remained. It was a cumbersome family talisman, not what I'd choose to represent my pilgrimage; a necklace, lucky coin or photo from the trip would have been far more meaningful. It was my only possession, and I didn't want to leave it there because I wanted it to make it to Border.

Rolliard carried the brigade patch in his hand as we approached the doors. The gates were twice my height and surrounded by souvenirs. Apparently, some kind soul came out regularly with a ladder and moved items higher above the doors to make space within reach of new travellers. A tin box on the floor held tape to attach anything to the bulkhead. I watched Rolliard fix his regimental patch into a gap.

A cup and saucer, several poems on scraps of paper, lip balm, a cigar lighter, pictures of children and elderly relatives, a crucifix, a prayer mat, a wig, a medal, a pet's collar, a condom, colourful beads, dried chilli pods, an officer's epaulettes and hundreds of other items decked the walls. Yet, I had nothing to add.

I stood back while Rolliard enthused over his addition and sent a message to his friends, and then I remembered it was the kind of thing I'd loved sharing with Annie. I'd long ago given Rolliard access to my inner eye feed, so I held still and watched as he talked through me to his hundreds of brothers and sisters in arms, giving them a quick rundown of what we'd seen and done.

Somebody with a sense of pathos had programmed the door to open with three knocks; perhaps it was the eccentric first captain himself. Rolliard insisted that I step forward and take charge of the ceremonial deed. When the doors opened, they revealed a small area with an ancient, grey airlock leading to the command habitation. There were no fireworks or bright lights to walk into, just a final stroll through the corridors of bureaucracy to have our passports finally checked, stamped, and our names entered on the roll of pilgrims in a similar way to the office of the *Compostela* on the Iberian peninsula.

'Field of the stars,' blurted Rolliard as the officer on duty took his passport, itself just a souvenir with no political travel value.

'What's that?' I asked.

'Campus Stella became Compostela, it means field of the stars. I only just thought to look it up. Neat, don't you think?'

When I thought of our walk along the gantry, I couldn't think of anything more appropriate.

The officer directed us to a captain's office. *New Osaka* had twenty-five captains, and tradition dictated that all pilgrims completing the walk be met by one. She politely asked us how we had found the journey and listened from behind her desk as we delivered a concise summary. A change in her demeanour indicated that her proxy had updated her with an interesting item.

'You're the two candidates for the Border programme?' she asked.

'That's correct.' I said. Rolliard appeared to have problems speaking freely in front of high ranking officers.

'I doubt you can imagine the resources diverted to supply Border—as well as transporting you and the thousands of candidates from every other star. Around Shang Lo, the debate is on a low flame, but if you went to Mandela or Earth, the Cannots have armies of people taking to the streets.'

Her mention of the Cannot Be Grouped caused a slight flinch from Rolliard. I was intimately familiar with the current state of affairs with the rising sub-culture. My proxy fended off a hundred death threats every day from them.

'The Cannots will have to realise that Border isn't to blame for everything. Equally, it isn't the solution to everything,' I said.

'Only a few decades ago, I would have agreed with you, Mr Evans, but, as I said before, I don't think you are aware of the size of support mounted for Border, a significant percentage of the total human resources available. You won't find out easily either.'

'Perhaps I misunderstand you, captain—are you saying that we are investing too much in Border?' I asked.

She leaned forward in her chair.

'No, I'm not. You said Border wasn't the whole answer or the whole problem – I think you're wrong. Everything will pivot on what happens there. The *New Osaka* believes that with every soul in its body.' She spoke about the ship as a person without the slightest hesitation. 'If by any chance you are not aware of the gravity of your candidacy, whether it is pure luck or skill, I urge you to consider it fully now.'

She waved at an ensign to lead us away without waiting for a reply. It was a relief to leave the oppressive atmosphere of her presence. *Arid responsibility.*

We ate in *Chow One*, officially the furthest bow-ward restaurant in *New Osaka*. Before the food had arrived, I started the inevitable discussion with Rolliard of our impending hibernation.

'If she's right, then all this messing around is a waste of time. We should be working on speaking Para now,' I said.

'Feel free to try—I have—but let me warn you that everyone who's tried learning 'from the book', so to speak, has failed dismally. We get to Border a year or two after Spindle's return, and he's the man all eyes are on: the CBG hate him.'

Rolliard bobbed his head about, trying to see if our food was about to be delivered.

'Rolly, can I let you in on something? If anything we've heard is true, then we're doing something important, and frankly, I'm not good at doing important things. Describing a girl in an alleyway, sure, pondering on the meaning of life, I'm your man. But put the world on my shoulders and I'm a nightmare. I won't fumble through—I'll jam up. I'm the kiss of death to anything of significance.'

45

Music started over hidden speakers, we were eating during a low customer ebb, and the proprietor was flitting about the tables and chairs, laying out cutlery and tweaking decorations.

'Didn't you tell me that all you did was be yourself in the interview?' Rolliard asked while still hunting for any sign of food being brought to the table. 'Granted, you may have known through your gestalt pals that you were a sure thing, but that's the whole point here, isn't it? If everything we hear out of Border is true, then you have to have a natural aptitude before you can even start lessons in Para—there's only one teacher and only one class. Don't consider the other stuff. It's irrelevant.'

'Context is what I do, or used to do. I don't think I'm capable of shutting it out. For Feng's sake, Rolly, it wasn't that long ago that I was walking out of Ray Green's hospital.'

The food arrived, and there was no more talk for a couple of minutes, but Rolliard gave some thought to my comments.

'Look, I know you feel you can't handle it, but let me give you some soldierly advice – sometimes it's nice just to follow orders. You're not a poet anymore, right? So just follow my lead. We'll get the train back to hibernation, go to sleep, wake up, get down to Border and get it over with. No fuss. Stop using your brain.'

His words would have had more significance if he hadn't had a bundle of noodles dripping out of his mouth and been gesturing at his temple with a spork. He had hit the nail on the head. I wasn't a poet anymore, and I knew it. I'd known it ever since the moment I entered the doors of that hospital. Green taught me new patterns of behaviour. Life is just a game of dress-up. Today a writer, he'd said, tomorrow a builder, a thief or a parent. What good is a costume change if you don't acknowledge and invest in the role? The wisdom in following Rolliard's simple plan without fretting over the hows and whys dawned on me. *Private Evans Reporting.*

We left *Chow One* after a few drinks and got the train down the spine of New Osaka. Rolliard's new approach had one benefit that was immediately apparent to me: things got done far quicker. I did not stop to consider whether I felt like doing paperwork or a medical examination.

My proxy notified every contact of my status change before going into a long, induced slumber.

So, after months of living and enjoying the company of the people of New Osaka, I obeyed their most common insult: 'go to sleep'.

One hundred interviewees stood in rows of ten, filling the airy, seatless auditorium, which looked more like a gymnasium in its current format. *Chances of winning zero.*

Each hopeful candidate dressed in grey tang suits waited beside a floor mat as if we were about to start a morning tai chi session. The slim woman on the teaching platform wore a similar outfit but with a dark red sash indicating her ambassadorial rank. Beyond her shoji, paper wall segments lit by the morning sun of Border, formed the side of the building. A few door panels were slid open, allowing a sea breeze into the room and revealing the palms at the shore. *In winter, a palm / flowers green on Border through / a white paper screen.*

As I considered the view, a grey-haired man passed by my shoulder. He walked down the middle column with so little noise that he startled me. He climbed the platform with a light step and cordially greeted the woman. So this was Spindle, the legendary professor.

In profile, his hooked nose and sunken cheeks gave him a cruel look. I saw his elfin assistant stoop in to share a clandestine whisper. Spindle was the reason we were all there: the only person who could teach this topic, Spindle cast his net so wide for students that he would even see failures like me. The cynic inside me tried to reject the en masse interview process as a soulless factory, like a civil service exam. At the same time, the rest of me knew that something important was happening on Border. *To thine own self be true.* My demons expressed themselves well, but I had to find a way to make them shut up and focus.

It was a clean test, meaning no drugs or memory aides were allowed. When we arrived on Border, we were issued with our grey outfits; mine had 'Evans' tastefully embroidered on the lapel and collar as if to prevent swapping with another candidate, though what advantage that would give I couldn't imagine. It would be difficult to see how anyone could cheat. Some robomone, manufactured hormones, might have been handy. *Elegant Repetition* would have been ideal. Spindle faced us, the paradisal sun of Border on his back, an air of foreboding around him, the slight rustle of excitement in the group turned to silence.

'Where to begin? This is the critical question with a task as vast as learning the Para language. Para speakers communicate in a far more complete and expressive way than we do. Every tone, gesture, stance - even silence is a part of Para. Let us be clear about the difference between this and what might be termed 'body language' in our culture.' He gestured with beautifully animated expressions as he spoke, roaming the small stage in front of us and filling the hall with his presence.

'My face and hands express emotions that can enhance or contradict what I am saying to someone familiar with my cultural background. These motions could be easily misunderstood, and they are almost all subconscious. I added them without explicitly thinking, "I will knit my brow to tell these students I'm serious."

He demonstrated with a comedically serious frown that caused the braver in the audience to chuckle.

'In Para, this weakness common to all human languages was addressed in some early epoch. A Para speaker *always* means what they communicate with every sound, gesture or position, and they can express something additional and different with each *simultaneously*.'

Spindle allowed a moment, then another, for his words to sink into the audience and took up his thread again, firing his points at the waiting interviewees like a machine gun.

'A Para phrase reveals history, opinion, fact, conjecture, location and feelings—all in a statement similar to musical composition. But critically, through the art of Para, he will be perfectly understood in all these facets by another Paraunion citizen or perhaps even by one of you, should you reach the final goal of becoming an Ambassador.'

Spindle held out his hand, directing our attention to his assistant.

'Let us examine one answer to the question of beginnings. The neutral position is used only by very young Paraunion children before they master the parallel nature of the language, but it is an invaluable tool for us. Paraunion toddlers soon move onto a joined-up Para where there is no hesitation between one phrase and another, which allows a fugue-like carry-over of context from one passage to the next. To avoid this complexity, we will begin with neutral, then attempt to say something and move back to neutral. Dr Broulé, could you show us a formal neutral, please?'

The delicate woman nodded and switched to a vacant expression; she relaxed her posture and hung her arms by her sides. She did look very neutral, if not corpse-like, but I thought I could mimic it.

'Now we want to deliver the phrase "I am pleased to meet you". Imagine how you do this in your home language. We limit ourselves to selecting a pronoun, a verb or two, a noun, the tense, an action, the object and imply formality. Simple and sing-song: two great powers of our degenerate language. It's resilient to loss. A beginner might well drop some of the words or slip the tense and still be well understood. Naturally, you might just use body language, a bow perhaps, to introduce yourself. In Para, a bow is a particle of speech, so these shortcuts are out of the question. Dr Broulé, please show us the open formal position, which should be easier for our students to read. Please pay close attention.'

The assistant tilted her hands very slowly, palms pointed forward, her head bent down then back up with an alert look. She appeared lighter, gravity-defying. Good grief, we hadn't even got to 'I' yet. I felt myself being drawn toward her. Something about the economy and deliberateness of her movement magnetically drew my eye.

'Crudely speaking, this is an introverted beginning, a foreword to a statement regarding something of the self. Please use the mats beside you to practice moving from neutral to open. Dr Broulé and I will come around and assist. We will spend some time getting these points right. I ask that you remain silent as we do, remember every action, noise—even timing has meaning in Para—you must master doing *only* what you intend. We will add to this a simple Para version of "I". A concept we reduce to a single letter, Para details how the speaker wishes to be addressed and their feelings on the philosophy of self. For now, you will just copy Dr Broulé's rendition until such time as you are skilled enough to fashion your own "I".'

He gestured to Broulé again, who had returned to the neutral position. She repeated the opening but this time gently sang or spoke—I couldn't decide which—a modulated note or word. There were definite consonant and vowel noises, but they rolled gently over each other in a wave. *E pensando di lei / Mi sopragiunse uno soave sonno. And while I thought of her, came to me a gentle sleep.* Yes, like damn opera. Fascinating but distracting as hell while I tried to memorize her actions. *I would have watched her soul and body both!* I had to get my demons under control.

She repeated the phrase three more times, returning to neutral each time. I tried the hand motions while watching her. The soothing action seemed to provide a bit of inner quiet, so I went back and forth a few times, and before I knew it, Spindle and Broulé were down from the platform, getting candidates to emulate the action. I was no Para master, but I could tell from Spindle's gestures that he found most of the attempts painful.

I decided the hand motion might just be achievable, but I hadn't a chance with the head and words too. Was it even a single word? I hadn't a clue, and it seemed impossible. *I can do this.* I honestly didn't think I could do it. *I can do this.*

The moment of judgement came closer as Spindle moved along the students. He arrived at my row, only two people away. He blanked a girl whose performance was clearly beneath him—didn't even ask her to do it again—so I tried not to watch the next one, reasoning that it couldn't help my chances. The memory of the Osakan captain looking at our passports at the end of the pilgrimage came to mind. *You can't imagine how much is at stake*, she'd said.

Keep hold of yourself, I thought. *I can do this,* my innards retorted. Ah, of course, the perfect time for an ill-advised sense of confidence. There wasn't time to follow Green's advice now and make friends with my hallucinations.

Spindle stood before me. The forbidding aura was undiminished. I heard Broulé announce me as 'Evans – poet'.

In a surreal moment of fear, I felt the breeze cool my brow and saw the hot palms sway outside as a sea wind gently rocked them. It seemed as if I'd made Spindle wait for an age, and when I saw him cock an eyebrow at me, I tried to jump into the hand action, then partially remembered the head movement afterwards and ended warbling out some toneless noise. Spindle twitched with a suppressed reaction, but Broulé broke out in a laugh that she smothered with her sleeve.

'I apologise for my assistant, Mr Evans. Had you meant to say what you did, I would promote you immediately into the Border University. However, by way of an apology, why don't you try it again? This time perhaps say it to Dr Broulé?' They exchanged another amused look as I tried to appear neutral to Broulé. *I can do this.*

'You're a poet, Mr Evans?' Spindle asked.

'Used to be.'

'Then think of the whole style of the message as you saw it. You are expressing 'I' to Ms Broulé here. Let's go again, shall we?' Spindle sounded almost kind.

Again, I waited at neutral for an age until, in despair, I forgot what I was doing and managed to begin and end all three actions at once. *See me! Here I am.* I couldn't critique it. It felt closer. The guts of it felt right. Spindle didn't laugh this time; he thanked me and moved straight to the next unfortunate interviewee.

We all stood there in the neutral position until he had moved on to the row behind me. It seemed unfair to turn around and stare at the other candidates as they went through the same humiliation, so I just looked out of the open doors. *Sad poets watch through a grate: Spindle's shore.* When the two adjudicators arrived back at the podium, I was surprised by how little time it had taken to process all of us. Eight years travel for an hour in the flesh. Spindle raised his hand for our attention.

'I'm afraid there isn't enough time for me to thank you all individually for your efforts and sacrifices. Bear in mind that Para is not a facile undertaking. Ms Broulé will come back around while you take some well-earned refreshments and put you into tour groups for the University campus. Please enjoy our meagre offerings with my compliments.'

With that, he passed a whispered message to Broulé and made his egress through a screen door. From the back of the room came the rattle of trolleys. Everyone relaxed and looked about as if emerging from a trance. The porters set up a buffet fit for a king and beckoned people to come and get started without any formality. I spotted Rolliard already mooning over the contents of one of the dozen heavily laden trolleys.

I looked for booze but didn't see any available. When I went to pass a casual comment about it to Rolliard, I saw the tears in his eyes. The ex-marine had taught me more about the Paraunion and Para en route to Border than I could have found in weeks of research. *All our righteousnesses are as filthy rags.* My attempts at study gave me less insight than Rolliard's throw away comments. He was a true paraphile.

I wracked my brain for some small talk to distract him, but it was clear he was wound too tight from the assessment to respond. Still, it was good to stand near someone I knew.

'We don't really know what he was looking for,' I said.

'I know what disappointment looks like though,' Rolliard replied.

Broulé hovered, aware that she was interrupting our talk.

'Mr Evans, you're on the last tour at 1400. Cadet De Griffen? You're in the 1100 group. I hope that's okay? Don't let me disturb you any further.'

I watched her walk away. *She walks in beauty, like the night / of cloudless climes and starry skies.*

'She walks in what?' asked Rolliard.

Shocked that I'd let my halfwit inner self out, I covered the comment with something crass.

'The 1400 tour, I hope,' I said.

If you were coming in the fall

After the grand buffet, we were free to wander as we liked. Some candidates mingled and found out who was in their tour group. I slipped out through the front screens of the building, drawn by the glimpses of Border's seascape through the doors.

A plantation of tap palms generated power from sunlight and passed it through their roots back to the university buildings. The purple sheen on the broad leaves gave them away as machine-plant hybrids. The path meandered through the grove and down to the beach. Once clear of the trees, I saw silhouettes of other islands on the horizon, a handful of the tens of thousands that dotted the shallow ocean of Border. It was a world reproduced from a South Seas fairy tale, and I fell in love with it at first sight, not least because it was everything that Movey was not. A twinge of sadness hit me when I thought of leaving on the next shuttle.

The orientation had mentioned that failed candidates could apply for work at the university, even though there was no guarantee that they would be involved in the diplomatic programme. Maybe I'd apply. The situation with the Cannots hadn't calmed down; if anything, it was worse than before. My proxy filtered out a dozen death threats every day, and I couldn't imagine being safe for long on Shang Lo.

What would it be like here at dusk or at midnight or dawn? *Mamua, there waits a land hard for us to understand. Out of time, beyond the sun, in Paradise, all are one.* The *New Osaka* had awakened a thirst to explore and see new sights, an urge the Crush had stamped out of me. I sat on the dusty, crystal sand and ploughed my fingers through the warm grains. From the folds of the tang robes, I pulled my lucky charm, the dandelion paperweight, a sphere of glass no bigger than my palm. My only real possession. Discreetly, I buried it in the sand beside me, leaving a part of me in Border forever.

Abruptly, my inner eye told me it could see the net again: the security for the exam had lifted. It struck me that this was the first time in decades that I'd been disconnected from humanity like that. *Years without quiet. Weak tides.* Rolliard insisted that the Paraunion didn't have an equivalent of the net: maybe it was time to be more Paraunion.

After half an hour, the sea had only moved inches back and forth, so I walked along the shore. The artificial moon, faint and hovering over the horizon of the zealous blue sky, made frail currents in Border's oceans. *Clone moon.* I tore my attention away from the sea and wondered how the tour could be better than being alone on that beach. I'd always found sightseeing too orderly – you never see the things you aren't supposed to.

Behind the tap palms, the paper doors and walls of the university buildings struck me as odd: the architect had created a delicateness about the structure, but at the back of my mind was the feeling that the walls couldn't hold up the four stories above it. It looked like a house of cards. I recalled Rolliard boasting that Border's system was full of debris that regularly tried to smash into the planet, but there were swarms of drones out there. A titanic computer in the moon produced and guided all those little cleaners while its lunar home swept away other harmful objects and dust. All the same, the university didn't take risks—the campus could probably defend against a head-on strike if it had to. At that moment though, visually at least, it seemed like a strong wind might blow over the facility.

Hexagonal rocks made steps down from the building next to the diplomatic department, and a rugged woman in coveralls with a broom laid across her knees sat upon them. I thought it might be a good time to check my proxy and see if I could find out who she was.

A lot of rubbish had built up since I was last online—an unkind description considering it was primarily well-wishers and feeds I had signed up for. A bead of rain hit my shoulder, and I saw a tissue of high cloud in the sky. The rain fell in an odd, spaced-out manner. *Thin rain, weak tides, stillicide drops lament the prince.* I scampered up the steps to escape the rain towards the stranger.

'Don't bother going in. The rain here doesn't last long,' the woman said without making eye contact.

'Good to know. Thanks. You work around here?' I asked.

'Here and about. I keep the place clean. They call me the 'buildings and university logistics operator'.'

'Doesn't the place pretty much clean itself? No offence.'

'None taken.' She looked at me with her chin propped on the end of her broom. 'Yep, the building takes care of itself, but something always needs moving or checking. You've got to have a role nowadays—you can't just have a simple job. They don't understand that I don't want to play a role, you see? It's just social credibility and total employment nonsense—I want to lean on a broom all day—I'm Jones, by the way, pleased to meet you.'

I suppressed a smile. Coincidence had no fear of comedy or distance, it seemed, and our common distant heritage might buy me a few more nuggets of information too.

'Evans,' I replied.

We shook hands, and I took a seat on the steps just as the rain gave up and ceased falling. I exchanged a look of satisfaction with the cleaner. It seemed a shame to leave that place so soon. My proxy warned me that the tour was about to start.

'I've got to get along to this sightseeing group, then I'm probably off. Good luck with the broom Jones.'

Just as I headed away, I heard her reply.

'1400 tour, eh? Don't let that weasel push you around. When he stamps his feet and says, 'I want an answer!' you just stare him down. He does a lot of judging in very little time. Too eager by half to be back off with the Paraunion, I suppose. You know he's got a thing against humans, doesn't like coming back for recruits, even though he knows it has to be done.'

I gave her a grateful nod. Jones, in my estimation, didn't seem the type to waste words. Her meaning was a mystery to me, but I filed the comment away to mull over later. *Blind oracles laden Border.* Jones had an air of weary solidity about her.

I ambled back to the interview hall and saw four people there, all in the same grey outfits as myself. They looked over as I entered and welcomed me back. Just one of the refreshment trolleys was still present, dispensing self-service drinks. Five people seemed like a very, very small tour group.

As I began to fiddle with the urn, Broulé appeared. *Fearsome as an army with banners.* She smiled as we gathered around her like primary school children.

'Let me put your minds at rest. You're not going on the tour. I'm afraid for you lucky candidates, the interview process is a long way from over. We want to keep you here for at least another month if that's possible?'

She looked about to see if there were any objections.

'The teaching process will be sustained and intense. This is partly to do with the requirement for immersion in Para and partly because of the need for Professor Spindle to be in other places.'

I remembered Jones mentioning how eager Spindle was to get back to the Paraunion. Broulé glanced at the interview hall still equipped with the hundred floor mats.

'Let's move to somewhere more appropriate for our numbers.'

She took us through corridors dappled with sunlight and the aroma of cedar. I was stunned that I wasn't being shipped off until it hit me that Rolliard, assigned on a much earlier tour, wasn't going to be staying, and a wave of survivor's guilt struck me. He'd be sitting on the flight or in the waiting lounge, and he'd search about and not find me. I sent him a quick note, not sub-verbalised but written, thoroughly against Green's orders.

Picked to stay – so sorry, speak soon. You deserve this more than me.

I put the proxy to sleep again but felt a drowning sensation creep over me as I closed the inner eye app. For a moment, my whole being wobbled, as if I'd walked on slippery cobblestones without realising it. That way lay hell.

Broulé waved us through a door into a spacious classroom with four wooden benches lined in two rows on the slate floor. A Japanese stone garden with sand and raked spirals lay beyond the teaching area. Above the stone garden, the ceiling opened to the sky, making the whorls and stones almost luminous.

I could see that a getting-to-know-you session was imminent for us. *You're nobody till somebody loves you / you're nobody till somebody cares.* I would have pulled up my bio, but I wasn't sure it was a good description anymore.

Broulé chose one of us, a tall candidate with soot-black hair, and introduced him to the rest of us as Dale, then asked if he would stand and tell us about himself.

'I'm a generationalist,' he said. 'Our family has seeded moons and lived outside the government or law for a hundred years. By the time I was eighteen, I'd been in six land feuds.' He told us his story in a low, croaking voice, he didn't have much cultural credit to splash around, and I felt for him when he laid out his options.

'I'm lucky to be here. I know that,' Dale concluded. 'Everyone on the generation farms has been for the aptitude test for Border—just on the chance that it's a ticket out. I don't know how I'm going to get used to this much sunshine and fresh air.'

Next was a poli-lawyer called Marna Malverona. She expected us to have heard of her, and almost everyone seemed to nod in recognition. I guessed that they probably let their proxy fill them in on everyone's background information, and only a few days ago, I'd have done the same without a thought, but I was reluctant to return to being an inner-eye addict so quickly. *I have no ambitions or wants.*

'Border is a tremendously important project. Consider this one fact: only seventy-eight years ago, this system was a rock infested wasteland—today it's this.' She made an all-encompassing gesture. 'I never dreamt that I would participate in the program, but since I was advised to take the aptitude test, I've had an iron belief that it is my manifest destiny to serve politically on both sides of the Paraunion-human border.'

Had Marna been advised by a gestalt in the same way I had? Or perhaps some secret government project had tipped her off? She was a career poli-lawyer to the bone. I shuddered to think what questionable uses she could put the g-Russ to if she somehow gained leverage over them. Her words were ladened with gravitas about finding a new calling and the complicated political situation with the Paraunion. She repeatedly dropped hints that she knew more than she could say.

Finally, she shut up.

Broulé gave me an expectant look. *I tell you about the billions gone, clouded out of sanity, / besotted with life and crushed like dots on spheres that collide.* Proxies had undoubtedly given the other candidates a summary of my recent fiasco leaving Green's care. I struggled through telling them about being from Shang Lo, writing a briefly acclaimed poem and signing up for the Para programme as a chance to move into a different relationship with language. *Words cannot say / I had a break down / and moved away.*

Next, the graceful, elderly-looking candidate sharing my bench stood up. He bowed and cordially introduced himself as Ho Chow-Lutsk from the Labyrinth Language Institute, where he had taught for forty years as the head of the morphology department. He remarked that it was his honour to meet us. I immediately felt outclassed; the Labyrinth Institute had turned me down when I had applied, and Chow-Lutsk was a god there.

Last, a young woman who'd sat behind us introduced herself as Nian Zhen Delaware, a twenty-two-year-old from Alta Texas. Her confidence was effortless and frightening. She was looking for something to do before choosing a career, and as there were no age restrictions on applications to Border, she threw her cares to the wind and went for it.

'The night before my test, I dreamt about meeting a Paraunion and would very much like to see one for real,' she concluded.

We shook hands and exchanged pleasantries, but there was something new in the air.

Competition.

10   Because I do not hope

We rose at dawn.

The first order of daily business for candidates was to exercise. Access to the net was banned again, and the energy my brain had saved was noticeable. An internal sense of time returned without needing constant updates from my inner-eye.

Each of us had different ways to achieve that first objective of the day, to activate the body so the mind could receive lessons. I ran around the beach peninsula. I hadn't enjoyed it the first time, but a hypnotic flow had emerged. My feet sought out the harder sand where it was easier to run, and my mind emptied while my breathing steadied. *Zen and the art / of archery / were never part / of this treachery.* Even my demons were more in harmony with my thoughts.

I passed the pontoon bridge to an adjacent island and kept my eyes open for Chow-Lutsk on his balcony. The previous day I'd had to go and wake the old bird, who was not a morning person, a common trait of great thinkers. I spotted him on the gallery going through some weary tai-chi moves, though the nodding palms on the shore looked far more in tune with the universe.

Sometimes, I would catch sight of Marna in the ocean, cutting through miles of water or Dale, who clubbed a punching bag senseless up on the roof gym.

The path by the low cliff took me around the back of the grand interview hall, where Nian practised gymnastics. Her speciality was the floor exercise, where she defied gravity with lift and speed. She tumbled and arched through the air, all executed with a look on her face so passive that you'd believe she had walked casually from one corner of the great square to another.

If Spindle was telling the truth, all of us could pass and become Ambassadors. The institute needed hundreds, but there were only two in existence: Spindle and Broulé. As the sand passed under my feet, I worried that the task of learning Para was so mountainous that none of us would make it.

We studied Para shorthand, Spindle's invention to make notes on a Para speaker without learning the incomprehensible and equation-like written language, which remained a closed book to human scholars. As so much was said in parallel, the observer only had a split second to see and note the elements, so augmented reality programmes helped us annotate movements into Spindle's eight-stave system and convert it into his coda notation, a pidgin Para. I'd become worryingly reliant on the coda, waiting for the programme to deliver a boiled-down human version of the dialogue rather than reading it directly.

In the complete eight-stave output, a fluent Para speaker might be able to record nearly all of what was said. Coda gave a crippled shorthand version that hinted at the gist of the conversation. The university's transcripts only appeared in the abridged coda because that audience knew almost nothing about Para, no matter how much they might protest otherwise. Spindle frequently made spiteful jokes about them in Para, none of which we translated. Being in a Para conversation was like listening to an orchestra; the coda was like reading a short review the next day.

I pounded along the last stretch of beach and looked out to sea to take my mind off my legs. Vertical clouds formed pillars above the ocean, hanging down from the sky to the water like thin statues. I felt a twinge of embarrassment when I remembered the Cannot in the crumpled suit at the partycast—an oasis for the elite—that's what she'd called Border. It looked precisely that way right now, but this was how the Paraunion had ordered their embassy planet to be built.

I upped the tempo of my stride and headed towards the outline of the embassy forum. I mounted the stairs, still running, and clambered my way to the agora platform, built to hold several thousand attendees for presentation ceremonies and meant, one day, to receive a Paraunion guest speaker.

Jones sat on a bench with a look of amusement on her face. A breathless nod was all I could manage, the blood pounded in my ears, and I bent double with my hands on my knees. She tapped me on the shoulder and handed me a glass of cold water. *Our ways so much less mysterious than Hers.* I gulped the water down and gestured my thanks, but she had already turned around and walked away, going about her business whistling some old hymn.

I'd had no time to consider events outside Border; my world became that of a disciplined student. I learnt. I obeyed.

Once recovered, I headed back to my room to shower and dress in grey robes. Spindle was always the first to the lecture room, and I wondered if he was gleaning something from our arrivals. *Paranoid punk no more.*

The stone garden room was sunny and pristine, and as usual, Marna, Dale and Nian had beaten me there. We waited patiently for two minutes until Chow-Lutsk arrived, looking like a confused first-year. There wasn't the slightest sign of impatience on Spindle's face, but he began the lesson immediately.

'From now on, we will immerse ourselves in Para. There will be no exceptions, not because I want to torture you, but because you must know how to respond while under pressure, a vital survival skill in the Paraunion.'

O Lord, I thought, the spoon-feeding is over. *I love the spoon.* I needed the spoon. Spindle set himself to the most obvious neutral I had ever seen him take. A sign of the opening of an era. *We few, we happy few.*

¤ Perhaps you've guessed how difficult it is for me to teach and not be in the Paraunion, but you are our greatest hope. Race and gender, as you have known them, are useless concepts. Danger in the Paraunion comes through movements and alliances, but they have no conception of individuals taking action based on race or sexual background. The difference between one citizen's genetic roots and another is commented upon only medically or if it were to pose a temporary impediment—like the shape of Evans's head. ¤

The only section I got was 'Evans's head'. The augmentation let me see it all again as a transparent ghost of Spindle with the stave and coda notation parsed underneath, but by the time I vaguely understood, I was seconds too late to join in with the laughter of Chow-Lutsk and Nian.

Spindle showed no sign of letting us catch up by waiting for the coda, the cheat notes.

¤ Today, I'll introduce you to the concepts of charges, masters and classic archetypes as the Paraunion use them. The Para terms charge and master can be troubling; you must listen carefully to the context in which this relationship is phrased to deduce if it is a downward or upward power connection. You must shake off any negative—or positive—connotations that you may have about these terms. We aren't considering human history or culture.

¤ The standard direct translation of a charge as "slave" may confuse and upset. Still, no other word in our language transmits the absolute power and responsibility that a master has over his charge. However, even this remains highly inaccurate, and only the Para phrase sums it up. "Child" is too optional and temporary and implies a genetic interest. "Ward" is too impermanent. Eventually, you must accept that the Para "charge" is a wholly new thing and tacitly learn the good and bad aspects. Equally so with "master". You should pity the non-Para speaker trapped outside these concepts.

¤ Our second cultural basic is the use of an archetype. The concept of a classical type is found in our ancient literature and philosophy but not in the all-permeating way that Para speakers use it. Aristotle was referred to in ancient texts as "the Philosopher" with the assumption that all readers would associate this role directly with his arguments. At the mere mention of "the Philosopher", a classical human reader should conjure up that incredible thinker with all his political and scientific opinions. These archetypes were assumed to be wholly understood by the reader, so it is with every Para archetype.

¤ William of Ockham, the theologian and logician, was known as "Worthy Beginner": *Venerabilis Inceptor* because the dean disliked his methods and refused to graduate him, ironically elevating him to a less fleeting title. "The Philosopher" himself and his student Theophrastus attempted to make a system of all the character types that could exist in drama and developed thirty general classes, beginning formal literary criticism and psychology. Imagine if the whole human race had taken part in that project and continued it for all the centuries since. For the Para, there are thirty-nine of these stock, dramatic characters and they are used primarily so that discussion can be impartial and without giving offence. It's common for a speaker to attack his central argument with these personalities to show that his logic is battle-hardened. ¤

I tried to keep up, but even with the augmented reality program ghosting him, Spindle lost me. I panicked, and my hands began to sweat. I switched to simply recording as he described Para's iconic characters and hoped that some of the hurricane of information was sticking.

The sound of Marna crying came from somewhere to my left, but Spindle didn't stop. She was escorted from the room by Broulé while Spindle paused and then returned to neutral. I looked at the remaining students, who all wore ashen expressions. Spindle launched into an explanation of the contract system amongst the Para where every person is another's master and also somebody's charge—creating a strange power network that harnessed self-interest and society's benefit. *Equally enslaved diamonds.*

¤ You see how this interweaving system of distributed masters and servants, each utterly answerable to the other, creates desirable natural results. In the Paraunion, if Mars declared war on Earth, Martians who have charges on Earth could stop them from fighting. This power network is referred to in Para as the "Graph", and it does not allow for such one-sided biases.

¤ In a citizen's life, they eventually acquire three charges and are legally responsible for the health and wealth of that person; the possessions of the charge are entirely at the disposal of the master. ¤

The compound noun used by Spindle to refer to the sex and position of the master caused my translator to stammer with an overload of possible meanings, which it tried to solve by suggesting hundreds of contexts. It ceased to be helpful as a real-time tool.

Perhaps that was the real intention of the lesson.

Spindle pointed at me and instructed me to sit over to the side of him. I slowly grasped that he was arranging us into a typical Para scenario. Some sat or stood at angles to the speaker, and some leaned on walls. Each position offered the speaker the chance to say something about what they heard. I wondered where Marna had gone, I'm sure the same thought tortured the others, but we were forced on and on by the relentless teacher.

In shock, I realised I would need to record everyone in the group and then replay them all in the coda to have any hope of understanding what was going on in the multi-layered conversation. Total failure was imminent.

Spindle began in unabridged Para, twice as dense and complex as before and a deluge of information that I lost track of within a dozen seconds. The AR programme eventually produced a stilted coda, which I tried to scan quickly and hoped would leapfrog me back into Spindle's lecture as it happened. It was a hopeless battle.

¤ The "Lucid Jester" considers things preordained, meaning that events can be looked at without a personal attitude, resulting in the ability to find any situation funny, no matter how horrific. All events are within scope for his clowning. He argues that by laughing at the details of the horror of life, the grand carnival, we attain an understanding denied to people who find it unbearable to deconstruct tragedies. ¤

Spindle guided us to confirm we understood some part of his speech by a gesture, a change of stance or a phrase. There were choices for using vocal, hands, full-body or the position relative to the group. Some "registers" were available to humans, but more existed for different body types. *Yacketayakking screaming vomiting whispering facts.* We had transferred without warning or precautions from a child's version of Para into something far more profound and complex, dumped from a paddling pool into the sea.

¤ "The Temptress", or with her full title "The Temptress In White Clothing", appears to be an outmoded sexual stereotype to our eyes. All of you would sway away from opinions backed by ritual virginity and sexual determinacy. Take a moment to consider some points. First, no archetype is deemed to be right or wrong in themselves. They are used to view the argument under discussion from different points of view. Second, the Temptress is respected as one of the most paradoxical figures and, therefore, a powerful tool for highlighting paradoxes. Third, sexuality as an aggressive movement is irrelevant in a culture where asexual, polysexual, transexual, hive and many other arrangements are all included—not just included but deeply understood with individuals migrating across sexes or changing sexual systems. So, though there is no sexual politics, there is a rich exchange of sexual philosophies.¤

Spindle leant one hand against a stone pillar and folded his arm behind his back. Para came from him so naturally that he could afford additional gestures.

¤ Citizens must understand the needs of others because they are masters and charges to people in other cultures and arrangements. The Paraunion is a society encompassing all walks and beliefs. Unfortunately, there is no time to initiate you in comparative cultural theory but consider, how would a driven businesswoman of our culture learn to decide what is best for a sensitive teenage boy? What goals might a male poli-lawyer set for a life-basic neverrider or glitterbeast while keeping their true best interests at heart? What happens if that sensitive teenage boy at his majority becomes the master of the polilawyer? I hope you see that cultural understanding and empathy are critical subjects for the Paraunion; not being tutored in their fine points is to lack one of the necessities of civilisation itself: the understanding of *other* civilisations. ¤

I lost hope of understanding the whole scenario, even with all the tools at my disposal, when the professor laid off meaning into the posed students, using their reactive attitudes to create a fugue-like argument that continued to state itself all around me. He conjured the opinions of the "Lucid Jester" and the "Temptress in White Clothing" against and into the conversation.

By the end, Spindle slowed to a near Para silence and then posed a very readable ethical problem of an orphan becoming the master of a pregnant adolescent.

¤ I want an answer from each of you immediately. In this case, who is correct? The Jester or the Temptress? ¤

I heard an answer from Dale, but as I'd long since given up trying to track anyone but Spindle, I couldn't tell which choice he'd made. At the same time, I sensed from our teacher's movements that he acknowledged answers from Nian and Chow-Lutsk. *I know that I know nothing.* I crossed my fingers behind my back and hoped to heaven that Jones knew what she was talking about.

It was a fifty-fifty question, the Jester or the Temptress, and I could have guessed. *Jones over gold.* Instead, I stood up from the stone bench and carefully stood at neutral, despite the waves of pressure I felt from both the students and the teacher. I thought I heard the crackle of time passing in my ears.

¤ Correct Evans! You have no opinion and very little understanding of this complex and heated subject to the Parunion. Now I must go and talk to poor Marna. 'Nothing' is the correct answer. Humility is highly valued by the Paraunion. All: please review this conversation for details that you haven't grasped. Dale, would you come with me, please? ¤

Chow-Lutsk came over and offered his hand to me in congratulations, which I shook half-heartedly. His face gleamed with sweat, and his frame bent from the strain of our baptism into full Para. I wiped a sleeve across my brow and noted the damp stain left on the grey material.

Behind him, Nian faced the sand and stone garden with her head bowed and her arms dangling at her sides. It was the only time I had ever seen her spirit broken.

Chow-Lutsk followed my gaze over his shoulder, and we both went over to give her a pep talk. Only then did I realise how jealous I'd been of this young, polite, wholesome girl and her innate ability. *What a piece of work is man.*

*

On the main island, there was a bar.

It was the only lively spot on the whole planet, not counting virtual places, of course, but then we trainee ambassadors had no net link. I might even have said that the withdrawal symptoms were beginning to wear off. The habits of a lifetime took a long time to fade. I realised how much of my time I had spent crafting mundane nuggets of information to share with my friends and the rest of humanity. *Once a day update tool / that publishes pictures of your stool.*

Since Spindle's lesson in humility, we had been allowed to relax a little. The campus bar was the only place where we could blow off steam and take a short-lived break from our total immersion into Para. Even so, slight gestures and cadences of the supra-cultural language sneaked into our ordinary conversations.

The bar contained the good and bad of human-on-human action. The customers elected music, and a virtual overlay of the bar would have shown which people were looking for others: for sex, food, discussion, or any other pursuit. I had to imagine that for myself without my proxy.

None of the Para candidates, cut off from virtual activity as they were, had a say in the songs or knew why anyone else was there. A minor niggle to everyone except Marna, who found the idea of not expressing her musical view unbearable. She seduced a middle-aged climatologist and then got him to describe the jukebox list so she could put his votes on her choices.

Nian and I chose to get our kicks from a mixture of coohlol and mematonin cocktails. Chow-Lutsk sat opposite and dispatched a respectable amount of whiskey without concern that we would have to be up again the following day for more punishing exercises and lessons. Detox pills only did so much, and there were no weekends for us. When I raised an eyebrow over the amount he was putting away, he smiled at me.

'Let tomorrow's problems happen tomorrow,' he said.

I saw Dale standing at the bar on his own. Nian paid him a visit to see if he wanted to join us but quickly returned after being told in no uncertain terms that he wanted to be alone. I caught his distracted profile in the light from the bar's lights: lost deep in thought, or perhaps he'd managed to reconnect his link or both.

Marna attracted a crowd of people around her, so we didn't feel the need to invite her to our little table, and she wouldn't wait to be asked if she wanted to join anyway.

The bar nestled in the basement of the giant university faculty building, a self-service affair with a long counter that could be staffed in case of busy formal functions. Unlike bars or clubs in Movampton, it had plenty of space for different groups to spread out, and with the dim lights and music, there was a reasonable amount of privacy. In Shang Lo, you would've been shoulder-to-shoulder with strangers and friends alike.

Some academics recognised Chow-Lutsk and introduced themselves, and he politely presented us as his fellow ambassador candidates. With them, I was delighted to see Rolliard.

He told me how he'd begged to get a role, anything, at the university and been given a trial on the team handling public relations. I took great pleasure in telling Nian about our adventures on the *New Osaka* and loudly made it clear that I thought Rolliard was far more knowledgable on Para than the linguists from the university.

'You probably haven't heard about the Jakobmann platform then?' Rolliard asked after we'd caught up.

'We're completely off the net, I'm afraid,' Nian replied.

'A small army of Cannots took over the whole installation and started demanding relocation.'

'Relocation where?' I asked.

'To a decently formed planet. Failing that, they wanted permission to board the *Rio del Estrella* and settle here.'

'Here? To Border?' asked Chow-Lutsk.

'Yeah, the same old argument: a whole planet shared by only a few hundred thousand people should be divided out to the needy. They don't seem to have thought about how they would get here or that there's almost no land on Border. They just want the institute shut down to make way for them.'

'If I understand the CBG manifesto, and I'm not sure anyone does, they don't care about the Paraunion. Don't they reject them entirely?' Nian asked.

'Luckily, the captains of the big twelve think differently. The *Rio* warned them several times to release control of the platform. When it became clear they wouldn't give up easily, it re-plotted its course to steer away from the whole system. So both *Rio* and the whole Piper system will be unsupplied for seven years,' Rolliard said.

'They're going to blackout? That's horrible!'

'It won't come to that, but there'll be years of information rationing. They have to make three years' worth of qubit material last for seven. Last we heard, the Cannots on the platform were negotiating with Ioline, the parliamentary habitat, for someone to send them rations. There's talk in the system of having a referendum over whether to outlaw the Cannot Be Grouped.'

Rolliard shot me a glance that said: you and I know this means trouble. I'd considered the members of the CBG a bit of intellectual fun up until that fateful party at Annie's, an odd bunch who wanted to be outside the norm, like other novelty movements. A part of me even sympathized with them, although I often used that part to lure hardcore believers into saying silly things.

'You can't outlaw the Cannots,' I said, 'it's like telling teenagers not to have weird thoughts and listen to bad music—they do it anyway and, very occasionally, they're right.'

'An underground movement would be a catastrophe,' agreed Chow-Lutsk, 'it would veil the conception of the CBG with a kind of mystique that it has no right to.'

Nian nodded her accord with the old lecturer and added in a hollow voice, 'Think of giving the order for the *Rio* to miss the star, knowing that you're dooming your crew to all kinds of shortages.'

I remembered the captain we'd met on the New Osaka.

'From what I've seen of them, the people on those ships will think of it as an inconvenience, but buckle down. The billions on the planets and habitats, well, they're a whole different question. They aren't used to thinking of themselves as a separate entity that can be cut off: I wasn't. With the net, we all seemed to live on the surface of one enormous planet; without it, the illusion fades, and you see how many poor souls there are in basic, how everything's built with the cheapest materials, and how little we all have.'

'You think there'll be a revolution of some sort?' Rolliard asked.

'You'd have to talk to Marna to figure that out.'

He looked over to the large group, listening to Marna grand-standing and then back at Nian and the rest of us.

'I don't think I'm that interested in her opinion,' Rolliard said, then a strange expression crossed his face. Something in his inner eye had caught his attention. The proxy was relaying information to him.

'What's up?' I asked.

'Some journalist who passed himself off as a Cannot has just released a load of new material onto the net. I hate to tell you, but the hijackers' broadcasts from the Jakobmann platform include a lot of *The Pollutant Speaks* in their double talk. There's a video of them having services where they sing verses like a communion prayer. It's pretty strange.'

Revolted, I wondered if this had been coming for some time. Had I known that the Cannots were gradually spiralling more and more out of control and mistakenly thought of them as a bunch of dangerous, experimental kids?

'So the CBG have found a different source for their required air of mystique anyway,' said Chow-Lutsk.

'This is crazy. They can't do this! They can't just bend what I write to say whatever they want!' Outrage gripped me in the stomach. 'What are they going to do when I denounce them? They must know I'm out here on Border!'

Chow-Lutsk stood and put his hand on my shoulder. I hadn't realised that I was on my feet and had shouted in Rolliard's face.

'Look, I know you're just the messenger,' I said to him. 'Sorry.'

Rollie graciously accepted my apology.

'I'd get on with that denouncement as soon as possible,' Nian commented.

'It's never helped in the past.' Rolliard noted, 'It's not just that, there's a counter-movement starting against everything that the CBG touches or mentions. It's pretty vague at the moment, polilawyers and the culturally well-to-do, but it's growing teeth. It isn't clear they're backing the Border project, but they want to put the Cannots down like a bunch of animals.'

'There's always some that feel the answer is to cut the heart out of their enemies,' Lutsk shook his head sadly.

The bar suddenly felt humid, so I excused myself and walked across the footbridge, then along the starry beach. Black wavelets nudged the shore. Everything about Border was peaceful. I loved it so much; who could blame those platform refugees for wanting to be brought there? The rage I'd lost control of in the bar was a symptom. I was sympathetic to the Cannot. *The Pollutant Speaks* was written for the likes of them. *...turned out on the street: Wingate, Henry, Johnny Po-lotti and Mayday Susie of the hundred tricks, / West gong, Lovedreary: masters of sex, dreams and escape.* Their problems were real. Without ways to pacify the population of the Piper system, others would realise that the rebels weren't crying over nothing. Even though every action the CBG took turned out badly, and the conclusions they drew from the problem of the Crush were wrong, they might just bring attention to the billions abused and neglected in life-basic.

It was easier to accept the CBG as lunatics than admit they worked from beliefs I held dear and used them to justify every action I was absolutely against. *Good seed / cold soil / bad water.*

I wondered whether to make a statement on the net about my opposition to their actions. If I said that I disapproved of the use of the *Pollutant,* I would immediately be cross-examined over whether I thought they were wrong. Any answer other than a straight yes would be seen as covertly adding fuel to the fire. At least being in training on Border gave me a reasonable excuse to be silent for a while. I put my feet in the wet sand and willed some of the peace of Border to flow up into me. What I had considered the happiest period of my life had been brought to an abrupt end. Try as I might, I could not persuade myself that I had no responsibility for the situation—they were, after all, my words.

'If you want advice, you should speak to Spindle,' came a voice from behind me. It took a while for me to make out the seated outline of Jones in the night shadow of a tap palm. 'He's been a figure of controversy for years. You've got to hand it to him. He plays the part well.'

'I don't think I'm ready to share with my tutor,' I said.

Jones got up with a groan and dusted the sand off her trousers. She started plodding back toward the training building and called over her shoulder.

'No man is an island, Mr Evans.'

11   And when the music stops

¤ Playing the game, ¤ Spindle announced with several adjunctive gestures, indicating this was an informal phrase. ¤ If you want to get something done inside the Paraunion, you need support. You have to play on the most complex board devised: the Graph. ¤

Each of us tried to pick up hints of subtext the professor threw into each clause of his speech.

¤ Support needs to be proportional to the size of the task. Say, for instance, you want a house built, a minor matter and probably only requiring two or three backers. But suppose you want to create a new exploration university. You might need hundreds or thousands of supporters, and then there's the possibility of opposition. Any opposition is deducted from whatever support you have, meaning that you need enough backing to out-weigh the opposition by the number required to approve it in the first place. ¤

Spindle looked up through the opening in the ceiling at the clean blue sky, then down at the patterns of sand around the rock just before his feet. Decoy gestures: not part of the conversation.

¤ It's easy to see that things can take centuries to be decided. When there's a stalemate on an important decision, the Paraunion refer to this as a vrys: there's no direct translation. I find it best to picture it as a long-term storm in the weather system of Paraunion politics. A vrys is as chaotic as a weather pattern. ¤

Dale seemed unusually animated over the discussion of vrys. He asked more questions in that single session than I could remember him doing in all the previous training. Marna was lifted slightly by the discussion of politics, even if it was of an alien form, but struggled to escape from stilted, child-like Para.

Lutsk, Nian and I observed.

It was doubly cruel that the truth boiled to the surface when speaking Para because of the expressiveness of the language. The most a determined liar could hope for in a conversation was to suppress information. Outright falsehoods showed up as inconsistencies in the speaker's context about their feelings, hopes and concerns. *I made my song a coat / Covered with embroideries / Out of old mythologies / From heel to throat.* The truth we could not avoid while watching Dale and Marna was that they were both failing, Marna far more so.

¤ What do the Paraunion do in the event of external war? Who decides how much to throw at the enemy? Can a master order all his charges and his charges' people to support it? ¤ Dale clumsily packed his multi-part questions into a few bulleted Para phrases.

¤ Internal war as we know it is unheard of, except among a few species that require it for reproductive purposes. War from outside of the Paraunion? I'm afraid that's one of the details we still don't know. Like so much that is at the most exciting end of studying the cosmically significant races of the Paraunion: it's not that we're being denied the knowledge, but we don't even know what to ask.

¤ As for ordering a slave to command his slaves and so on, it is considered a breach of rights in the Paraunion constitution to interfere with your slave's own master-slave relationship. ¤ Spindle reflected all the questions onto Marna so he could see if she was keeping up.

Learning Para was like walking into the eye of a storm. One moment you're half-blind and struggling. The next, you're in the calm epicentre and you see the cyclone raging around you. What happens if you don't find the middle of the storm? I wondered. What if the cacophony of meanings and suggestions never made sense? You would stumble around and around in ever more confused circles.

That was happening to Marna.

Lutsk, Nian and I sat to one side, safe in the knowledge that we had found the quiet heart and, as much as I disliked her for being arrogant and self-important, I couldn't bear to watch anyone so lost, slowly losing their mind.

Marna was a painful sight because Para let everyone see her confusion. Everyone in the room knew that Marna was on the verge of being dismissed from training for her own mental wellbeing as much as because she hadn't made the grade. We watched it come into the conversation, slow and inevitable.

'That's enough, I think,' said Spindle, switching out of Para as a small mercy to the defeated candidate.

Marna sat down on one of the benches, hollow-eyed with exhaustion, too expended to cry or protest. Nian got up to comfort her but stopped just a few paces away from the poli-lawyer. There was a strange aura around Marna, like when you pass a boyzoid in Movampton. You don't know whether they want to stab you, sell you something or just haven't noticed you at all.

Spindle called Broulé into the room while Dale went down on his knees in front of Marna. He looked into her eyes, but there was no reaction at all.

'I think she's loaded *Alone*,' he said.

Far too late, I stepped in and tried to help.

'Marna,' I shook her by the shoulders. 'Marna, come on, it's over. Look how far you got. You should be proud. I know you can still feel a little of what's going on. Come out. We'll all go over to the bar—would you like that?'

There was no response, just as if she were an instant coma patient. *Or etherized upon a table.*

'It's me next, isn't it?' Dale growled. 'Look at you three, smug and safe. You never gave a crap about Marna or me. You knew we'd never make it, didn't you?'

'That isn't how it is,' Nian said.

'Don't think I didn't see you helping each other out. So I'm not in your little club, eh? No space for a moon-seeder in your gang—is that it?' Dale had pulled himself up to his full height, and he seemed to fill the whole classroom. 'I thought we were supposed to *drop all cloaks,* Evans?' Dale quoted *The Pollutant Speaks* at me. 'No special favours, no daddy's girls, no "sorry but you weren't born in the right place"?'

Through broken teeth / the pollutant speaks. I tried to adopt a pacifying pose. Was this something that Dale had thought all the way through training, that we were against him? Or had it popped into his head under pressure? I thought he'd hit me when he moved forward, but he pushed past and out of the door.

Spindle was forced to back peddle and re-enter the room to avoid being flattened by the exiting generationalist. Broulé followed close behind, dauntlessly set on calming him.

Nian sat by Marna and told her quietly how much we all cared about her and how worried we were. Lutsk kept his seat in the back of the class; we exchanged a Para gesture, which might translate roughly to "I don't want to be in the way, and I don't think either of us can help".

Lutsk looked at the doorway through which Dale had so recently disappeared.

¤ There's more going on with that boy than it seems. You appear to particularly aggravate him. I'm also sure he's better at Para than his progress suggests, ¤ Lutsk noted.

¤ I didn't realise I'd made so many enemies, ¤ I said.

¤ Oh, worse than that, I'm afraid. ¤

I looked at the chunky old academic to see if he was making a joke at my expense, but his expression was severe, and a flood of weariness rolled out with his breath. He adjusted his grey tunic before continuing.

¤ If not very nearly, then very actually, he loves you. Perhaps not in a facile physical way, but unrequitedly and without stint. Haven't you noticed how he never talks over your opinions but is quite happy to go headlong against everyone else? Even Nian, who, as we both full well know, eclipses us in wit, compassion, beauty and intellect, is nothing in his eyes. ¤ He glanced across the sunlit stone benches to where Nian knelt.

I was, not for the first time in my life, blindsided by the idea that I was somehow special to another person.

¤ Maybe Dale's got a point? The three of us are a mutual admiration club. We could have unintentionally left him out in the cold. Why didn't I spot it before? ¤

¤ You see that? I give you an answer, and you swallow it whole! Think Evans! There's more at work here than just that. Life is a gruesome play. Our road is likely to be precarious. We must find out what's going on inside us before we meet with the Paraunion, ¤ he paused in thought and then said with a wink, ¤ It's easy to be wise in love when you're a dried-up old fruit. ¤

I patted Lutsk on the shoulder and went out to search for Dale along the beaches and pontoon bridges in the quiet afternoon. Wherever he had gone to be alone, none of us managed to spot him for the rest of the day. If I'd spoken to him, perhaps I could have saved us.

12   In the well of a wave

I ran back across the pontoon bridge between the training institute and the main island. My bare feet made a different note every time they landed above one of the support tanks. *Pap pap pap pum pap pap pap pum.* I had switched to barefoot running a week before. Now I couldn't return to running in shoes. My efforts to predict Border's weather had turned out to be less reliable than tossing a coin. There weren't any of those eerie head-shaped clouds about at the moment, just a few high white sprites. I predicted it would be hot with patches of thin rain in the afternoon. *Weather, whether, weather.*

Training had carried on since the incident with Marna, and none of us spoke about it, though it was frequently a Para subtext, even in Nian, though most commonly in Dale.

Running gave me a lot of time to reflect, and this was its greatest downfall. Over the months, I'd fallen in love with Border: it wasn't to everyone's taste, but I liked the simplicity: run, learn and rest. *Repeat.* There were no days off. *Three hundred and fifty Wednesdays a year.*

My route turned off the bridge, along the beach and up to the ceremonial platform, keeping the pace constant, eating up the distance.

Jones sat with a glass of water beside her. I gave her a word of thanks before I picked it up and drained it; no more was I bent double on the finish line. She plodded off about her mundane business without a word. I wondered if that was so that I didn't hear an un-Para syllable and spoil the immersion we had endured for the last few days? Was Jones under orders? *Orders, proffers, Jones.*

Shortly after exercise came classes. Classes in such a relentless regime that soon it was oddly uncomfortable to be anywhere other than the sparse half-open teaching area with its simple benches and sand garden. It was only in that room that you weren't rushing to get to, coming from or revising for work. All life was satellite to the hours spent listening to and trying to gain approval from Spindle.

Nian came the opposite way along the corridor. She wore the grey tang suit with a savour-faire I put down to her annoying youthful adaptability. We arrived at the door of the stone garden classroom precisely at the same time and struck up a conversation in Para, having both recently cracked parallel phrases. We talked while the other spoke, which would have been odd to hear in our native tongue, both chaotic and rude.

¤ Again! Exactly to the stride. Did you speed up, or did I slow down? Synchronicity at work. ¤

¤ To the stride. Again! How many is that – five days? I didn't speed up. I tried to ignore you to see whether it would still happen again. Synchronicity at work again! So, to work then. ¤

I gallantly waved her in through the door ahead of me, and we saw Broulé and Spindle deep in conversation with Jones.

'Have you seen Dale?' Jones asked.

¤ Not since last night, ¤ we both replied. Then dropped the accidental Para and repeated ourselves so that Jones could understand.

'Not only is he missing, but there is a strong chance he plans to do something destructive,' said Spindle. 'We found this in his quarters earlier today.'

Jones held up a metal tube as thick as a finger, with holotech coding across its surface.

'It's black market qubits, half-used, allowing Dale to exchange messages with an unknown contact without any chance of interception. Judging by the amount spent, he's been talking to someone for at least an hour a day since he arrived,' she said, 'The container is rigged to make data recovery extremely difficult.'

'He's a Cannot,' I said with sad realisation.

'Without doubt,' Broulé replied. 'We all know that Dale was about to fail the training. If someone has kept up a stream of indoctrination and persuasion, he may think this is his last opportunity to execute an attack.'

'And these, we presume, were to keep his motives a secret, even from himself.' Jones held up a bag of pills marked with chevron stripes, almost all of them red and black, but two or three were green and black. Engram mematonin—*slice*–like the coachgirls took in Movamption. Dale could suppress his beliefs during the classes until the drug wore off.

Nian sat down on her bench. The thought of a colleague attempting to harm her was difficult to handle.

'They'll be looking to make a symbolic gesture,' I said. 'It isn't the loss of life—Border's not that densely populated—it's the notion that the Cannots have people dedicated enough to reach out into other systems and cause chaos.'

Jones nodded her agreement.

'With no way to smuggle a traditional weapon onto Border, we're left with sabotage. But the ground-based parts of the institute, the tap trees, the Headström generators and the launch area are designed so they can't be made unsafe. That only leaves the off-world equipment. This system still contains a staggering amount of shrapnel. When the Paraunion named the location, we assumed it was a test, or perhaps the abundance of raw material was necessary. The blueprint gave several possible solutions, only one of which was within our technological reach, so we made drones, worker bees, as the engineers call them. The blueprints told us to wait until they'd done their job, but events forced our hand. People want to see results for the billions spent here, so we had to start without waiting years for the system to be cleared.'

'They're autonomous, like a swarm? Can they be hacked?' I asked.

'No. Bees are a sensor array, replicator, engines and basic machine intelligence. They redirect asteroids, nibble comets and make more of themselves. But the "queen" ensures they arrive in the nick of time, an arrival only made possible by their collective knowledge being processed and extrapolated by her centrally on the artificial moon.'

'Can Dale get to the moon?'

'Not a chance. Transports are infrequent and restricted to engineers,' said Broulé.

'But he doesn't need to.' Jones looked horrified at the sleek tube in her hand. 'The qubits are made here, on Border, at the equatorial generators because an orbiting factory wasn't safe in the early construction. The moon is tidally locked, so everything it says to the workers is relayed from here.'

*

Half an hour later we discovered Dale holding a gun to the Queen Bee's head.

The bees' defence was communications-heavy and used many dedicated qubit generators to synchronize its workers. These had backup factories in the event of their failure. Still, no one had ever really considered what would happen if the active storage tank was polluted because that simply couldn't happen by accident.

Dale, or perhaps the CBG handler pushing his buttons, had thought of it for him. His right hand gripped a nanite tube that he had already locked into the side of the smooth storage tank. He stood on a stone dais on which four tanks were arranged in a diamond. Around the tanks, a short ruff of sand separated them from the lightly fluctuating sea of Border. Lying on the concrete at Dale's feet, a device periodically flashed that hid him from the facility's sensors.

Chow Lutsk and I approached slowly across the pontoon bridge. We couldn't stop Dale from delivering the fatal dose to the Queen Bee unless we lured him away from the tube. *Samson, tear out your hair.*

The ray of hope was that Dale hadn't yet injected the corrupting load into the tank; perhaps he was scared for his own life? If he was, then maybe we could persuade him to reconsider what he was doing.

Lutsk was still trying to catch his breath from the run across the bridges. We'd split into pairs to check the possible sabotage points around the institute. This storage island was the furthest from the main building and institute shields, an uncomfortable thought. I glanced over my shoulder at the main island and its paper buildings bathed in sunlight and guessed they were about two kilometres away via the bridges.

¤ Welcome to the show! ¤ said Dale with a grin. If he was worried about his own life, it certainly didn't show. His Para was unnervingly fluent.

¤ Don't do this, ¤ I said. ¤ You're better than this. Somebody from the CBG has wound you up for months, but give me a chance to talk you through my side of it? ¤

Lutsk was bent over, puffing hard, but raised a single finger that indicated he wanted to speak. Luckily, Para lets you laugh, cry or wheeze while continuing to talk.

¤ We all want the same thing—we want the poor out of the hovels, we want the poverty-stricken elderly not to vegetate in pain, we want space of our own. You're angry because you look around at Border and see the privileged few in all this room? Why partner with the Paraunion so urgently? Because once allied with them, we can make thousands of new worlds, heal the sick and pull down the hovels. We're on the same side. ¤

¤ So we rely on the charity of aliens? ¤ Dale replied, his hand gripping the nanite tube. ¤ Tell me, did these aliens look at us and take pity when they saw how crowded we were? No. Did they find mercy in their hearts when they saw billions go mad in the Crush? No. What makes you think they'll see things differently once we send a few trained monkeys? Do you know how much human productivity is currently being spent on Border? Do you know how many big ships are making trips to Border instead of real planets? ¤

¤ It's a lot, ¤ Lutsk agreed, ¤ but the evidence points to humanity as a floundering culture, stagnating. You can see that, can't you, Dale? It's at a point in its evolution where it must either integrate with its neighbours or fail entirely. It's not the Paraunion testing us; it's nature itself asking, do you have the self-control to survive?¤

Dale shook his head in pity for a deranged old man. His Para was more lucid now. I realised he'd failed in some part because he'd had to suppress the fragments that the slice couldn't cover. *Forget I took a drug to forget the drug.* Loaded on the green drugs, he was more certain than he'd ever been in his life of his convictions.

Dale turned his attention wholly upon me.

¤ You're following orders from an alien culture that doesn't give a damn about us, that just wants to see us in a grave, or maybe just likes to play games with other races. I wanted to talk you around, but Crossley said you wouldn't listen: that you'd been given a free pass out of life-basic so you'd conveniently forget what you knew when you were young and poor in Movampton. You were bought out. I forgive you. But we should *fear the dreamer in the day*, shouldn't we, Evans? *Fear the dreamer in the day.* ¤

¤ I'm listening now, ¤ I said and stood at neutral.

Dale looked up into the crystal clear blue sky as if a chime had sounded. He glanced back at us with regret, a messianic look of forgiveness for our misguided actions, clicked the qubit tube button, and then detached it and dropped it on the floor.

¤ Don't you see I'm giving us all the chance to be better? ¤ Tears welled in his eyes. ¤ Not just to survive but to be better, not just to escape into a different culture but to be the humanity we should always have been fighting for. I'm here to restore a nation, Evans. ¤

Immediately, the clear, bright sky streaked with a single long trail, some small debris burning up in the atmosphere. The CBG had timed the crippling of the Queen Bee at a pivotal moment. Hundreds of thousands of bees suddenly lost their instructions and floated purposelessly on. Ten thousand black missiles were never averted or mined for material. Sooner or later, they would get through.

I looked at Lutsk. He'd need help to make it back in time. Dale began clambering down from the high stone dais that the qubit containers were mounted on. He clearly intended to try to save his own skin; this wasn't an intentional suicide mission.

The flat ocean far to our right was speared by something moving at incredible speed. The waters bucked up wildly. Lutsk and I started running straight away. The size and power of the concussion wave built as it raced towards us. Dale looked at the pontoon bridge and decided that the generator island was safer to weather the mini-tidal wave. Ultimately, that decision would prove to be short-sighted.

We ran until we realised that the little distance we could cover wouldn't get us to safety. The next island was more like an atoll, so low that the wave would pass straight over it. In fact, most of Borders' islands were like that. It was as if the whole place were built as a shock absorber for meteorites, which, of course, it was.

However, the pontoon bridges were not designed with such events in mind. I knew that the floating spans were tethered to the sea bed with enough flex to account for the slight shifts in Border's weak tides.

Lutsk didn't panic. He was still the quiet, impressive man who would surely make the best ambassador of all of us, better than even Spindle. He stopped me.

¤ Grab the pontoon, lay flat and hold on, ¤ he ordered.

I got down and gripped the slats, ramming my toes between them. Lutsk did the same just as the wave struck us. I felt the split-second rise as the pontoon was thrown up and torn free of the anchors, then we spun and were consumed by the water. The bridge's body shielded us from the full force, but the undertow tried to tear us away from our shelter. I felt my wrist twist and pop while my legs flailed under the water, unable to keep their purchase. When the bridge dropped back, unmoored but still unbroken, I looked over to see Lutsk hanging off the edge in the water, one mangled arm locked between the slats. Half his face bled where it had smashed against the bridge. I pulled him up and freed the jammed limb. He lay on his back with his chest heaving.

¤ Get running, Evans, ¤ he said.

I started to try and get my good arm around him to pick him up. My other damaged hand was seizing up quickly. I'd be damned if I was leaving him, but he pushed me away.

¤ Look up! The sky is falling, and I will cling on here. Get running. ¤ Had those words not been in Para, I might not have listened, but the implications were so clear: it's OK, I have no chance, you have very little. It was like a long, drawn-out argument summarized and then tied up with a conclusion. I put my hand on his chest for a moment and couldn't bring myself to say anything. So I stood up and ran.

As I ran, I saw that Lutsk's description was more accurate than I had imagined. The horizon was scarred with trails, and somewhere beyond, a deafening boom heralded the oblique entrance of a fireball.

Though torn from its moorings, the pontoon bridge network was still complete. I hurtled along as fast as my feet would carry me, though the surface was less stable than it had been on my morning runs. The things you can endure while running for your life and the pains you can endure are astounding. I waded across to the next bridge section at the atoll, hoping that another tsunami wouldn't suddenly pull me into a watery grave. I didn't look at the sky or the sea around me. *I fear thee, ancient mariner!* I focused on my feet, on moving and clambering. The institute building was proofed against any disaster, natural or man-made. If I could make it there, I'd be safe.

There were two more sections to cross, each half a kilometre long, typically just a couple of minutes running, and beyond, I saw the scintillating dome of the institute protective shield flickering around the island. It struck me that they might not take down the shield to let me in. They might not think I'd survived and locked the doors. I tried to shake the thought off; all I could do was run and hope. *Without Lutsk.*

The construction of Border was always more sophisticated than I could guess, and I continued to underestimate its designers, both Paraunion and human. What looked simple seldom was.

A pair of orange boxes streaked out of the dome. One flew directly towards me, and the other veered away on a different vector. At the same time, another strike hit the ocean only a few hundred metres from me. I fell on the bridge decking, unable to grip the planks with both hands and thinking I would be torn away and drowned in seconds.

The orange emergency drone made it to me first. It locked onto my back and threw up its protective shield with a deafening power hum. The spherical shield sliced through the pontoon bridge millimetres below my feet and above my head. The reverberation and noise inside the shell were deafening, but the tumult of water, bridge and air outside the globe passed harmlessly. As soon as it was safe, the drone dropped the shield and lifted me into the air. It accelerated hard and returned to the institute in a matter of seconds. As we were about to strike the barrier, it flashed on its own shield for a moment and passed straight through.

An area in front of the main entrance acted as a mobile hospital. Four more orange emergency drones hovered over patients while a few people, whether doctors or concerned onlookers, I couldn't tell, stood around.

The drone rotated and lowered me onto a waiting gurney, then injected me with a cocktail of medicines as a general-purpose survival tactic.

The drone's twin brought in the body of Lutsk. His eyes were open and glassy, but his body was broken like a ragdoll. The drone attached ventilators and electrodes to the body, but it was clear that the spirit was gone. Whatever drugs had been pumped into my blood let me take all this in with a strange sense of detachment. The drone straightened my forearm and wrist before setting them in hardening foam. I didn't feel a thing. *I didn't feel a thing.*

My attention was drawn to the other side of the triage area, where Spindle shouted and refused treatment as he followed the unconscious body of Nian being pulled away on a gurney. Two drones operated on both her legs as the trolley moved. They drilled and weaved a lattice of ceramic pins into each of them. A scaffold held the shattered parts together. I guessed that if they were operating on her legs, her chances of survival were good.

Behind Spindle, the frosted smear of the shield lit up with red flashes of impacts. No sound penetrated our shelter, but it was clear that the CBG had known exactly when to damage the Queen Bee to cause a colossal amount of damage. Perhaps there were more sympathizers on the inside of the Border institute? They managed to get a qubit container and drugs onto Border without detection; not an easy achievement.

I lay my head back down on the gurney, the sensation of being covered in thick blankets passed over me even though the drone had just cut off my grey jacket.

Soon the news of what had happened would be reported everywhere on the net, and the CBG would get precisely what they were looking for: publicity, notoriety and fear. No matter how many ideologies the Cannots took on board, and mine was not the only work that they had cobbled into their philosophy, they would never escape that they were fighting over the oldest warring issue: land to live on. As Dale had said, or more probably whoever had been talking through him for the last months, he wanted to restore a nation.

The flashes beyond the shield boundary slowed as I drifted into sleep. I heard the words of Dale and Lutsk over and over again but knew I'd lacked the skill to persuade Dale or save Lutsk. *A new heaven and a new earth.*

*

Spindle's study looked out over the dark sea and away from the main islands of the university. He sat at a tilted desk, tracing out curving motions with a stylus. A genii globe floated beside him: a paper lantern without the paper, just the light source. It dropped honey light on his back, arm and face.

I tapped on the open doorframe.

¤ Come in, Mr Evans. What can I do for a former poet at this late hour? Have you spoken to Ms Delaware? Dr Broulé has taken Lutsk's body to the main island to arrange its return with honours. ¤

The in-roads and out-roads of Para questions had ceased to aggravate me. I thought I could glimpse their usefulness on the horizon, but at that point, I handled each question in logical clumps and then tacked additions onto the end in a cack-handed style.

¤ My apologies for disturbing you. You know 'Former Poet' would be a good archetype. I realised this afternoon how little I really knew about Lutsk. You were there for almost every memorable story I recall about him, except when I was his human alarm clock. ¤ I sighed, not in Para, then continued. ¤ Jones told me about Lutsk's condition. I thought he was a lazy academic, but sleep must have been difficult. Every morning, he got up in pain. I think Nian went over to the university to get hammered—her words—at the bar. ¤

Spindle reflected on my comments, and in Para, even reflection had different flavours. There's no awkward silence in Para unless it's intentional.

¤ He had neural turbulence for years. He must have thought that becoming an ambassador would probably be his last achievement. Our eminent friend couldn't face the dumbing-down of a surgical cure and didn't believe in upload. Jones knew but wouldn't tell me, but I suspected from glimpses of things he said in Para. ¤

¤ Jones the cleaner? ¤

Another problematic concept in Para, a person in hails of laughter can continue to answer you and comment simultaneously on the nature of their amusement. It demands practice.

¤ Jones, a cleaner! The Athena—no, the Mycroft of Border! You think the holder of the purse strings to a planet is a cleaner? Ha! She's the calculating machine that burns whole ships of quantum bits answering questions from polilawyers on foreign policy—and who knows what else? A cleaner, ha! Evans, you have a talent for comedy, ¤ he paused. ¤ God, I wish Chow-Lutsk was here for this. ¤

The final statement destroyed my annoyance at being played the fool. So I got to share in the joke, laughing more at what Lutsk would have thought of it. That was one of the deepest changes that Para makes in you, throwing arguments into the archetypes, losing or transforming your feelings about things so they can be viewed objectively. Now Lutsk became an archetype I could call up whenever I needed his opinion.

We talked about him for a long time. As I bid Spindle goodnight, a question occurred to me.

¤ What are you working on there? ¤ I asked, pointing to the odd graphic on the desk, full of angles and looping knots. ¤ Cracking the secrets of written Para? ¤

¤ I'm flattered. No. I'm just practising my signature. Good night Evans. ¤

He turned back to his work and adjusted the genii globe directly over the desk. I realised that as the display on the desktop was self-lighting, the genii globe must be present to light something else, perhaps his hands, which were laid carefully on either side of the diagram.

I felt I was disturbing Spindle by hovering, so I turned and quietly walked away. Over my shoulder, I heard Spindle call out.

¤ If you see Jones in the morning, please tell her my floor needs a good brush. ¤

13   Nor for the towering dead

The graduation ceremony was no hat-throwing affair. A year had seemed a short time on Border. The platform was populated with professors from other departments and polilawyers sent to talk about the importance of firing emissaries at the Paraunion and forging new agreements. There were thousands of academics and students, and there was Rolliard. *There walks my friend.* His administrative work helped him stay close to the source of all Paraunion knowledge. We chatted in a corridor before I had to kowtow to the dignitaries. Rolliard shook my hand as I apologised for not being in touch more, and what struck me was how proud he was. There wasn't a hint of jealousy.

He was a stout defender of my character against the avalanche of hate and controversy the Cannots and their supporters stirred up. Rolliard was interviewed countless times during the months of enquiries after the sabotage. His opinions changed the general feeling from the CBG being the underdogs to the Border institute being the embattled good guys—constantly fighting to survive and achieve its goal. He even tried to liberate *The Pollutant Speaks* from the Cannots' ideology, but without success.

The Cannots still used the *Pollutant* as a revolutionary *I Ching*, dipping into it for punchy phrases, raiding its vocabulary of discontent, all the time claiming that I, the author, had been pressured into denouncing it. They claimed that I had divinely channelled *Pollutant* for them and then fallen from grace.

Rolliard: another friend I was about to leave behind. I had stolen his adventure in many ways. He had convinced me to see the mission of Border as more than just an escape from life-basic, so I resolved to make up for my lack of gratitude and pull him into the limelight as much as possible in front of the detail-crazed audience.

Chow-Lutsk's son received an honorary ambassadorship on behalf of his father. He reminded me a lot of his dad, calm with a hint of sharpness. A mind-boggling number of people attended over the net, many of them wannabes for the following interviews, a lot of them trying to escape life-basic as I had. I tried to forget about them constantly watching us. *Spool on / Cue and rewind / I won't mind.*

Spindle and Broulé took the brunt of the speeches while Nian and I tried to smile and nod as much as possible. Mid-speech, the professor, who was the object of envy for the other learned men packing the seats, thanked those same gentlemen for their support—and in one of the most subtle displays of Para—also doubted their parentage was legitimate. *I heart Spindle.* He was a cruel and utilitarian human but a very likeable Paraunion.

With the advantage of Para training, I looked at Spindle with different eyes. Even when he wasn't speaking the super-culture language, I could sense that he was constrained and his thoughts crammed into the little boxes of human words. He hated being back on Border so much because he felt claustrophobic in our tiny language.

Nian and I were presented with pebbles from the shores of a Paraunion world—the stones looked as if seawater was turning over inside them. We held them out so the gnat-like cameras could get a good look for the viewers.

I tired of shaking hands and smiling, *Don't deserve (thanks),* and there was no sign of Jones anywhere to find out how long we were expected to remain on view. I wondered what the Bleeding Soldier would think about the pompous affair, probably that the lack of humility would ultimately lead to the mission's failure. Finally, I spotted Jones out of the corner of my eye. Polilawyers surrounded her, and lecturers queued behind them with some axe to grind. Nian tapped me on the shoulder. A broad red sash blazed across her kimono, giving the outfit a definite suggestion of the ambassadorial, depressingly cunning for someone so young. I immediately wished that I'd thought of doing the same or asked her what she'd wear ahead of time.

She walked awkwardly on her replacement muscles.

¤ Had enough of the circus? What'd the Bleeding Soldier say about it all? My mother is over there in floods of tears: now she's decided she doesn't want me to go. Jones is lost in the mix, I see. No wonder she stays over in this faculty most of the time. Let's bow out as soon as possible, brother. Say your adieus to Border. ¤

¤ Yes, exactly. I was just thinking about the Soldier. Without Jones, I think they'd have had Spindle in chains years ago. Right, a drink and a toast for the viewers, then we'll get to the airport. Don't blame your mother. She doesn't know where you're going. *We* don't know where we're going, honestly. Do you know what scares the polilawyers most? They have no control or idea what we'll be doing out there. ¤

We didn't speak for more than a few seconds, but that was enough for a good deal of the physically present audience and all of the net viewers to get their first real glimpse of the mystifying Para in action.

The hush was oppressive.

All day, I feel alien.

I switched back to my smile-and-wave tactics, and Nian followed suit. From nowhere, Broulé appeared beside us and made a song and dance about time pressing on and so many preparations.

We managed to look like we were leaving reluctantly.

Jones took us to a side office, where she sat us down and made a show of closing the door.

'Since the sabotage, we have come to a single conclusion: humanity is not safe.' Jones inspected the flimsy windows for dust. 'Dale said Crossley had told him what to do, even what to think. That could explain the behaviour of the Cannot Be

Grouped. Crossley's god complex has been spread out amongst billions of followers using the *Pollutant Speaks* as their holy text.'

'I still can't believe that works,' I said.

'It's cult-thought, isn't it? Why do you expect it to make sense? I mean, Crossley is clearly mad,' said Nian.

'We have a specialist working on that side of things. Since we woke him up, he's got another couple of years onboard the *Río de las Estrellas* to help us make sense of things from a position of safety.'

The university network had a high level of trust with students and staff and opened an impromptu inner eye call to show the figure of a grumpy Green sitting on a chair. An orange outline showed his addition to reality, then faded after he'd become the focus of our attention. He looked at me, gave a comedic roll of his eyes and a shrug.

'There really is no rest for the wicked, it seems,' said Green.

Jones paced up and down the room between us, not waiting for us to exchange pleasantries or catch up with each other.

'We fight an ongoing campaign to ward off attacks from the Cannots, both in the physical sense and politically. The resources required by Border and its mission to the Paraunion are significant. Our support with the polilawyers is a fragile majority, but the ships' captains completely back us. Our support is far from unanimous, and ambitious parties look at the billions of Cannots as a populist wagon to ride into power.'

'Surely no one in politics is taking the CBG seriously?' I asked

Green shook his head at my woeful innocence.

'Oh, but they are. Someone is taking the crazy out of the Cannot arguments and spinning it into polilawyer talk—and her name will be worryingly familiar,' said Jones.

'Marna?'

'Exactly. Ever since Marna Malverona came out of *Alone* and left Border, she has tried to convince anyone and everyone that the programme needs to be shut down. She took being rejected very, very badly.'

Jones waved at Green to take over the point she was making.

'And that is behaviourally very interesting,' Green said. 'Looking back on Marna's political career, you can't deny that she's been ambitious and cut-throat, but she's never changed her philosophical viewpoint, and she's never been a huge friend to the life-basic citizen. She's had several major failures but has never changed her political stance to overcome them.'

'What did she do?' Nian asked.

'The usual; deflect, deny, blame circumstances.'

'So suddenly she's a life-basic protester?' I asked.

'Quite Evans, *suddenly*,' Green noted, 'the most suspicious word in the history of mind-body studies. She spent eight weeks in *Alone* and then snaps out of it with the sudden urge to embrace the cause of the neverrider.'

It dawned on me what Green was getting at. Jones nodded and then looked out of the window, her hands gripped each other in a tight knot behind her back. At that odd moment, it occurred to me that I had never seen her sit at her desk.

'So *Alone* has been spiked to turn people on to the Cannot propaganda? If you need to brainwash someone, solitary confinement is the best place to do it.' I said.

'I've constructed a possible history,' Green said. 'It suggests that Crossley's delusions happened after his second relapse, and he'd discharged himself from my hospital in Movampton. The *Alone* program had large, complex updates soon after, and unfortunately, they were passed as security patches and applied to every user. We estimate the current impact to be nearly a quarter of the adult population. I'd bet the programme that once edited every person out of reality now edits out everyone except Crossley, and god knows in what form he appears to the victim.'

'Hold on. We're saying that a quarter of humanity is being mind-controlled?'

'We can't prove it, and honestly, we haven't a clue about Crossley's methods. Surely someone would have protested if the victim had been aware of the process. Maybe it happens when they sleep? This is all circumstantial,' said Jones. 'I've tried to make a case with the government intelligence services to have the programme banned or at least marked with warnings, but they say their investigation has turned up nothing incriminating. They also say that behavioural modification like this isn't achievable with current medical and technical knowledge.'

'Come on! They can't imagine it being made?' I snapped. 'Crossley's an augmentation genius. For all we know, he's had it up his sleeve for years.'

'What's the point?' interrupted Nian. 'I mean, what does Crossley really want?' Her comment caught us all off guard.

'Power?' I suggested.

'No,' commented Green flatly.

'Revenge? Money?' I offered.

'No, no. You misunderstand Crossley completely. He's going to fix the world: the Crush broke him, and now he's going to save us all from it. First, he tried to solve it virtually with the *Alone* program. Now he's resorted to changing reality.

'Don't you see? He's a messiah. He will do whatever he thinks needs to be done in his holy crusade. He's going to relegate or shut down anything else that doesn't, as far as he sees it.'

We took some time to come to terms with Green's description of Crossley, hidden behind a shield of crazies. If Jones suddenly announced that Crossley was a government construct or a cover story spread by the Alten-Earth far-right, I'd have been more comfortable with the idea. But Green hadn't said that, and how typical of the Greenian philosophy to view evil as good from another angle. Jones decided to put the weight of the world on our shoulders.

'One-eighth of the population may not sound like a majority, but that's an incredible amount of block voting power in our political environment. As the Cannots' arguments become laundered by Marna, that force will increase. We won't be shut down, but we're beginning to be crippled, without resources to scour the population for new ambassadors, without regular ships to Border or funds to defend our position. Every cog and wheel of the Border programme has one final output: to produce ambassadors like you two. That will become decreasing likely until it's impossible. I'm not exaggerating when I say that the pair of you might be the last ambassadors we produce.'

'But there's Professor Spindle and Broulé too,' Nian said.

'Spindle, yes. Broulé, no, I'm afraid.'

'Why? She's a far more experienced speaker than either of us.'

'There are personal issues that prevent Pazaana Broulé from returning to the Paraunion', Green intercepted the question. 'She does all she can here as an academic tutor, but she'll probably never return to active duty as an ambassador.'

'What happened to her?' asked Nian.

Green looked uncomfortable talking about the details. He looked into the air and chose his words carefully.

'An ambassador's voyage into the Paraunion can be isolating and disorientating. Our hosts ensure the physical safety of ambassadors, but the envoy's ability to withstand the *otherness* of the many cultures inside the Paraunion is part of their assessment.'

Jones turned and looked at her new, possibly last, ambassadors.

'This is why you, as the third expedition, will be assigned with attachés to support and help you with any duties that don't require Para. Before we get too deep into this point, let me come to the main reason for pulling you both aside like this.'

'Spindle has spent more than three years in the Paraunion, and he knows more about it than any other living human. His primary contact is a being called Meletrus. They have an excellent working relationship, and Meletrus heads up a small group that thinks humanity may gain entrance to the Paraunion. This would come with all the life-saving and world-shaping technology we've dreamt of and quite a bit we haven't imagined. However, Meletrus expressed concerns that our preparations haven't been fast enough. When Spindle asked why, Meletrus implied that she couldn't tell us but that the Paraunion might be diverting its attention away from new members.'

Jones's last line was typical of a Para conversation described and translated to a non-Para speaker. In my mind's eye, I recreated the scene where a Paraunion told Spindle through context the effects of a circumstance that Spindle wasn't even aware of.

'Did he say how long we might have until this embargo?' I asked.

¤ Meletrus used a notion from the Martyr with Five Keys. I hope you're familiar with him? ¤

Jones looked annoyed at being cut out of the conversation, but Spindle had already briefed her on the matter, and the professor knew his comment would be more meaningful in Para.

The ice on gates falls first. Nian's expression told me that I hadn't misinterpreted; every argument in the archetype of the Martyr involved loss and self-destruction.

Jones saw the worry on our faces and clapped her hands together.

'Still, Meletrus is a great friend of our cause, a creature more intelligent than any human, thinks that all humanity is in danger from ourselves or some other power. We must find a way to persuade them to let us in.'

'But with the Cannots and Crossley,' asked Nian, 'Can we be sure that the assembly will vote to join the Paraunion?'

'The home front is my responsibility, and with a little help from friends,' she nodded at Green, 'we'll keep order, but all of that will be for nothing if we don't get invited in. We must imagine that somewhere in an unknown room, someone has set an alarm clock for the extinction of our species. All we can hear is the ticking and even that faintly. We must not confuse how faint the sound is with the consequences of the alarm ringing. You'll leave Border immediately and take an unlisted transport to the nearest hub. Once there, you'll be shuttled away beyond the reach of the CBG; if they can kill our ambassadors, the show is over.'

Jones looked at the apparition of Green for closing comments.

'God help us all,' said Green and flickered out of existence.

14   Sorry I could not stay

'Unlisted transport' turned out to be more complicated than I'd imagined. All automated craft were coordinated and logged by Queen Bee, which Jones considered potentially unsafe. Spindle, Nian, Rolliard and I took a runabout to a distant island that appeared occupied by a hulking sea monster. In fact, the beast was a vintage 609 Dipper, with long, concertinaed fuel umbilicals dipped into the sea.

Rolliard drove the skiff right up onto the beach and cut the engine. It reminded me that gentle Rollie was trained for something other than desk work—he was the perfect choice to make a secret drop-off. The main belly hatch of the dipper was like a black cavern in the bright Border daylight.

'Move that fucking toy boat out of the way!'

The voice came out of a black engineering bay, quickly followed by the epitome of a crusty pirate. Tools dangling from the loops and pockets of his flight suit and jangling as he clumped towards us. He moved straight up to Rollaird and eyeballed him.

'Peace core, eh? You should know better then! Stow them,' the space dog pointed at us, 'then get it out the bloody way!'

His voice was like an engine misfiring. Rollaird, although a head taller than the other man, cowered and apologised.

'It's ok.' I said. 'He's taking it back anyway, so it'll be out of the way before we launch.'

'Oh, really smartarse? Then why are all your names on the flight manifest?' He threw a clipboard at my head and stomped back into the cargo bay. Spindle laughed and walked after him with his flight case.

I checked. He was right.

'Surprise…' said Rolliard meekly.

'Why didn't you say! This is great news, you're going to the Paraunion! Honestly, there's no one I'd rather have with me.'

Rolliard looked sheepishly at the ground and shook the sand off the manifest he'd just picked up.

'This is why I wasn't sure how to talk to you about it. I'm not assigned to you. I've been teamed up with Nian,' he made an apologetic shrug.

Nian came over and mockingly hugged the giant in a possessive way. I was put out, but I had to admit that they would be a great team. *Green, Green, the match up machine.*

'So *who* is my aide?'

Spindle's voice came out of the dark bay.

'They don't know.'

'Can I know?'

'Jones says there's no need. In my experience, it's best to trust her to take care of everything this side of the Paraunion border.'

The captain stomped out into the sunlight again, then looked at us as if he'd never seen anything so ridiculous.

'Why are you still in my way?' he bellowed.

*

In a few minutes, we'd loaded our luggage and pushed the skiff back out to sea, where the wind took it further and further into the limitless ocean. The captain announced his flight once we were strapped into the acceleration seats.

'Welcome, blessed passengers,' he rasped. 'We will be travelling to an undisclosed destination which will take an undisclosed amount of time. Those unused to space travel in the old fashioned way, please keep hold of a sick bag or take as many pills out of the dispensers as your heart desires. I'll be your pilot, so if you have any questions, please shut up and keep them to yourself as it's a tricky job with lots of switches to flip and gauges to check.'

The Dipper's passenger bay was exposed steel and carbon fibre without ornamentation because of the cost of pulling it in and out of planets' gravity wells.

'Is this safe?' asked Nian, who, unlike the rest of us, simply didn't seem to understand the concepts of fear or intimidation. The captain scowled, but Nian's innocent look got the better of him. He leant in and spoke at a fraction of his average volume, somewhere close to a normal person's shout.

'The stars are in my blood, young lady. I'm one hundred and eight years old in three days....'

'Oh, happy birthday, Captain...?' Nian beamed.

'Transom. Thank you, but that's not the point I was making. I've flown Dippers and Heavy Lifters for seventy of those hundred-odd years and even did a spell on Interceptors for a while, but I've never ever lost a vehicle.'

'But why risk it?' she asked.

'Ha! Why not replace me with a box of wires or a little remote control? You'd be amazed how much work there is for a pilot that doesn't log flight plans, ask questions about who goes where or what needs doing on the quiet,' he pointed to the heavens, 'up there.'

I wondered why I hadn't included the unemployed space workers, the vacuum dogs and the noleggers, somewhere in *The Pollutant*. They were the kind of displaced misfits that would have been perfect. *Fight, fight on against the dying of the light.*

Despite the captain's assurances, we were thrown around and deafened in the windowless hold when the Dipper took to the air. Spindle smiled to himself during the conversation between Nian and Transom, clearly delighted to be leaving Border, but during launch took on a strained expression.

The only person who didn't look worried about the idea of travelling on a manually-controlled, explosive-powered craft was Rolliard. He was back exactly where he most wanted to be, part of a team, almost a family, but this time headed to the place he'd been dreaming about for years, into the heart of the Paraunion.

On a needle trip, the ascent is so gentle, acceleration and deceleration so controlled, that the period of zero-g during the carousel load is mundane. Not on the Dipper. We experienced it for two days. Spindle and I were nearly perpetually crunching the anti-nausea meds while I don't think I saw Rolliard take one. Nian seemed to get special dispensation to sit up in the co-pilot's chair on the flight deck. *Little sisters go elsewhere too.*

There was nothing to do in the cargo bay, so we spent quite a long time floating behind the flight controls, the only place with windows, each of us supplied with a passenger tether so that we wouldn't get stranded in the relatively large hold area. After a while, this seemed to irk the pilot.

'Stop watching me! Go and amuse yourself somewhere. There's a micro-galley and a pack of cards back there.'

'Why would you want a pack of cards? Feng me, you don't have an inner eye, do you?' I blurted.

'That's why there are so many switches and screens. Imagine how much all that instrumentation weighs,' said Nian, fascinated. 'I knew there had to be a better reason.'

'You can stop wetting your pretty knickers. This,' Transom indicated all the screens and controls, 'has worked for seventy years. I've had fewer failures than my silicon replacements and enjoyed the experience far fucking more than a box of flashing lights.'

We left Nian and Transom to the window and clambered back to our seats in the hold. No one went to find the cards.

After several hours, Spindle became noticeably more animated. As the only one of us privy to our destination, he clearly thought that our unconventional flight was about to end. We did what generations of commuters have done before us, like sheep worried at being left unprepared; we checked our luggage and started peeking out the flight deck to see if the destination was in sight.

The excitement was evident on Spindle's face as he addressed us in Para.

¤ This is *Bleak House*, a qubit factory way off the ecliptic plane. It's useful that we can take a prodigious amount of material with us for communication with her ladyship, ¤ Spindle implied Jones, ¤ and that our departure will be a quiet and private affair. "The boat" seems to have been here ever since my arrival, skipping away on odd errands. We'll be on it for around two months passage time, awake. Also, please try and be polite to the boat, as its opinion is not without weight in the Paraunion. ¤

Spindle motioned that he was open to questions. Decorum and impatience collided with each other, impatience coming out the winner. Nian and I talked over, with and across each other in a way Para does allow but is still poor etiquette, a style reserved for children who have eaten too much cake.

¤ Two months isn't going to get us anywhere significant, is it? Are you telling me there's a Paraunion colony just around the corner, somewhere in the dark? Is that what all the secrecy is about? 'Her ladyship,' you mean reporting to Jones? Isn't that spying? Won't the Paraunion be upset? You said "the boat", not "a boat"? ¤ Nian said.

¤ Be nice to a spaceship? I'd rather sleep through the journey if that's an option. Anywhere significant, I should think not. I don't have the net, but two months will put us bang in the middle of nowhere. I'm sure their machine intelligence is better than ours but are you saying that this 'boat' can play fast and loose with the laws of physics? ¤ I interrupted and argued with Nian.

¤ We'll be awake because our classes in Para have to continue. Also, the Paraunion don't hold with avoiding consciousness, so there are no hibernation units on board. You didn't expect one of them to waste his time coming out here to greet us, did you? The Paraunion have very little interest in what we personally discuss with Jones or anyone else. Look, if you have more questions, just ask the boat. ¤

107

*

The 'boat' as it wanted to be known, a noun, not a pronoun, was at the time of our first encounter only a hundred metres in length and thirty tall and wide. It lay alongside the gargantuan, ugly factory on its dayside. A spectral gleam shone on its rounded corners, and deep grooves hatched the hull in a strange pattern. A section large enough for the entire front portion of the Dipper to enter was open to space and brightly illuminated. To my surprise, I saw furniture and other human comforts clearly visible within. It was a bizarre sight, as if a living room had been cut in half in the middle of space. *O stranger, I am home.*

And there stood Annie Bugatti.

She leant on a red velvet sofa, oblivious to the void of space. The Dipper came in from the dark into the sparkling interior, and we saw her scrunch up her eyes, trying to make out some detail. When the Dipper's cabin came into the light, she made out our faces in the cockpit.

Once the shuttle halted, Transom opened the airlock with a magician's flair. We walked without choking or freezing onto the boat. I rushed out to greet Annie.

'How on Shang Lo did you get here?' I said after trying to hug the life out of her.

'Haven't you heard? I've got an alien super ship,' she laughed, 'and since the Cannots keep trying to kill me, I was on my way to Border anyway. That Jones chick arranged it.'

I introduced her to the rest of the gang. It went without saying that I'd found my new ambassadorial aide. Nian took an immediate shine to her. Who doesn't want to be like Bugatti? Spindle even seemed to thaw slightly from his normally pompous formality. When Rolliard met her, he was awkward. The two had heard so much about each other on the *New Osaka*.

'What's up, Peace Core?' she said, shaking his hand.

'Nice to finally see you in real-time.'

'Have you kept my boy here out of trouble?'

'I want to say yes', Rolliard paused, 'but if I'm honest, he's still in trouble.'

'As always, as always. He nearly got me killed while he was on an entirely different planet. Well, Envoy De Griffin, let me welcome you to an all-singing, all-dancing Paraunion mega-ship.'

'Nice. Do we both get one?'

'I don't think so.'

'Shame.'

We unloaded the Dipper and gently closed its lock, then it floated backwards out of the boat's infrastructure. Transom grinned through the pilot's window of the Dipper, gave a little wave and then tumbled the ship's nose over its stern to return on the same course it had arrived on.

I have often wondered how well calculated the boat's first words were to us. How those words set us at ease and began an outline for the kind of relationship that we could expect from it.

'Now, is anyone hungry?' it asked.

15   The whine upon the rail

The Paraunion suggested the concept of Border University and its location as a casual offer, along the lines of "if you can do this, then we'd be interested in meeting you". The location set it next to a tiny dark flow, part of the cosmos where the boat informed us that the universe was under the influence of another universe. *Get that.*

I watched as an avatar of the boat, a three-foot-high monopod with a broad cranium and black, globular eyes, explained the mysteries of the universe to the Para speaking portion of us.

¤ These 'rivers' of the universe allow travel without enduring long flights across static space. Some Paraunion consider the existence of these conduits a pointer to indicate the presence of an absolute being. Others side with the Crippled Thinker that there is no implication to be made. ¤

The boat provided answers to whatever we wanted to know and critiqued our Para in a nurturing way. It fashioned its interior to whatever layout we desired, but I struggled to get to know it and build a relationship. It asked me if a permanent avatar would make me more comfortable, but I refused. When it asked why, I said objectifying it would be tantamount to superstition. *Talk to the glove puppet child.*

It agreed and sounded relieved.

Spindle taught his classes assisted by constructs of the boat, and he'd asked for the classroom on Border to be reproduced, complete with its sunlit Japanese stone garden. I watched the boat conjure a thousand tiny suns into the air above the sand and dim the lights, so that glowing rivers of indigo were clearly visible streaming among them. A cluster of seven stars were haloed, indicating the systems that humanity clung to.

The professor addressed us flanked by two strange Paraunion controlled by the boat, intended to acclimatize us to the more extreme species. The monopod on his right and a fiery plant structure inside plasma spheres on his left. I wondered if the flames were clothes on the branches or an integral part of the creature, and what would be the diplomatic way to ask?

¤ Humanity's worlds are close to a dark river, and, ¤ Spindle gestured at the chart, ¤ according to the boat, no miracles are involved in travelling one. Mankind isn't surrounded by a protective moat or in an unreachable backwater, so anyone who takes an interest could come looking into our precious corner, and all they need to do is turn off the river. ¤

Nian looked at me and made a downcast context change. She was thinking of Jones's warning about the Paraunion shutting their borders.

¤ Our species is open to incursion from any group that can launch a modest number of vessels. One thing is sure about our society: we have no defensive capability. Our gigantic city ships are delivery boys, not fighters. ¤

Through the plasma colour tones, the boat made a Para side comment. I struggled to distinguish the meaning as it used inhuman registers I was less familiar with.

Nian echoed it for me.

¤ It did a little laugh at the gigantic ships. ¤

¤ Not impressed, huh? ¤

Spindle continued. He zoomed the system map out to show the eleven thousand systems of the Paraunion within our galaxy, all veined with dark rivers.

¤ The Paraunion consider themselves in a middling stage of development. They speculate about cultures who have mapped all the rivers of the universe, even somehow found a way to cross into the universes whose influences are assumed to make the dark flows occur. In this, at least, they are adorably humble: seeing themselves on the border of a transformative age, they term it the 'dimensional revolution', already benefiting from creating small higher dimensional spaces, many within their own bodies, to store not only power but also information. ¤

The blazing plant added, ¤ The computation and energy held in these pocket universes may be impressive, but more importantly, they include a Paraunion's identity and self. They protect us from physical harm and allow us to expand our minds beyond the physical limits of biological predestination.¤

Spindle took over again.

¤ It's a far more intimate arrangement than our proxy butlers and neural laces. The Paraunion would find them distasteful, the butler too crude an approximation of the will and the lace like medieval surgery. ¤

The boat made an expression of disgust, noting in a context that it was fake and put on to demonstrate the term.

The classes continued on and on.

Every time I believed I had conquered the language, Spindle revealed an aspect had been simplified to get us started, and we were required to begin again. Trickier and more eloquent Paraunion were conjured out of thin air for us to practise with, and the boat pulled their strings and tested our skills. Multi-limbed, clawed, gaseous, stony, scaled, rooted, feathered, diaphanous. They were all paraded before us. Just a tiny sample of the thousands of races that glued together the Paraunion.

I had little time to miss Border. The continuous revelations about the Paraunion from the boat and Spindle made life exciting. *A privilege to be alive.* My days of living half-immersed in the net and twitching from the Crush were almost forgotten.

We were a strange family looked over and cared for by the boat, who occupied a stoic, parental role. Annie and Rolliard weren't excluded from Para lessons. Rather than watch our classes, the boat arranged for their own dedicated instruction in culture and lingual basics, which it taught simultaneously to ours. Rolliard cried when it told him he'd be able to learn some Para. Bugatti was less enthusiastic.

Something odd happens when you meet people you'd thought life had taken away from you. The care and admiration I had for her were still there, but that impulse to touch was gone. I could see that it was the same from her side, too much water under the bridge. Had Green and Jones known that we'd feel this way? Or had they chosen her for more controlling reasons? Or just to keep her safe? Still, if there was anyone I wanted with me in a clinch, it was Annie.

After classes, we dined together in a stateroom that the boat had generated and dubbed 'the galley'. It was clear that, with some warning, the boat could create objects, not projections like the creatures in its lessons, of almost any complexity. The galley boasted a long mahogany table, chairs and a large window with an ever-changing view over an alien harbour. I watched the scene, wondering if it was all a fantasy or if I saw events through a camera on a distant world, then the boat interrupted my thoughts.

'Just had some news of our destination if you are interested? We're heading to the Lemniscate, a recovered stellar age fortress,' the boat said, with the disembodied voice it reserved to represent itself.

'What's a Lemniscate?' asked Annie.

'During the stellar age, many species struggled for supremacy during the pre-history of the Paraunion. Some built large military installations attempting to make impenetrable defences.

'After the foundation of the Paraunion, the installation was brought back into use by an artist named Lonyard, who re-mastered its environments over four hundred years. The artist left the fortress to evolve, claiming it would be the height of artistic achievement in a hundred thousand years. He disappeared, suspected of arranging a vast circular light-speed journey to return to his masterwork once the aeons had rolled by. The installation can be visited and has a few full-time inhabitants. Its purpose now, other than as an artwork, is a repository for the Graph. Students and opportunists sometimes choose to stay and collaborate there.'

'They want to live on a database?' asked Nian.

'The Lemniscate is said to be a place of great symbolism, ¤ the boat sounded neutral on the matter, ¤ and as the author, Meletrus, says, "everything has to live somewhere". The Graph documents all the relationships in our society, and some argue the Paraunion *is* the Graph. It retains all masters assigned, both past and present. Individuals seeking to exploit power patterns inside the Graph have to be very careful not to contravene the laws of usage, which carry severe penalties. The Lemniscate is otherwise used as a place of solitude for academics.'

¤ Can you show it to us? ¤ asked Spindle.

I was about to translate for Annie when the boat dimmed the room further and created a representation of itself approaching a star system, which quickly expanded into a red giant with a black hole extracting a wisp of material from its bloated partner. The boat highlighted a twisted figure of eight, which rotated around the stars, constructed of billions of linked, curved elements.

'Fuck me. Look at the size of it. That's one mother of an art gallery,' Annie shook her head in disbelief.

'Lonyard said the idea behind the creation was more important than the work of art itself,' The boat replied. 'The fortress is just a single instance in time of the real work of art. The size is irrelevant. If Lonyard returns, he hopes to be justified by the aesthetic machine he has set in motion. We'll land at a section known as the Gun Wharf, roughly translated, so you can judge what you think of his oeuvre. I hope you enjoy it. I have to say it's not really my thing; overly grandiose and very Ottapita. Please remember that the underlying construct is of a crude bygone age. Even the alterations you might see are just the ramblings of one artist.'

The boat sounded genuinely concerned that we would think badly of the Paraunion for using this gargantuan necklace around a black hole and red star.

¤ I don't understand where you would get enough material to construct it? ¤ Nian did enough thinking ahead for the rest of us. Her mind was a little more flexible.

'This used to be a three-star system. The early clans thought a little like the Burnt Tinker.' The boat did not sound happy. *Stellar vandalism, far out.*

My belief organs went into meltdown as we approached the planet-sized Gun Wharf, a single link in a larger structure.

¤ None of the original vessels were intended to stop or land here, ¤ the boat explained, ¤ the wharf provided ammunition and fuel, readily available with the judicious use of a tame black hole, to passing vessels. The resupply was accelerated to them while under the relative safety of the Gun Wharf ordinance, now long since dismantled. ¤

While the past was mind-bending, the present was fantastic as long as you sat back, relaxed and enjoyed it.

The boat had made an observation balcony for us, shielded from the vacuum of space, and lowered the balcony gently to the ground on landing. Lonyard had introduced hundreds of bound ecosystems to the structure. Otherwise, the Gun Wharf was a grey landscape of tunnels and slabs with vast curving intakes and cannon mouths. At that moment in the evolution of the artist's project, the wharf was dominated by jade vines, colossal pineapple-shaped plants and a variety of avian life. Gravity at our landing point was close to standard, although the boat informed us that this was a seasonal factor on the fortress chain. The wharf was visible for a tremendous distance, and I saw great amphitheatres with birds strutting about them, with cliffs and ravines all a little too square or too circular to be natural.

Over the rise came my first native Para speaker. Being acclimatised on the boat helped to bypass being star-struck and dig straight into the essential details. A good Ambassador can't afford to stand agog every time he meets a new VIP.

She was Meletrus, a type of "she" untranslatable into human but the pronoun approximation recommended by the boat for Annie and Rolliard. She seemed overdressed for the steaming jungle draped over gun-metal surfaces. Her genetic makeup appeared aquatic, breathing channels dashingly slung over each shoulder, her two thin but wide eyes, clearly not rotary orbs, and the striking colour of fresh-cut copper. She had no pupils, but the occasional blink revealed eyelids.

Her splendid cobalt, floor-length robe had billowy sleeves for her four arms, the lower set clasped below her chest with the hands linked. The upper arms were visibly more powerful, and she swung them gently as she walked. I couldn't tell if she had feet under the robe as it hung down to the ground, but her poise suggested irresistible solidity.

Spindle strode out to greet her.

¤ Good day, Meletrus, or is that inappropriate in these climes? Our thanks for agreeing to meet so informally. Have the vines become more mobile than the last time I was here, or am I anticipating too much in Lonyard? Let me introduce you to our two new speakers, Nian Delaware and Evans Ezra Evans. ¤

Spindle gestured towards us while we stood as nonchalantly as possible in the neutral position. The boat whisked Annie and Rolliard off on a private safari around the Gun Wharf to give us some alone time with the dignitary. Meletrus addressed us formally and referenced herself to Spindle in the style of a work colleague.

¤ What a pleasure to finally meet you and have names to attach to you. In discussions, you've only been referred to as "the candidates", which has a chilly indefiniteness about it, don't you think? You may be right, Professor Spindle, about those vines, but it seems unsporting to take measurements to find out. Impatience is the enemy of art, isn't it? Now that we've met, we should begin talking about your placements. You should be proud that the literary, artistic and historical records circulated about humanity have tickled some Paraunion fancies. Let's take a walk and see how your lessons have gone; after all, "the language is the people, and the people make it daily," as I once heard someone say. ¤

Meletrus was modest and impish simultaneously, evident in her subtext to Spindle. Later, I discovered that she had published a distinguished work on the changes in the Para language traced through the generations of the Graph.

Spindle trailed behind us as we walked around from one view of the Wharf to another, while Meletrus encouraged us to talk freely with her. Nian demonstrated her virtuoso talents without a hint of nerves. I followed their conversation, but my own performance was cloddish. *The puppet strings are tangled, and we cannot dance.*

As we walked, I saw the boat drifting slowly above the canopy of tall trees in a ravine, having left the aides to explore somewhere. In a comment to Spindle, who shared my fascination with the boat, I unwittingly also mimed my thoughts in Para.

¤ Do you think it's lonely or just admiring the art? *Is it grieving over a lost star?* ¤

Meletrus, who I'd thought was deep in conversation with Nian, was startled by my observation and joined us, watching the boat drift, a solid cloud afloat above the trees and towers.

¤ How sensitive of you, Mr Evans. We must place you somewhere they appreciate the soul of a romantic like the River Swimmer. ¤

¤ It's my pleasure to go wherever you think appropriate, ¤ I said, embarrassed. ¤ When you've experienced as little as I have about your culture, one place is probably as good as another. ¤

She inclined her head sagely at my remark.

¤ If the purpose were only exploration, I'd agree, but we are thinking of the larger agenda, aren't we? Where can the most impression be made in the fastest time – it's less what you learn from exploring than what the Paraunion learns about you that matters. ¤

She came closer to all three of us, the tone and register of her speech like a symphony compared to our own stumbling notes, trusting us, assuring us that she cared for humans, resolving to stay with us and making a subliminal promise to be a constant supporter.

¤ If it has not already dawned on you, ¤ she said, ¤ You should realise that you are a shop window for your race. ¤

Meletrus indicated a set of steps down toward a level plain covered with a drifting powder mist, a pair of hexagonal pillars the only thing in the empty space.

Nian shielded her eyes to survey the edges of the plain where the bountiful jungle and plants stopped abruptly.

¤ Why don't the vines grow on here? ¤ she asked Meletrus.

¤ Maybe this area is developing something new. Maybe the zone defies the reconstructive power of Lonyard's work, or perhaps he omitted this part deliberately. Interesting, isn't it? ¤

Nian walked around one of the pillars. The dust moved slowly, almost politely, around her in whorls. She stopped, waiting until it settled again. Carefully, she made her way to midway between towers and then swept her arms around and clapped her palms in front of her, creating a high, sweet echo. Two vortices grew and climbed before her, then fractured into spirals of spirals, going on and on into the distance, filling the whole plain before her.

¤ You said she is how old? ¤ Meletrus asked.

¤ Twenty-three. Soon. ¤ Spindle answered while taking a seat on the steps.

¤ Remarkable. Very impressive. Very intuitive. ¤

I remained mute, aware that I was playing a justified second fiddle to my colleague's language and adaptation skills. I felt like a neverrider caught outside the gates of a Marketoria school. Meletrus seemed to notice and turned to speak to me over one shoulder. If we were a shop window for humanity, one of the toys was much shinier than the other.

¤ You've come to see our culture, and I start you out inside a dusty piece of art. How selfish of me, hardly an ideal education in the workings of our society. Maybe my focus on the Lemniscate as the Graph store biases me? Still, I think we need to see some less abstract sights. We shall visit the origin world, the joint capital of the first two species to unite in the Paraunion. There you'll really discover more about us. ¤

We watched Nian turn and walk back towards us, still favouring one leg.

¤ You said I was like the River Swimmer? Do you want me to save a lover from the tides? ¤ I asked, showing I was familiar with the story.

Meletrus laughed and didn't answer for a while. She pointed to a tower block rising slowly into the misty daylight for reasons beyond my comprehension. *Cryptic alien art / who melts away zoo / judges winter poet anew.*

¤ It's been some time since we last lost anyone to drowning. However, the Graph and the dark flows can produce treacherous conditions of their own. I'll try to find you somewhere sufficiently similar to your own culture so interaction will be easier. Still, I'm disappointed to hear that we won't be receiving any poetic epics of your adventures? ¤

I looked at my feet in embarrassment, not a Para gesture but seemed to be understood by Meletrus, perhaps through Spindle's reaction.

¤ No, ¤ I replied.

A series of Para subtexts went on that I didn't understand. Meletrus looked at me with an aspect of sympathy and helpfulness, those copper eyes regarding me sincerely, examining my soul, but with a note of reluctance to intrude. Spindle hummed nervously to himself and put his hands deep in his pockets.

¤ You do bring the most interesting candidates, don't you? ¤ she said.

¤ We work with what we have, ¤ Spindle replied. I felt slightly insulted.

¤ Oh, and just a note, if I may, on the *River Swimmer* ambassador Evans? ¤

¤ Of course. ¤

¤ The lover drowns in the air after being removed from the river. ¤

¤ Really? ¤

¤ Trust me, that's rather close to its hermeneutical key. ¤

The boat drifted beside us and opened a regal stairway to allow entry. Nian had returned from the plain and regarded the three of us with curiosity.

¤ This place is amazing. Did I miss something? ¤ she asked.

¤ Just an invitation to the centre of the universe, ¤ I said.

¤ Is that far? ¤

¤ Just around the corner, ¤ said the disembodied voice of the boat. To those with a working knowledge of dark flows and spacetime, its tone implied that it had made a cracking joke.

There was Bugatti and I, Nian and Rolliard, and Spindle on his own. It was easy to see style differences when arranged around the polished galley table.

Nian and Rolliard looked capable and serious in their silver-grey ambassador garb, waiting patiently for the next step from Meletrus. Rolliard, nearly a foot taller than Nian, could have been confused with a military bodyguard if it wasn't for the looks of innocence and delight on his face. Nian remained impervious to fear and doubt. She fretted about the downfall of humanity, but she never questioned her own capacity to complete the mission.

Spindle remained a tiny, compact and inscrutable figure. Utterly more self-sufficient and experienced than the rest of us, he constantly spoke with Meletrus. The granite professorial attitude he had on Border softened now he was back in the Paraunion, but he talked only Para, even to the untrained aides, letting the boat translate him.

That left us. I couldn't get comfortable in the grey ambassador uniform, and Annie simply refused to have anyone else dictate what she wore. I copied one of the suits I'd seen the g-Russ wearing, though it looked ironic when I wore it. *Poverty doesn't wash off that easily.* Annie stuck with her signature glitterbeast-gothic look. She said anything else would be "inauthentic and unworthy of a delegate for culture".

So, in short, we looked the least impressive of the delegations.

Jones called in to wish us well. Or at least that's why we thought she'd called. She looked as if she hadn't slept since we'd left her weeks ago on Border. Her projection paced up and down beside the galley window that the boat was currently providing us.

'Before Meletrus takes you through the visitor protocol, I'll update you on the situation at home. I don't expect you need reminding again that you aren't here to explore and make friends—you're here to get that invitation into the Paraunion sealed.

'Cutting to the chase, there isn't any good news. Shang Lo, Movampton and Feng have contracted with private law and order companies to handle civil disobedience and rioting. Cannots have destroyed retail outlets and public amenities, sites they claim are "thought farms", involved in a conspiracy against them. As far as I can tell, targets are chosen at random.

'Shang Lo isn't alone either. There are signs of unrest brewing on Earth, Xin and Nuova. The political wing of the CBG has a name now: the Human Rights Party. It's tearing the old polilawyer system apart and reverting most of the assembly back to party politics. Very clever and very dangerous.'

'Do people know they're in danger? I mean, have we warned them about *Alone*?' Annie asked.

'Green and I have contacted the department of information. We keep them updated with every piece of information we have, and they do their best to get it out there; however, Crossley has this disastrous talent for getting seemingly neutral commentators to dismiss all evidence as a conspiracy theory.'

Meletrus made a gesture indicating that she would like to comment. The Para speakers immediately gave her their attention, but Jones, Annie and Rolliard were surprised.

¤ At this point, it is inappropriate for me to directly comment on your internal cultural affairs. As a neutral overhearing such an event, you'll excuse me if I remark how this seems a classic case of the *Squire Presidium*? ¤

Meletrus drifted away as if she had clearly said too much. While the boat whispered his translation directly into the ears of the non-Para, I saw Nian and Spindle make worried looks at each other. Jones, tired and unused to not grasping everything first, let some of her frustration loose on Spindle.

123

'Alright then, what's the Squire Presidium? New information is of little use if only the three of you understand it!'

'Meletrus's position is delicate. Let me try to distil the Presidium archetype down to the elements that I think our host is trying to highlight.'

Spindle looked at me, then moved on to Rolliard. I think he was aware I was almost always the stooge in his examples, and he was knowingly sharing the experience.

'Let's say Rollaird here is the squire. The squire in this scenario is an ambitious but not-so-capable figure. The squire can use anyone who owes him a favour or whom he can get leverage over. He can make promises of future gifts and influence, anything except figure out the path to power himself. So Rolliard, what would you do?'

'Well, if it's politics, I suppose I'll need someone who's an expert in politics?'

'You've got that: Marna,' I said.

'What else?' Spindle pushed.

'I want to beat the opposition, so I suppose I want people to make me look better than I really am, perhaps even tell me what I'm doing wrong?'

'Of course, you do,' said Jones, 'you're not used to persuading people. You've got *control* of some people, but you don't know anything about inducing support.'

'Oh dear,' Annie sighed from across the table.

The others turned to hear her out, but I'd already started to unpick what she was thinking.

'Evans and I know someone exactly like that, some people exactly like that,' she said.

'The G-Russ, yes, but they're totally opposed to the kind of anarchy that Crossley's madness represents,' Jones said precisely as if she'd considered this possibility several days ago.

'"Opposed" is a strong term for five heartless marketers that can be made to do almost anything when their gestalt mental well-being is on the line. One little bit of psychological turbulence, and they go pop. I mean, they sorted out Evans's life here just because they had some conflicted feelings over me that I let them work out.'

Jones looked as if someone had punched her in the spleen. *For just a hand / the rain it raineth.*

'Not only can you get the kings of spin to do whatever you want if you have the right leverage,' Buggati noted, 'but they also won't even feel terribly bad about it. They are just doing what they need to do to survive. No wonder our side of the story isn't getting any traction.'

She looked at our depressed faces, then picked a grape from the bowl on the table and looked at it thoughtfully.

'I'll tell you one thing. God help the "squire" once the G-Russ work out a way around whatever mucky secret he has on them. Spiteful little gutties they are.'

'I'll tell Green what we're up against,' Jones said, 'Now get those rings on and get this job done before there's no home to come back to.'

With that, she disappeared. There could be little doubt that the home front wouldn't be won first.

'Rings?' asked Rolliard.

Meletrus, sensing that it was appropriate to return to the conversation, joined us at the glossy table.

¤ Yes, rings indeed. One for each of you. Your safety is essential to us. Boat if we could have the devices? ¤

Whether summoned into existence by the boat or stored inside the table, I couldn't tell, but before us, silver rings emerged from the wooden surface, each patterned with black pictograms.

¤ Every Paraunion environment will be in some way dangerous to your health, not to mention many of the activities a citizen might innocently invite you to take part in. The visitor rings are designed to prevent any harm from coming to you. With them on, you're effectively immortal... that is until the batteries run out. ¤

Spindle, Nian and Rolliard had already picked theirs up and slipped them on. I was about to do the same when I heard Annie clear her throat.

'What if I don't like the symbolism of the Paraunion giving me a ring?'

Meletrus laughed. Spindle audibly sighed in frustration.

¤ Anything close to your person and secure will do. The device can adapt in size, shape and texture, whatever pleases you most. If it offends your aesthetic, it could blend seamlessly with your skin or embed inside your chest if you prefer? ¤

'I suppose a ring is fairly practical. Just don't get the idea that I'm your fucking fiancée Evans,' she conceded.

I gave the room a few moments to settle; a little discussion went on about the merits of letting others see that we were ambassadors, perhaps making the rings more ceremonial. Annie and I had made our peace over the last few days; we weren't going to be romantically involved again. Too much time had passed. *Time to be naughty.*

I whispered into her ear, 'We're not engaged. You work for me, lover.'

At which point, the indestructible properties of my ring were immediately tested.

18 Burning out of season

The halls of history are littered with poets' ramblings; a bird, a vase, a boy they picked up last night or who just left them. Generally speaking, the idea that poets are big thinkers is a crime. Frame a thing: keep it small and detailed. They dream small and hope it means much more. So, it is unfair to show a poet the actual gates of heaven.

Onis glowed, dimly black-red, in space. A hooded lantern in the satin of the night. Each solar pole was crowned by aurora, where the flux and light of the captive star within emerged. Everywhere else, Onis surrounded, enveloped its host star, captured every sunbeam and even moved the star at the will of its creators. Imagine a sphere with the top and bottom thirds removed and the remaining shell as big as the orbit of Shang Lo or Earth. *Dyson's fear.*

The boat took us through a polar opening, diving in and around the lip of Onis so that we cruised above the internal atmosphere and could see around us the colossal bright landscape. Meletrus pointed out one of the original planets, held just above the surface of Onis like a moth pinned to a tile.

¤ This is the cradle of the Paraunion, ¤ the boat said, ¤ where two opposing factions lay down the first cultural rules and broke a cycle of conflict that had plagued them for centuries. ¤

¤ We'll start here on the capital world, ¤ Meletrus added, ¤ which is under special conservation and preservation orders. It includes significant artefacts from many of the five thousand species that have joined the union. ¤

¤ My god, ¤ I said. ¤ The whole human species could live here and have all the room they need. ¤

¤ An entire country each, ¤ said Nian.

'That would be typically human,' Annie remarked after waiting for translation by the boat, 'dividing things up just as soon as we've managed to connect them all together.'

Spindle nodded approvingly of that comment as he set off in search of his jacket. My heart and stomach turned. Before me was the answer to all humanities problems, but the Cannots wouldn't even look at it. They didn't even believe it was on offer to them. *Drowning, not waving.*

I think the boat mistook my emotional state for something else because it whispered in my ear.

¤ You know we don't vandalise every domain we live in. I can assure you we've come on significantly since this primitive time. ¤

*

While Annie and Nian stood in front of a molten-looking monolith. Rolliard obsessed over the visitor ring.

'Don't you find that things smell and taste different once you've put it on?' he asked.

'A little, but I put that down to being somewhere other than the boat.'

'Yeah, I thought about that too. You know the boat was a kind of cleanroom? It can print furniture, food and clothes straight out of thin air. It was a totally safe environment. And that first meet up with Meletrus, on a remote art installation, was a first interview which you must have passed, and then we got the rings, and we're let loose to do anything we want.'

'Not *anything* we want, Rolliard. There was a pretty big list of activities to be avoided.'

That focussed his mind on the task at hand. Nian stared over her shoulder at her aide fraternizing with me.

'This plinth is a million—one million—years old,' she said. 'Don't you think it deserves a little of your time rather than the gizmo on your finger?'

'Yes ma'am,' Rolliard snapped back into cadet mode when chastized, even by someone significantly younger than himself.

I wanted to touch the stone. The forbidden always attracted me. *The gravity of the subway tracks.* Million-year-old rocks are common, but this monument was the first object crafted by a Paraunion.

It stood forlornly in a broad grey-grassed plain that extended to the visible horizon. A horizon imperceptibly different from any planet and had never known a sunrise or set. Meletrus eased us into the sights of Onis. Was she worried about whatever had happened to poor Broule? Or perhaps she was thinking about my own problem with the Crush? Whatever her concerns, wherever there are cultures, there are meeting places, and where there are meeting places, there are cities. Our next stop was the largest city in the known universe, and I hoped it hadn't developed in the same soul-destroying manner as Shang Lo.

I still wasn't thinking enough like a Paraunion citizen. The monkey brain inside me continued to expect everything to be a slight alteration of things I had already experienced.

¤ That building is rather lavishly known as the "Sword of Heaven". It reaches beyond the atmosphere and is used nowadays as a community hub for administration on matters of sentient creation. ¤

We gathered around Meletrus as she enthused with all four of her arms. I tried to take in the grand plaza with one hundred and eight sculptures, the nearest a weeping figure bent over a dead, twisted beast on a crystal plinth. The wondrous buildings of the Paraunion crowded around the edge of the plaza in every direction.

Avenues formed chasms sprinkled with pedestrians that led away from the plaza. There were no taxis or security vans, no whisps of ferrite clouds in the air. No bearded prophets wailed madly in the bays of shops, while no multi-adverts scarred the sides of the buildings. No flumes sucked the fetid air out of the street.

Tranquil but not empty. The streets were broad enough to accommodate the dozen walking titans and dots of other citizens. One long beast seemed to pause in meditation before the balcony of an arboretum. The lack of hurry was almost suffocating to the human mind. *Crushless void.*

¤ The colosseum opposite is the children's art institute. The walls you see beyond are the exploratory planning society, a powerful organisation, as you can imagine, but sometimes used for academic research. Over there is the "Long Perdition Approach" of interest to those studying the pre-union leaders and a site of historical significance. The grey pillars you see are the drive cores of decommissioned warships.¤

Annie looked dizzy. I couldn't decide if she was better off not hearing the additional Para information that Meletrus was laying into the context or not. We had trawled through several hours of the capital's significant and mind-boggling sites, whisked from site to site by the boat.

'Need a break?' I asked.

'I don't want to sit on the floor in front of *them*,' she whispered.

In and out of the statues wandered Paraunion citizens, some with children, looking at sculpted scenes from the archetypes of their culture.

We all had varying degrees of culture shock. Still, with the assistance of the visitor rings, which could help moderate the metabolism, it was possible to recover rather than fall apart. There were limits, though.

¤ Is a rest out of the question, Meletrus? Or somewhere like a Hotiocha, or a café? ¤ I asked.

I saw our host was disappointed to break off the tour and not delve deeper into the miracles of her society's five thousand races. The concept of a café caused some difficulty, or maybe I'd translated it as a caffeine-den.

¤ The wall of song, maybe? Ah no, that's a bit too stimulating as well.¤

Other visitors slowed as they passed our group, intrigued by our species and discussion. A pair of Carshanid shaeks, delicate carapaces twinkling like wet bone, approached directly.

¤ My ward here is very excited about your guests, ¤ he said, embarrassed, ¤ she is due at the shaping grounds for her certification and would like to know if you want her to generate a 'café' for them? It might be instructional for our ambassadors? ¤

The master's context revealed that he was not the child's progenitor and that the young shaek had pressured him to ask. Meletrus sympathised with the guardian and made the best of things. She looked at our weary faces and came to a conclusion.

¤ Maybe it would be good for you to see a demonstration and get out of the city? That sounds like a worthy plan. ¤

The boat descended on us rapidly from far out of the sky, which caused more excitement for the young shaek. It spoke far too quickly for me to catch what it was saying, and it was at that point I realised that Meletrus and every Paraunion had been talking to us very, very slowly.

 ¤ The boat is *famous*, ¤ Spindle explained to me as we boarded. The actual phrase merged the concepts of unique, celebrity and shy.

*

Kap, the little shaek, minnowed up to me and flexed its skapulum. I'd been surveying the wrecking yard around us, which looked like a Hieronymus Bosch painting brought to life. Half-built things issued from the ground, copies of the archetype statues stood in disarray next to primitive shapes of unknown purpose and delicate helixes. Apparently, a school party had recently left.

 ¤ Would you like to share with me a café you like? ¤ she asked.

Meletrus and the instructor, a powerful-looking cube of muscle, both immediately joined the conversation.

 ¤ Oh my dear, ¤ Meletrus quickly jumped in, ¤ he cannot. Let me find some source material for you instead. ¤

 ¤ It'll be better that way, ¤ the muscular block noted.

The mode in which the little shaek had said "to share" confused me. Kap had used all the elements that a human is familiar with but added layers of permission like the bank system had those years back in Movey when it wanted every detail of my life.

Having overheard the information passing between Meletrus and the shaek, the muscle block looked at the surrounding vista and addressed Nian and Rolliard, who were examining broken relics.

 ¤ Could all visitors please return to the observation area, ¤ it said impatiently. Nian immediately pushed Rolliard back to where we were standing. The meat block summoned a flattened metal circle with dainty chairs to emphasise its point.

¤ Now, we'll need a little space to start working with, won't we? ¤ it said to the shaek.

The litter of buildings, statues, machines and curiosities was levelled out immediately for hundreds of yards in front of us. Beyond that area, stranger things still loomed on the landscape.

¤ And a little backdrop to keep things pleasing. ¤

A surround of trees shimmered into existence, not growing up but coalescing out of the atmosphere. They were too far away for me to tell if they were natural living plants or just sculptures. The open ground inside the tree line looked like volcanic sand.

Kap—keen to get on with her project—began plotting out the edges of the construction like a sketch artist putting in the first lines. What started as a rectangular tracery of orange lines was supplemented with arches, lintels, windows and doorways. As she drew, the air filled with the smell of hot sand.

Around the building, a street with pavement was outlined and quickly filled with generic stone material.

¤ The area is seeded with construction motes. All the elements you could ever need, so students can express themselves without waiting for the nodes to gather or transmute materials, ¤ Meletrus informed us.

In the meantime, under the instructor's guidance, Kap had moved on to correcting and solidifying her design. On Shang Lo, we used building printers, but the Paraunionists controlled unseen forces and machines to do the same job without the actual printer. Miraculously, a Parisian café appeared. At first, dimly out of rough masonry but then with doors and windows, awnings and tables, out of thin air. The instructor guided her in refining details, developing the whole construction from primitive shapes into convincing facsimiles.

Perhaps they didn't know that none of us had ever been to Paris, let alone sat in a café on the Boulevard Raspail.

Odder still to see a human building and street so large with no one in it, as if the apocalypse had struck and left a single grand feature untouched. The student and instructor moved inside to refine their work, deducing as they went how items should be finished, turning grey sculptures into brass, cloth and wood. Finally, they beckoned us in.

I couldn't say how accurate the reproduction was, but it convinced me. I had watched in a dream until that point, but as I sat down on the soft green booth seat, I was surprised to find it wasn't just light and illusion.

'Impressive,' said Annie, 'but still missing a key ingredient.'

I stared at Annie as I feared she was insulting our host.

¤ Indeed! What is a café without coffee? ¤ laughed Meletrus. ¤ But as that might be a little unfair for our young constructor. Please allow me. ¤

On the table appeared cups and saucers and then eventually coffee, the aroma of which filled the three-minute-old building. It tasted, as far as I knew, like the real thing.

¤ We print clothes, objects and buildings, but this is something else, ¤ I said.

¤ It's less a case of technology and more of economics. Can you afford the energy and entropy of what you want to create? Do you really know the detail? We have endless libraries of prototypes, but if one wishes to construct something new, something of our very own, then skill, imagination and training, ¤ she nodded at the shaek student, ¤ are essential. ¤

¤ And bodies? Can you just summon them up too? ¤ Nian asked.

¤ Yes, though switching bodies entirely rather than changing what one already has is a lengthy process. The individual's mind with the *anamata* must be carefully transplanted. ¤

Meletrus could tell that the translation supplied by the visitor ring wasn't doing the word anamata much justice. Both Rolliard and Annie looked confused.

¤ The anamata makes us truly Paraunion; it is the keep, sanctum sanctorum, and deep, unmoveable well of a Paraunion entity. Only a few races naturally have access to these "cached" dimensions in their brains. Most are gifted at birth so that everything they are and want to be can expand and flourish into it like a budding garden given boundless safe fields to grow into. Once utilized, however, it can never be unused. The gate to that unlimited land can never be moved, which is why you'll find so much importance placed on physicality, proximity—even possibly a fear of being unconscious—in Paraunion behaviour. ¤

At that moment, we overheard the instructor mentoring the shaek and pointing at us.

¤ Observe the fragile biped frame and how they rest from a precarious state of balance. A wise architect can make many assumptions about the items we see around us. The brass rail around the bar for leaning on, the couches and booths. Note the lips and digestive nature of *homo sapiens*. The astute observer links them to the lip of the wine glasses and possibly even hidden rooms around the structure. The building materials suggest the life span and outlook of the species at this time in their history. ¤

We enjoyed our drinks in the strangest coffee house in the universe while being behaviourally dissected by a gruff block of muscle. It should have antagonised the onset of culture shock, but the instructor explained the human way of life simply and objectively, and it was what we were here to "sell" the Paraunion.

Spindle eventually tried to get the group back on mission.

¤ Meletrus, would it be possible for us to keep this construct? ¤

¤ Are you sure, Professor? It's only a student project? ¤

¤ I think I speak for all of us when I say that the hard work Kap has put into it is a credit to her. We'll need a place to meet and entertain visitors, conduct our ambassadorial duties and recuperate. I can't think of a better start. There are only five of us, ¤ he waved at the fifty-odd tables around us, ¤ and this location appears to cater to more than that number.¤

¤ It's my duty to remind you that you are visitors at the moment. You have no rights to an embassy with any sovereignty over the land it stands on. On the other hand, I do see your point. I'll seek permission for a suitable location elsewhere on Onis. ¤

The little shaek was very excited at this development, the sour instructor less so. Nevertheless, humanity gained its first tiny foothold within the Paraunion.

Unfortunately, it did not please everyone.

They say that all publicity is good publicity. The G-Russ would undoubtedly have said it, and our application for a tiny amount of space somewhere on the vast inner surface of Onis caused a scandal. While the dispute raged, the Cafe Des Humanes—a title Nian came up with after browsing pictures of ancient Paris—remained preserved on the training grounds. It could have been wiped out and rebuilt from Kap's original instructions, but Meletrus said gifts in the Paraunion weren't discarded lightly.

There was a short-lived *vrys,* an argument in the Paraunion network, over the appropriateness of allocating space on the vast interior of Onis for a human meet-and-greet centre; after all, Onis had a preservation order on it as the capital of the Paraunion. The vrys made more people aware of our existence.

It was a pro-human master of the master of the child Kap who clinched the deal. It suggested a derelict site that held no cultural importance, a location that was more of an eyesore waiting for renovation. Not everyone was happy about the decision, but an unexpectedly large number of Paraunion took part, listened to, and voted on the debate. As a by-product, the complete history of humanity and its achievements compiled by the Border Institute was distributed to a wider audience.

Nian, Spindle and Rolliard thought the whole escapade had been a roaring success, but Bugatti looked at the issue from a different angle.

'They might be interested in humans now, but one thing's the same between the Paraunion and us, the public loves controversy and entertainment, but it doesn't mean they'll do anything for us. You heard Meletrus: this isn't an embassy. We need to prove that we're worth taking in, not that we're going to cause trouble and act like pricks all the time.'

'Who says we're acting like pricks?' I asked.

'Evans! It's your favourite tactic. Who was it who vandalised the flipride station *joytime* dispensers every Lost Soul day?'

'People need to wake up and see the state they're in once a year, not get blazed on commuter drugs every day, and I was never caught doing that.'

'But you did it.'

She pointed at the others as they prepared for a new batch of visitors to our not-an-embassy.

'These guys are the feel-good-fluffy type. You and I know how the little people get left out in the cold after the amusement has worn off, and the purpose of this mystery tour is to *not* get left out in the cold.'

'Alright, I hear you,' truthfully, I had thought the same myself.

'Look, you and I aren't the shiny goody-goody crew, are we? What do you think that sneaky shit Jones put us together for?'

'Fashion tips?'

'Don't be a Feng artist!'

'Ok, ok. Dirty tricks, Critishins side door stuff. I hear what you're saying, but we need to be careful. If we try and add a little zip to this campaign, Nian or Spindle can't be involved or hear about it. I'd say we could get Rolliard on our side, but he's pretty wound up about the duty of being an ambassadors' aide. He just might tip off Nian.'

'Believe it, brother. There's nothing about Para or being an ambassador we can teach those three.'

I looked across the dozens of empty tables at the real ambassadors: Spindle, Nian and Rolliard. Annie was right. I'd never be as good at Para as Nian or Spindle. *Or Lutsk.* I never had the open nature of Rolliard or Nian. Movampton had screwed that out of me and chocked me full of prejudices and fears. Occasionally, I felt a twinge of guilt for the civil disobedience of my youth, unlike Annie, in whom the light of anarchy was perpetually lit. Mostly though, I was grateful that the same spark wrote the *Pollutant*.

Wasn't I just what Border had been forced to send because so few candidates had passed the test? *Few serve from outside.* I swirled the remains of my replicated belle epoque coffee in the bottom of the china cup.

I saw through the window the boat touch down without a sound on the street, without troubling the awnings shading tables and chairs from the everlasting daylight. A vast bluish mountain loomed on the horizon beyond the boat, where our road was incomplete. *Our own Fuji-san.*

¤ Do you see that? ¤ I pointed.

'Come on, Evans, don't make me listen to the translator.'

'Sorry—do you see that?' I pointed again to the mountain.

'Sure, really big hill, what about it?'

'According to Meletrus, it's a living being, one of the few completely sedentary entities in the entire Paraunion. I want to go and see it.'

'Ok, let's go.'

'We're not allowed.'

'Why's that?'

'She said it would be genuinely dangerous to our minds to speak to it.'

'Feng me.'

'Yup, but the more I look at it, the more I still want to go anyway.'

Several Paraunion disembarked from the boat as we spoke. Nian and Spindle had gone out to welcome them. Rolliard signalled that we should go and join the greeting committee.

The boat formed a tented opening like the exit of a grand iron marquee, and out of it came the three visitors. A camera fish led the way; its long, rusty pipe body was tipped with a single vast eye, a popular body format for Paraunion acting through an avatar. It politely approached the waiting human ambassadors while the other two Paraunion ambled out, still deep in discussion. They made no attempt to hide their comments from us.

¤ Promise me, D-t-arr, that you are approaching this with an open mind, ¤ said the glass prowler.

¤ I assure you, Pontus, that's all I wish to do. I'm just asking you to not try to sway me before I get a chance to see things for myself, ¤ D-t-arr replied, his spectral black face shells grinding as he spoke.

D-t-arr's pace matched the glass prowler but not its fluid movements. Instead, curtains of slick muscle jerked and coiled to propel the black-green mass along.

To make the café less solitary, Meletrus had sketched in the rest of two streets, almost a twelfth of the old arrondissement, complete with lampposts and trees. Her plan was to populate the area with great articles of human art. At the moment, only Rodin's *The Thinker* was in the centre of the junction in front of the café, acting as a reminder to us that we needed to do something more there.

D-t-arr took this in with an underwhelmed air. At the same time, Pontus acknowledged us cordially and joined the conversation with Eteri, the camera fish avatar, who was eager to hear what we had to say.

¤ Now, has anyone talked to you about the rights to your form yet? ¤ it asked.

¤ Meletrus mentioned it but said it was too early to be discussed, ¤ Spindle replied.

¤ Oh, never too early! Never, never! You should think about it now. There's a lot of appeal to these cultural knickknacks and folk stories but giving people the chance to *test drive a human* is where the interest and excitement are. ¤

Eteri said "interest and excitement" with the same lip-smacking tonal resonance an old Movey banker might have said "liquid capital". Nian guided it into the café with Rolliard following behind them. Aides had to keep as expressionless as possible. A fraction of the conversation was translated to him via the visitor ring.

Spindle greeted Pontus with a tone of familiarity. It must have been their third or fourth meeting judging by their context, and Pontus clearly held the visiting professor in high regard, perhaps even verging on calling him a friend. D-t-arr had quite a different attitude.

He approached with a truculent posture and inspected me as if I were a static part of the exhibit.

¤ Thank you for taking the time to come and see us in person, ¤ I said as a formal and appreciative greeting. Annie took up position several steps back from me.

¤ You're the mental patient they sent to explain the wonders of humanity, aren't you? I don't mean to be cruel but this process is probably unnecessarily stressful for you. ¤

His condescension was palpable. It was a pet owner's tone without any affection, a disenchanted veterinary nurse talking about a stray cat. It caught me off-guard, and my reply was stuttered and hesitant.

¤ It's a privilege to be here. Can I show you some of the exhibits inside? ¤

D-t-arr roamed around the statue of *The Thinker,* considering it, ignoring my question, until he came to a stop and leant casually against the figure's knee. He looked down at me and sighed.

¤ Alright then, I suppose that's why we're here. Again, I don't mean to be rude ambassador, but I'll bet that no one else has talked to you about the disappointing biography your race provided us, have they? No? I thought not. You'll find that a lot in the Paraunion: nothing is secret, but a lot remains unrevealed. ¤

D-t-arr examined me closely for any reaction to his comments. I'd managed to recover from his initial blindside and realised that his intention was to get to the bottom of human nature as soon as possible, even if it was with blunt force.

I guided him into the café whose doorway had been enlarged to a Paraunion standard but kept in the era's style. The back walls of the salon had been removed and led into two wings that looped to make a large quadrangle, each side lined with exhibits. The pieces on display were mostly replicas of important cultural objects. A few rare cases were the real deal, shipped from Border. Our guests had no need for explanatory texts or infographics and seemed intimately aware of the details of human history, science, and literature.

Such a museum of humanity could have easily been virtually fabricated by any half-competent augmented reality designer, but Spindle assured us the Paraunion had high regard for authentic, not virtual, experiences and a suspicion of simulations. Our role as ambassadors was curating stories, summing up the tragic romance of all human endeavours. *6.373 The world is independent of my will.* The selected items were rich in narrative potential to fuel the Paraunion penchant for debate. Even D-t-arr was not immune.

We stopped before a clay tablet. It was an authentic artefact with verses of the Odyssey etched into it by a long-dead Greek. D-t-arr didn't appear to be paying my tour guide patois much heed, but he was gravitationally drawn to the object itself. I saw it was a good time to shut up and let him enjoy himself without my interruption.

¤ You say it matched the story that had been handed down? ¤ he asked.

¤ Almost exactly. ¤

¤ And this was only a few millennia ago? You certainly have come up quickly, haven't you? These items transmit how busy you humans are, so creative, why it'll be no more than a few more centuries before you'll be able to hold your heads up high and deservedly seek membership. ¤

¤ I don't see why we shouldn't be seeking membership right now. As you say, we're a creative force, and we can't ignore what we know is outside our own borders. We ticked off your first requisite: we made the Border planet. We're adventurers and makers; you can't show us an undiscovered country and not expect us to set off into it. ¤

D-t-arr considered me, his context reflecting genuine sympathy, not just to me but towards the exhibits around us.

¤ I understand. But is that what all humans want? To sign up and collaborate as part of the Paraunion? To be consumed by the burden of the tasks it entails? You still have many more fascinating little folk journeys to work out of your system. Most of your population walks around in a virtual dream, a fantasy that you and your party are disconnected from while with us. Haven't you grasped what the Paraunion find so essential? To be alive is to be as awake as possible. Someday, soon perhaps, you'll genuinely become conscious as a people, and I think then you'll be ready to join us. ¤

¤ Why not help us? Why not teach us? You seemed concerned that this interview process was cruel to me, but am I not the *Sister who Rises from Misfortune*? ¤

I think my use of the archetype caught D-t-arr off guard. He hadn't counted on the level of preparation that Spindle and the boat had given us and didn't expect to enter into a paraunion style debate.

¤ The *Sister*? I suppose there is that way of looking at it. Who are we to deny you your dreams and stories? Now let me concentrate, please. ¤

We walked on; past an invisibly suspended copy of the sculpture *Nocturne in Black and Gold* and a performance of *Kitsun no So*. We passed an arrangement of priceless Roman, Venetian and Centaurean glassware, then stopped for a few moments in the infamous *New Musical Fugue* vorticism with the original recording and tryptic. We slipped by the silver nitrate portraits of the members of the Manhattan Project. On and on we went: through science, history, language and art, but nothing occupied my visitor for more than a handful of moments.

As we passed each epic achievement, I was lifted by my race's accomplishments and a fraction disappointed when I realised there was nothing from Movampton. *I am Movey.*

When we returned to the Salon, I saw the others discussing matters under the awnings, looking happy and relaxed. I reminded myself that D-t-arr was just one of many people who would be judging our membership. There were bound to be naysayers.

¤ Did you enjoy that D-t-arr? ¤ asked his prowler friend.

¤ Some elements were amusing, I won't deny, but I think your hopes of gaining a unique indigenous thought or idea to bring into the Paraunion are in vain. Lots of interesting distractions, nothing altogether new. Nothing original. ¤

¤ You lack the patience to dig for diamonds, D-t-arr. ¤

¤ Time is something we should be spending wisely now, don't you agree, Eteri? ¤

The camera fish was caught off guard. Something about its attitude reminded me of a worker taking a sneaky day off.

¤ What? Oh yes. Well, who's to say what tomorrow might bring? The dark oceans might turn out to be harmless or simply unnavigable. How can there be any harm in familiarizing ourselves with another candidate? Let me remind you that finding new life is still not to be squandered. ¤

I felt a sharp dread as the camera fish mentioned dark oceans. Whatever they were, its context revealed how concerned the Paraunion were over the point. This was the issue that Meletrus had hinted might consume all Paraunion attention. Spindle seemed to want to jump into the conversation and drill Eteri for more information, but D-t-arr was still holding forth, and he wished to push home his argument.

¤ What's the point, though? Should outsiders come right to our borders, as many suggest is inevitable, we will regret having spent any time at all upon a candidate species and not making our own preparations? ¤

The prowler became annoyed at D-t-arr. His embarrassment projected in Para like speaking in front of a condemned man about his own lynching.

¤ The Paraunion brings peace and order to the universe D-t-arr. It provides guidance and protection. ¤

¤ Of course. But there are limits, ¤ D-t-arr pointed at my visitor ring. ¤ We give them a source of immense power, but they can only walk around appreciating its passive benefits like a dog resting in the shade of a missile. We could drop a universe of scientific advancement on them, and it would do no good until they are ready to receive it. It is better to leave them as if we had never found them, separate and unanointed by our well-meaning unionists, and return to them when the time is right. ¤

Spindle finally found an opening to put forward a point.

¤ You speak as if we were unconscious—as if we didn't know that our civilisation was on the verge of an enormous choice—but we are! We've come to you to enter into the family of the Paraunion. ¤

¤ And is that really how *all* of humanity feels? Have you given them all the facts? ¤ D-t-arr ground his silica faceplates as he spoke.

¤ It is how the majority feel. ¤

¤ We shall see, shan't we? I will study the information you've provided and add some research of my own. Then I'll have a more balanced opinion than my two giddy comrades. I am a realist professor, and I know better than to accept the first story I'm told as the truth. ¤

D-t-arr gave a curt, folding bow, then turned and made his way back into the boat without waiting for any response. Nian looked at me with a furrowed brow. She wasn't used to that kind of negativity, and it was a good thing that I had pulled the short straw of guiding D-t-arr. The camera fish and glass prowler gave far more civilised farewells and thanks, although underlying their calm surface was a bitter trace left from being derided by their colleague.

As the boat took to the air, a figure appeared in the street, solidifying quickly like a time-lapse of a statue eroding in reverse. It was Meletrus. When she spoke, the rarefied dust on her lips showed how the thin construct continued to aggregate itself even while it was used by the owner.

¤ Apologies for not being present, ¤ she said. ¤ How are your tours going? ¤

I took on the unfortunate job of relating the details of the visit. Meletrus's reaction was sympathetic.

¤ With almost every membership process, there are three schools of thought. The Paraunion are nothing if not philosophically predictable, maybe due to the same old archetypes in their arguments. Firstly, there will be those who see value or advantage in adopting a new race, maybe from absorbing their cultural richness, a unique engineering approach, or a distinctive biological feature. Remember that in the vast exploration of this galactic neighbourhood, the wellspring of life is still rare; almost every race is eventually accepted when it matures to sufficient levels, with only one or two strange exceptions. That means that virtually every species has some unique twist to bring.

¤ The second contingent considers the Paraunion as the salvation of the universe. They push for early and forceable appropriation of the new member as soon as possible. This zeal has caused difficulty in the past. The Paraunion way of having your fellow citizen as your master is difficult for the wild heart to accept; for some, it will always look like universal slavery. That led us to the union drawing up minimum standards for qualification; a Paraunion language centre, for instance. ¤

Meletrus noted with disapproval and a sideways glance that the avenue still only contained a single exhibit. She continued with a sigh.

¤ Finally, some say membership is for the circumstantial advantage of the existing Paraunion. There's a lot of early history to back that up, especially from the early years when the masterhood system's main achievement was to prevent wars. To paraphrase the *Lucid Jester*, sometimes it isn't the right time to load more gold in your canoe. ¤

I laughed, but Spindle and Nian both looked disturbed. I recognised the sensation they were going through, the same creeping realisation that comes over you when a lawyer or doctor, dispassionate and friendly, lays out the details of the process to you. *Reasons more terrible than tigers.* There are no certainties. This could happen, that could happen. Meletrus was being kind but clear.

¤ If these dark oceans are the reason the time isn't right, ¤ said Spindle. ¤ Why didn't you tell us more about them? ¤

¤ Facts about them are difficult to come by. I didn't want to mislead you, but I also didn't want you to be completely unaware of the situation, so I briefed Jones. We've lost exploration vessels without a trace. We track the distance into the unknown before losing them, and it seems to edge closer every day. Are we being targeted? Is our knowledge of what's between galaxies flawed? Who can say?

¤ If I could tell you, I would. Some assume the worst: that outsiders will be at our gates. The Paraunion has begun defence and research operations the likes of which history has never seen, at the cost of its other interests, including recruitment. ¤

Rolliard and Annie looked so worried and frustrated by the translations that I sat them down in the Cafe Des Humanes and clarified everything with them. Meletrus gave Spindle and Nian a pep talk and got them to choose more items for our surreal Parisian Avenue. As she summoned the imposing winged female figure of *Victory of Samothrace*, I slipped away to go for a walk.

*

Nian found me in the scrubland on the edge of our little preserve, seated on what looked like the concrete remains of a pillar laid on its side. I was, I admit, in a foul mood. I felt the mission was slipping away from us and that I had let the others down by not persuading D-t-arr that we were worth taking time to consider. Worse, I didn't like that he'd been able to shake me up with a few basic facts. I mean, you hear worse than that in Movey when you're ordering a sandwich. *The blind tackle kills.*

From where I sat, the mountain looked like a pinnacle of glass. It glowered grey-blue, thinking its long, universal thoughts.

¤ Is this a private brooding, or can anyone join in? ¤ Nian asked.

¤ Just spending some time with my new friend. ¤

I pointed at the great mountain.

¤ You always liked the strong, silent type. What have you two been talking about? ¤

¤ Glaciers. Skiing. The usual. ¤

She chuckled.

¤ Melly has put up twenty more statues. You should come and see. It's pretty cool. ¤

¤ No thanks. ¤

Nian kissed me on the cheek. It did make me feel slightly better. *Whose least amazing smile is the divisor of unequal souls.*

¤ You know, three influential people came to see us today, and two of them walked away convinced that humans should get to join the Paraunion. ¤

She made a good point.

21   Molon labe

Spindle repeated it.

¤ A private conversation. ¤

Meletrus looked perplexed for a few moments.

¤ Of course, you're entitled to secrets—you aren't Paraunion yet. No doubt our transparency is alien to you—just as you'll understand that privacy is an old-fashioned concept to us. It will take some time, but we can arrange it. ¤

¤ I certainly appreciate it. We do as our masters ask, and our masters may be slightly more eccentric than yours, ¤ Spindle said.

¤ Isn't it private onboard the boat? ¤ I asked.

¤ Oh no, quite the opposite. I hope we haven't given you the wrong impression. An integral part of the boat's make-up is its unceasing dedication to public duty. It cannot ignore anything it sees, hears, or senses for a great distance. It may even *want* to ignore you, but its conscience won't allow it. ¤

'Feng. That sounds awful,' said Annie.

¤ You should ask it, ¤ replied Meletrus.

Despite the unexpected nature of our request, it only took an hour or two for the clearance and construction of a room-size box, which the boat lowered into place. The location hid it behind the period facia from the casual observer. *I hear they eat their young.*

As far as we could determine, without genuinely offending our hosts, we would be able to communicate securely with Jones and Green whenever we wanted.

Perhaps that wasn't quite as useful as we'd hoped.

Projected via the inner eye, Green walked up and down. He'd clearly lost a lot of weight since I'd last seen him, while Jones sat back in her office chair, bowed but as yet unbroken.

Spindle gave me a worried Para gesture; he didn't predict joyful news from our superiors.

'They want Border closed.'

'Can they get a vote through?' I asked.

'No, not yet, but both Green and I think that by the time the next budget comes around to being agreed, they will have enough support to stop the search for new students.'

Green nodded.

'It's an easier approach from their point of view. They aren't shutting down the exploration or culture of Border, just making sensible savings. Then they can blame the project for lack of results, make more savings with the staff, and suggest that the whole planet could be put to better use. If they successfully divide the opinion against them, they will have the majority of influence amongst the polilawyers, and then the whole game is up. Time to empty out my desk.'

I returned Spindle's concerned gesture so that Nian could see it. Our leaders were looking worn out. Maybe now wasn't the time to give them the full story of our Paraunion mission.

'We recruited two definite supporters from the visitors we saw today,' Nian said encouragingly.

'And more visits booked in for the next few weeks. Bringing some genuine artefacts really paid off,' I said.

'We've Spindle to thank for that idea,' said Green.

'Our problem,' said Spindle, brushing off the praise, 'Is with the Paraunion sense of time. However urgent we feel this is, they are used to taking decades or centuries to decide anything. Pushing them into the timescale of a year will be challenging.'

'We'll need a win then,' said Green. 'Somehow, we've got to stall the Cannot movement and its political wing. Border is a requirement of membership. We can probably give you another eighteen months before it looks like a sham to the Paraunion. I mean, I hope we can.'

'Maybe we can get some Paraunion funding before then,' Nian asked.

That comment caught Jones by surprise.

'Maybe you misunderstand: we can't use Paraunion funding. Our cultures are incompatible for trade. If it were gold or silver or shells even! The Paraunion could produce boatloads of it and ship them to us. But culcap is issued only by our exchequer. Everything is valued by that. We can accept food or a shiny new ship from the Paraunion, but the one thing we can't get from them is money to pay our workers. It's a problem that we've thought through several times. It also might come with a stigma attached. Nobody likes international charity.'

'The Paraunion capital is energy and opinion, neither of which we have any significant sums of,' said Spindle.

'What's it like back home?' Nian asked.

'That depends where your home is. Our problems are exponentially worse wherever there were large populations of the poor and desperate,' said Green, 'Anywhere were multitudes might take to using the *Alone* program for a little comfort or escape. Shang Lo and Xīn are particularly bad, the social care infrastructure has collapsed, and local authorities are turning a blind eye to the areas they cannot help in.'

Movampton, a thousand tiny shocks is not enough. Green took no joy in telling me that our local neighbourhood was now a lawless ghetto. In fact, he may have understated the case. My improvement in Para had the side effect of making me several orders better at reading human subtext. Was it possible that a proto-Para was evolving in humans naturally?

The dark privacy box seemed to me like a bunkered war room. Perhaps it would be the last hiding place of defeated generals. Would we be forced to turn ourselves over to the victorious Cannots? I was sure that Spindle would take his own life first. He was so much a Paraunion already, and it was evident in his expressions when he heard about the terrible human suffering; he sympathised, but not as one of them. Spindle regretted that *those* people would do such a thing to each other.

151

We agreed to meet daily for updates, but that first meeting ended under a bitter, black cloud.

I didn't look forward to filling Annie and Rolliard on the news from home, but they had equally bad news for me. It seemed that most Paraunion have an appointment fetish. The more distant the arrangement to physically meet, the more gratifying it is to them. It's like showing off the ability to prophecy.

D-t-arr had just booked a return visit.

*

I waited through the intervening weeks, guiding curious Paraunion of every form around our growing museum. My knack for binding up all their questions into one grand narrative of the ascent of humanity became better and better. I didn't feel too bad about it either. When has history not been dramatized? Eventually, the day of D-t-arr's return came.

We decided all three ambassadors should accompany him this time. Little did we know he intended to bring support of his own.

He arrived alone. No sign of the prowler, Pontus, or the camera fish.

¤ Greetings, Ambassadors, ¤ he said, grinding faceplates.

We all reciprocated. D-t-arr looked at the long avenue that hosted replicas of every conceivable sculpture and statue that might interest our visitors.

¤ You seem to have created a lot of clutter since I was last here. Never mind, there's one thing that Onis is never short of, and that's storage space. If you think the interior is big? Consider the amount of unused volume *down there*. ¤ he rubbed a section of the street with a black curtained limb as if he saw into the ground.

¤ Would you care to see what's changed since your last visit, D-t-arr? ¤ I asked.

¤ No ambassador, I would not. I have made my summary of humanities achievements already. I'm not here to revisit that question. I'm here on a livelier debate, one left open at our last discussion. Is engaging with the Paraunion what humanity really wants? ¤

¤ Not only wants but badly needs, ¤ Spindle said.

¤ You see, this is the issue I have put my effort into solving. Is everything you show us here really a fair representation of your kind? I took the liberty of examining the situation in your government, on your streets and in your homes. ¤

The great black Paraunion lifted a baleful arm and pointed at the blank facia that hid the private room the boat had provided.

¤ You make your communiques in secret: to what end? It doesn't really matter. You'll be scurrying back inside it to whisper messages when this conversation is finished. In the meantime, allow me to present some colleagues. ¤

D-t-arr summoned two human figures on either side of him. Projections in mass, like Meletrus's avatar, allowed the user to feel and sense through them. The left form became recognisable as our former colleague Marna Malverona. The one on D-t-arr's right was a tall, gaunt man with a shock of blonde hair. He wore an ivory kijin-suit. His sulphate blue eyes took in the street of wonders, the Cafe Des Humanes, the endless summer sky above us, his expression one of rapture until he cast his eyes over us, after which it twisted into disgust.

'Don't you recognise me? Not surprising, not being a celebrity like yourselves. I'm Lucian Crossley.'

D-t-arr drank in our shock and distinctly moved himself to the side of the conversation, seating his spectre of a form on the pedestal of *Le Grand Van Gogh*.

¤ Good, I see there's no need for me to handle the rest of the introductions. I bring two examples from many I could choose, who represent a large section of human society who rightly wish to leave human progress as it's always been, a human matter. ¤

D-t-arr ground his faceplates together in a gesture of satisfaction. His context projected his feeling that everything had now been set right. With a gesture, he signalled for us to proceed with our debate. Marna wasted no time engaging.

'It appears a one-sided view of humanity is being put forward here,' she gestured at the cafe, 'as to the nature and wishes of humanity. There isn't a mention of the great revolution currently occurring in human thinking, a movement that holds our untimely relationship with the Paraunion to be unhealthy. As a political representative of just one of the parties representing this viewpoint, I demand that we be heard.'

As Marna made her remarks in a typical polilawyer fashion, all eyes were locked on the effete, skeletal figure of Crossley wandering among the new features of the avenue. *Why listen to the mon-key sing? / Behold the grinder sight-see-ing!* Annoyed at the lack of attention, she crossed her arms and waited for Crossley to speak.

'Unaccustomed as I am to being summoned, I would like to thank our gracious host for ensuring a balanced debate takes place,' he nodded at the reclined D-t-arr. 'He assures me this discussion will be broadcast to any Paraunion interested in the "human issue".'

'We'd be delighted to air our views, and how good it is to finally be able to do that face to face, Mr Crossley,' said Spindle, never easily taken off guard.

Crossley brushed some dust from the corner of the *Venus de Milo* and continued his stream of thought.

'Would you? That is decent of you, professor, especially since your clandestine flight from Border and your refusal to engage with members of Marna's party on policy matters. Of course, you leave such things to Jones, don't you? I understand. It can be difficult to attend to every little matter without some,' he waved his hand in the air, '*flunkies* at one's disposal. Tell me, Marna, what party does Jones represent?'

154

'None at all. She's part of the civil service,' Marna noted.

'A bureaucrat, a paper-pusher. Yet she takes upon herself the reform of the entire body politic under the beady eye of a foreign power?'

'The Border project was fully approved by our government,' Nian objected.

'Oh yes, *was*. It was fully approved, naively, many would say. A first step gesture, a toe in the water. But how far have we come from building a meeting station to handing over our sovereignty to this cultural machine? This beast that eats freewill for breakfast?'

'And what political party are you here representing, Crossley?'

'Marna is political. I think of myself more as a philosopher. Don't you see? Our friend D-t-arr, a true thinker in the Paraunion, knows he can't rely on self-published reports, so he sought different viewpoints on our race. Marna deals with fair, majority politics. D-t-arr and I care about what is right Very, very laudable. We have enjoyed a great deal of dialogue. Hence – I am here.'

I appealed to D-t-arr.

¤ You couldn't find anyone better than this con-man? ¤ I asked.

¤ Say what you will, but his opinions cause more action than any other person in humanity. Any discussion without him would be wholly inappropriate. ¤

Spindle decided to take the debate head-on, not in Para, so as not to exclude D-t-arr's star witness.

'The majority of humanity wishes to pursue this course, including the captains of our fleet. It's been useful to hear your views, but we are duty-bound to do our work until the house of representatives revokes our status as ambassadors. Besides, the Paraunion does not "eat" races. It takes the individuals who are ready and capable of entering.'

'An individual can join without their race being accepted as suitable for candidates?' Crossley asked.

155

'It's possible, though unusual. There would be ethical issues of egality,' D-t-arr commented, 'Entrance cannot be limited to the privileged.'

'Egality, exactly, equal opportunity for all, not just those who managed to flounder to Border by chance. Why should the few be raised up as gods while their brother rests in chains in the gutter? Do you know what struck me as most unusual when I was invited to participate in this debate by this remarkable individual?' Crossley bowed to D-t-arr.

'I'm certain we won't be able to guess,' said Spindle, exasperated at Crossley's grandstanding. *I sense a trap.*

'Your mission for membership in the Paraunion has cost humanity its privacy. Simply by glancing around, D-t-arr can read every message exchanged in confidence, our every dream or plan, the actions we wish forgiven and more. Isn't that true, D-t-arr?'

'Of course.'

'This isn't just a welcome pack. It's an encyclopaedia of humanity and a free pass to see and judge our every thought. You have sold our right to privacy and dignity.'

Marna joined in.

'And that is a legal matter. The government can't break its own laws. We will see the Border mission suspended until a full enquiry has taken place and a reformed Contact Act is passed to lay down the correct way to enter diplomatic relations with other species.'

'Marna, you can't be serious. You wanted to be an ambassador yourself only a year ago!' said Nian.

'I am completely serious, and as a friend, I'm pleading with you to accept that you can't carry on without oversight. You've accepted the word of your seniors up until now—you're without blame—you all need to come home and be safe, be controlled.'

The last phrase seemed particularly out of character for Marna. A tiny portion of Crossley's power over her had crept out of her subconscious. *Creatures from the id.*

'We agreed to be an open book to the Paraunion when Border was first founded,' Spindle said.

Crossley held his hands, palms out at his sides like a saint.

'We didn't expect a dissection. The Paraunion should respect our laws as we do theirs. In a few moments, after we depart, you'll be summoned to your secret meeting room and told that an injunction against further activity has been placed on the Border mission. We look forward to welcoming you back.'

He stared at me like a cat looking into a goldfish bowl. D-t-arr raised himself back up again.

¤ Well, these seem like internal matters to me, and I have far more... ¤ D-t-arr was cut off immediately as Crossley raised a hand to silence him. Such a small gesture, but the wraithlike man held complete sway over the black leviathan. Crossley couldn't have cared or understood what he was saying in Para. He took a deep breath as if about to start out on a long country walk and looked at me in triumph. Not only had he acquired control over a Paraunion, but he dared to tip his hand in front of me, showing that he had all the aces. *Who controls god?*

'I look forward to reuniting you, Mr Evans, with your therapist Doctor Green who has been taking an unhealthy interest in marketing nowadays.'

I have many faults, I'll admit, but under strain, sometimes my better side comes out. I need the pressure to cut through the baggage I carry and get to the essential me, that other Evans Ezra Evans, who doesn't care about the size or number of the opposition.

'You're an evil, manipulative man Crossley. I'll see you exposed and the Cannots freed. Whatever you've done to Marna, I'll undo. Every soul in Movampton and Feng will know what a parasite you are because I'll tell them. While you don't have me, you don't have complete control over *The Pollutant,* do you?' Immediately after I said it, I felt I had just listened to Lutsk speaking.

157

'Oh, Evans. Haven't you heard? They wail your words in the streets, the neverriders scream it while they beat their tattoos, the bunkhouse dollies whisper it to the terror behind the wall, the marketeers floss with it, the lost chant it as they stumble through the deepwalks. It's a universal, unlimited source of anger, comfort and rebellion that you created.

'But listen to you! Clinging to fear and paranoia, you claim I have an outlandish virus that stops people from being open to arguments other than your own. There isn't a shred of evidence. Isn't the best solution the simplest, that people want new leadership? You can't cope with this,' he pointed at the floor as if it were a moment, 'the most glorious time in human history, a species-wide revolution, for the poor, by the poor, through a virtuous leader. Give up your terrorism! No such virus exists. There is no puppet master. Join us on the barricades of humanity. Until then, I bid you adieu.'

Crossley's grin grew even wider as he spread out his arms. The man had no limit to his megalomania. Green said that Crossley would believe he was right. Perhaps he genuinely mistook his control over the *Alone* victims for faith.

D-t-arr seemed unruffled by the encounter. He cast a sideways glance at the avatars of Crossley and Marna to disperse them to the winds.

¤ Now, I believe you are due at a meeting in your private chambers? ¤ the shadow said.

22   Trippers and askers surround me

In that meeting, all our bad news was confirmed. The long grey box had never seemed so depressing. We sat around a conference table, each angry and frustrated. Our time limit had dropped from a year to a few days, only being spared from immediate extradition by the last pre-booked expeditions that Meletrus had arranged. According to the edict from home, there were no new activities.

Green wasn't present, and Jones had no idea of his whereabouts. She feared he'd been killed or fallen under Crossley's control, but there was no time to mount a search for him. According to Jones, Border was flooded with enquiry teams and polilawyer investigations. Every branch of study was suspended until further notice.

'We underestimated Crossley, or possibly the G-Russ. It's difficult to tell which. Somehow they invited D-t-arr to a complete inspection of humanity and showed the extent of the sentiment against Paraunion contact. In doing so, Crossley may have managed to expose him to the control program or possibly a newer, more potent version. It seems a risky gambit even for him—so perhaps the exposure was an accident.'

'Then we let the Paraunion deal with him. He's attacked one of them,' said Nian.

'There's still no evidence, and D-t-arr has already made remarks to cast doubt that Crossley is controlling anyone. Whatever he does, he hides it well enough that a Paraunion can't find it or simply doesn't recognise it.

'The consensus of Paraunion opinion is that it isn't possible on one of them. Even Meletrus didn't believe us. Exactly what our own hackers said: it can't be done.'

'So we're being sent home?' asked Rolliard.

'Immediately after the last cultural visits, the Paraunion are never keen on cancelling an appointment. It seems like a sign of weakness to them.'

'Jones, come on, tell me you've got something left up your sleeve,' I pleaded.

'I've called in every favour to stand firm on these cultural exchanges for each of you; otherwise, you'd be on a flight home now. Make the most of that time.'

Jones glanced at Spindle. The skinny academic had developed a thousand-yard stare over the last hour, peering into a future where he might be ordered to leave the Paraunion, exiled outside the Para speakers he loved. Spindle revealed little about it to Nian or me, but it was evident in his context he'd consider death before being caged inside humanity. It was a shame that the Paraunion culture didn't entertain the concept of asylum; he'd have been the perfect candidate.

Jones's attitude suddenly became stiff.

'Meletrus will be with you in person on the boat to brief you on details of your final postings. I'm afraid this is the last opportunity we'll have to talk. People are waiting at the door to take me into custody. Good luck, only you can save us now.'

She disappeared.

We were being picked off. Dissenters were being detained, but how long would it be before Crossley started moving the people who disagreed with him into concentration camps or disappeared them entirely?

Nian was counselling Spindle while Rolliard failed to calm down an incandescent Annie. I headed out of the door as fast as I could.

If I only had an hour left on the Paraunion homeworld, I knew what I would do with it.

Where the industrial ruins around our allotment ended, a scrubland began. At first sight, it appeared empty with low, simple vegetation, but on closer inspection, it seemed more complex with microscopic streams of water, sandy patterns and winding thumb-width ravines.

I passed over the terrain, leaving it untouched as the visitor ring lifted me and amplified my walking motion a hundred times. It knew that I wanted to travel and formed an invisible moving walkway for me. I focused on the misty peak of the mountain. From a tooth on the horizon, it grew to fill the entire landscape in front of me. Here was the quietest being in the cosmos, and despite warnings against it, the chance to share one of its long, sedate thoughts compelled me to it. *Another oracle stat.*

Over the past weeks, whenever I felt our cause slipping away, I'd come to the ruins of a disassembled building on the boundary of our allotted ground and puzzled over our problems. I projected my thoughts over the miles to the great silhouette, using it as a quiet sounding board for my worries. Was it delusion? Did the mountain, whose name I didn't even know, know I existed? Was I an ant passing under its feet?

Once over its foothills, the sandy earth turned to translucent stone. As I came to a halt, the visitor ring eased me down onto the floor, only a step away from where the body of the mountain began. *I too am not a bit tamed.*

Luminous rock led me along the base of a ravine. A hundred paces ahead, the sheer faces of the mountain began. There was a cave, little more than an indentation, where the gorge ended. I set my eyes on that enclave. Inside, a boulder was the right size to use as a seat. I imagined myself sitting on it, offering a plea to my imagined friend to help me. I took my first step.

Time stretched out as my foot moved from the first pace to the second, and a frisson, like sunlight, edged into my mind. As my heel rolled back to swing my foot into the third step, I wondered if I was doing the right thing. Perhaps I should turn around? A series of colossal shapes moved through the curtain of my psyche, pushing in, their bulk displacing my thoughts, confusing me. *Nine steps and death.* When I stumbled on the fourth and fifth strides, I was confused about why I was there. I bent down and held my head at the temples, taking my eyes off the little cave and forgetting entirely about seeking help from the thinking glacier.

Wanting to turn, I looked at my feet, but they wouldn't move. I dropped to my knees, but still, there was no relief from the soundless juggernauts that trammelled unknowingly through me. *Tread softly for I...*

My vision spun. I grabbed at the air for balance like a drunk on the tracks of Movey as trains hurtle by in the blue-grey night. Just missed, just missed, just missed. And when his luck runs out, he senses the thundering dark engine in an eternal lull, the air is drawn back, and there is a last weightless moment.

The world broke and roared:

QUINCUNXCOUPAUCOEURBALESTRADJINNKWI
FLECHEBOLTMINHKOWONHBLACKCARDTEPTEPT
EPUNSINGMORTHORLEANZORNHAU

And I dropped to the ground dead.

Nian looked furious. Meletrus, Rolliard and Spindle only slightly less so.

I recognised my surroundings as the elegant living quarters of the boat. I lay on one of the couches. The boat spoke as if kneeling beside me.

¤ The visitor ring alerted me the moment that its ward, who was supposed to be immortal and immune to all physical harm, had inexplicably died. Luckily, no passengers were aboard, and I travelled to your location at maximum displacement while the ring projected your corpse on an intercept course towards me.

¤ Discovering your state, I debated the ethical issues and considered whether this was a suicide attempt. On balance, I put aside the concerns of interfering with a lower-dimensional mind and used the visitor ring to execute an emergency anamata. The anamata, as a gate to pocket dimensions, allowed me to superimpose thousands of states of mind back and forth between your real brain and others stored in the anamata's alternate reality. ¤

¤ You see, ¤ it said apologetically, ¤ once you have things like body regeneration, you don't tend to keep basics like bandages and splints. Though there were many ways to save you, this was the only one available to me at that moment with these facilities. I think the alternative of letting a guest of the Paraunion die is unacceptable. If you want to do that, you can always do it when you get home. ¤

¤ So I'm a Paraunion now? ¤

'He's a feng idiot,' laughed Annie, the only one not huddling around me.

¤ I'm afraid not, ¤ the boat said. ¤ You're a halfway house between human and Paraunion, far more towards the human end than Paraunion. Some might consider what I've done ghoulish: a gruesome act but necessary to save your life. ¤

¤ Why Ambassador? Why would you do such a thing? I told you that it was dangerous! ¤ Meletrus sounded mystified.

¤ I thought that if anyone could turn around an entire civilisation heading into the dark ages, it would be a mountain-sized mind. I thought I could put my toe in and step back if it got too much. ¤

While explaining, I realised that my impulsive mission had failed, which struck me like a bolt to the heart. The mood around me changed from one of concern and anger to partial forgiveness.

¤ Well, come on then, ¤ Nian said impatiently. ¤ What *did* the mountain say? ¤

¤ I'm not sure. It's like trying to remember the details on the front of a truck that ran you down. It knew me, though. It cared. ¤ *He's afraid he'll blow our minds.*

¤ If you'd discussed it with me, I'd have gone instead, ¤ said Spindle, his hand on my shoulder. I realised that the more I knew him, the more I found in common with my tutor. The impression of a dusty professor and a grey civil servant hid a radical from the glib eyes of the world. Meletrus was stunned by Spindle's comment.

¤ This has not made my work any easier! I know you have to go back and deal with a brutal regime. I would help you, but my masters and their masters are clear on this matter: you are to return and deal with these things amongst yourselves. ¤

It clearly upset her. Her demeanour showed a surprising amount of affection, even to me. All the Para speakers reflected that respect back to her. Those listening to a translation missed the undertone.

Nian and Rolliard thought we'd both lost the plot, maybe even made things worse. Annie was less alarmed. She'd seen me be reckless before, and annoyingly she had a stoic faith that those acts were entirely valid.

'Looking good, Evans,' she said once the others had dispersed.

'You know, apart from failing to recruit the mountain, I feel good,' I said.

I meant it. Whether it was the encounter with the mountain or the Paraunion lobotomy, the static in my head, the shakiness and the drowning feeling had gone, swallowed up by an underground river. What might happen next? I had no idea, but I knew it was critical to wait for the flash of opportunity. Win or lose, I would play the game until the end. *You'll have to catch me if you want me to hang.*

After all, risk is a relative term when trying to save your whole species.

We left Onis, the great lantern of the Paraunion, the same day. Diplomacy is a two-way street, where each courts the other, regardless of who considers themselves the most advanced. We did our best to present our culture to them, and our hosts, in the spirit of reciprocation and an eye on the long game, had arranged for us to sample different parts of their society. Perhaps not of immediate use in the face of the humanitarian crisis, but then we were dealing with a culture that sowed seeds for future centuries.

This meant that each ambassador and aide would go separate ways. We'd only meet again on the return journey to Border, where we would be immediately detained and imprisoned just as Jones had been. I'd heard no news from home since Crossley's appearance, and the Paraunion had ceased inquiring into human affairs.

¤ Our dear professor will be coming with me to study the politics of the Graph and meet the scholars researching its protection and evolution, ¤ Meletrus said. ¤ While Nian and Rolliard will go to the edge of our regions to meet the newest species to become members. We hope that you record your experiences with them and the changes they have to adopt, and that record can inspire and encourage your own kind. ¤

She focused her conversation on Annie and me. As only Para can, she projected several conflicting attitudes about our assignment.

¤ Evans, Annie. Your visit has been altered after some discussion. You'll be spending your time on Vould, guided by and learning from a young exploration officer whose master has volunteered his assistance. The boat will remain with you to see to any needs you have. ¤

It was evident the boat would watch us. I took it as a fair judgment following my reckless actions, similar to the *Strange Trader* in Paraunion lore, who lays down all his goods on the floor in front of the fortress gate.

Nian looked at me with her stern, sisterly, russet eyes while Rolliard loomed behind her, both immaculate in their grey robes and crimson sash. She had no concern that Meletrus was sending them to the very edge of Paraunion civilisation, but she worried about me regardless that I was half her age again. More precisely, the harmony of her stance arranged in front of her aide said clearly in Para that she was worried about what I might do.

¤ The *Strange Trader* bargains away everything to the outpost he walks into, ¤ she said.

¤ He accepts the terms of his deals without a grudge. ¤

Spindle nodded in agreement with me, his posture closed. I knew the old teacher's heart was lost in the Paraunion, had been for years. One way or another, he wouldn't go back to humanity.

¤ Good luck to us all, ¤ was all he said.

*

Annie and I watched them depart across a glinting bridge in space, extended by the boat to another less elegant and brutish-looking vessel. I was sad to see them go. I'd thought that we'd find a solution together.

The experience with the mountain haunted me. I was worried that the recovery process, where the boat had sifted copies of my thought patterns, made me recall it differently. I caught myself sounding out parts of that last thunder word with my mouth, but who can speak out a thought? Even in Para, it wasn't as gratifying as that immanent *thing*—the flash that filled my head. Was I building a ladder in a cupboard and failing because my brain was too small?

'Boat, what can you tell me about Vould?' Annie asked as we ambled back to the living quarters.

'Vould is a site of outstanding natural beauty. It's the origin world of the Vuro who maintain some aboriginal societal traditions when in their native form. Like most Paraunion, they aren't naturally gifted with anamata, but I'm told that it's a very pleasing body shape. Paraunion visitors come to Vould to look at the world through Vuran eyes, as they have great empathy for the environment around them.'

'What do we know about our chaperone? How did he draw the short straw?'

'Ah, that's more interesting. Your host is Yvin, and you see, he's very, very much in love,' said the boat as if it were the most natural thing in the world.

Which I suppose it is.

Nowhere has clouds like Vould.

The sky was deep and wide. Impossibly broader than anything I'd imagined on Shang Lo, let alone on Onis. On Border, the clouds were little Easter Island heads drifting regally across the blue ocean, but on Vould, you looked up through canyons, fortresses and cities of cloud. The close sun was a burning lake among the scintillating reefs of metallic gases, and everywhere the atmosphere teemed with life. A firmament a thousand oceans deep.

Once you descended to the ground, it was no less bizarre. Red fractal hills rose on either side of stratified valleys where dust flowed back and forth, singing with speed, sometimes bucking up only to be battered back by the racing sky.

I made out the shapes of creatures in the jetstreams and the green shadows of nitrogen whales far above in the heavens. The scene was a theatre of nature, a wonder in motion, everything going about its daily business: everything except Yvin.

Yvin pushed his equine head against the wall in an expression of tragedy. *The sphinx redux*. He couldn't have been more dissimilar from his master Pontus, the glass prowler we had been introduced to at the Cafe Des Humanes. Thinking of the cafe put me in a dark mood, as I imagined it being entombed forever in the infinite storage space under Onis, but if I hoped to ever resurrect it, I had to remain alert. I was still watching for anything that might save us.

He was young and precocious. His lengthy vuro body rippled with agitation and shed reflections from its surface. Much to his chagrin, he was in charge of my well-being and guidance around his world, which distracted him from his full-time occupation of moping over his love life.

The other masters of Yvin had agreed to Pontus's proposal in the hope that I would broaden his horizons. *Buck up, young buck.*

I fiddled with the visitor's ring on my index finger. The boat had assured me that it could protect me from almost any environment; it was a store of immense power if only I could learn to utilise it properly. I remembered Kap, the young shaek student, and wondered if I could ever manipulate matter the way she had. If the ring were removed at any moment, I'd turn into a shower of dust under Vould's pressure and heat. How many minutes would it take for Yvin to notice my disappearance?

With the boat's help, I explored the section of the Graph that mapped the master-slave relationships around Meletrus, Pontus and Yvin in the hope of finding some loophole to delay our repatriation. Half of Paraunion culture was the many-to-many, the remainder was the language. To achieve great things requires influence and respect, to save our race would demand immense backing. Esteem and talent are the currency of the graph, not just for the individual but for the bonds-people in your care. Every Paraunion manages their family and their non-blood kin with indistinguishable duty, hoping to cultivate respect.

Yvin was only a cycle away from being allocated his first indentured charge. He had graduated from a nearby academy and returned home. His parents and masters hoped that the foal might return a stallion, wizened by intensive education and ambitious for the next hurdle of his life. In just a week, his secret was revealed. He was smitten with another young officer.

¤ I think even to your eyes, she would appear beautiful, Evans. When she speaks, it's a delight. Not like our caged and sharp Para here: you can see all the way into her soul. You have to understand how perfectly patient she is. She won't suffer as I do from all this indecision. They have sent our petition to the third tier, which means more interminable waiting. But what would you know about this form of torture? You're a Ronin, a river without land, a wild corsair! ¤

Yvin was delighted with his descriptions of my master-less status. He commented on it frequently, sometimes with envy, but mostly contempt. Meletrus was right; he was immature. He clearly looked up the 'Ronin' reference in an attempt to pique me. The object of his affections was Arbaun-Da-Felentual, who he gendered race-opposite from himself despite Arbaun being a totally different species. I'd been told that race was no boundary to the Paraunion in such matters and could be changed or manipulated. It made me wonder what they might have been able to do for poor Lutsk.

"Can we go to Bareggen and watch the flux riders today? There's plenty of time."

Buggati stood with crossed arms staring at the Voru in unbridled frustration. I translated the request to our host, even though I knew full well he could understand my envoy.

¤ I cannot think correctly today, Evans, ¤ Yvin sighed. ¤ Didn't you hear me say the decision has been raised to the third tier? Why should they do that? You've looked at our Graph, haven't you? Everybody knows that there are *vrys* on that scale that have persisted for centuries. It's cowardice! They won't decide, so they have thrown us into the void.¤

Vrys, the circles of opinion within the Graph rage like weather systems, sometimes for centuries, Spindle had told us. *And who can tell when the rain will stop?*

That was enough for Annie. She looked back to the boat, muttering about "bastard alien children".

¤ I feel an obligation to be out seeing things, Yvin,¤ I said. ¤Why don't you tell me about the academy's mission into the dark flows? How are the crews selected? How long have they been exploring? Maybe you should be grateful that the decision has been moved up to the next tier. After all, they haven't forbidden you to join with Arbaun-Da-Felentual, have they? ¤

Yvin motioned towards the ground beside him. Furniture was shunned by his kind. Annie tutted and turned to look out over the far more entertaining Vould world scape then seemed to think better of being around entirely and stomped off back inside the boat.

¤ You must be uncomfortable, Evans. Come sit by me, and we'll tell each other everything we know about love, eh? You know we're nearly the same age, or do you look down on my years because my kind thinks of me as an adolescent? Ah, but I imagine you've had many lovers, and I just the one. Come, come over here, and we'll whisper to each other what we know about the affairs of the heart. ¤

I looked over the low ruined walls of the kletch, a vuro resting place. Yvin's people had no conception of a roof or even rooms in the human sense. Their meeting places looked much like the final traces of medieval castles, but then the kletches were only meant to provide high perches, storage and perhaps a little temporary privacy. The kletch we occupied had a view across a great plain with three parallel ravines scarring it, each running with streams of hot dust. I saw a handful of other kletches on the landscape and a distant opal streak that marked one of Yvin's kinsmen crossing the desert through the heat-haze.

I went and sat with him. How could I not? We ruminated over liaisons from my past, even my fruitless gambits with Broulé. He teased out some poetic recitations from me—all the while humming and aligning himself in a long Para phrase that implied "Yes, it is like that, isn't it" or "These things you and I both know".

He was a painful romantic but brilliant, insightful and clever beyond my imagining. What must he have thought of my history? What would he have made of my life in Shang Lo? Yvin was due to join the crew of an experimental exploration vessel that would map the furthest reaches of the dark rivers. According to Meletrus, Yvin was a serious young scientist and leadership candidate only a few years ago. That was all before his relationship with Arbaun-Da-Felentual began.

¤ Tell me about yourself and Bugatti again, ¤ he asked.

¤ I don't know what more to tell you, Yvin. ¤ I was a little tired of giving him details of my life for him to tweeze over. The danger began there: he knew me too well and could manipulate me, distracting me when I needed to find a way to solve our problems—*MINKOWONH*.

¤ When you first saw her, you must have known that she would be important to you? You were a poet after all, weren't you? You should be sensitive to that kind of thing. ¤

I sighed and tried to recall the moment when I had first seen Annie. It had been when I'd managed to get enough credit together for the apartment.

¤ This agent, a real scumbag, gave me the hard sell after showing me around, and we were standing just outside the front door. Annie sat smoking in the sky plaza on a bench in that god-awful dressing gown. She just looked out: not down at the traffic or the other towers, not even at the sky, just blankly out. She had one leg crossed over the other and bobbed one foot up and down. ¤

¤ Oh, come on, Evans! ¤ Yvin tutted in frustration. ¤ You can do better than that. Spare me the bare facts: give me the dirt. ¤

¤ All the world passed her, missed her. And the bruises, the dressing gown and the smoking just exaggerated what a creature of grace she was. All cheekbones, legs and neckline. ¤

After all that time, I couldn't really remember my first words to her. I remembered the things she'd said to me, but then we had never really been star-struck lovers. We were friends with passion and then strange pen-pals. *Gone, lost, in the box of misremembered things.* I was glad she wasn't around to hear me. It wasn't the sort of thing she was a fan of.

¤ You are a flavourful race, Evans. ¤ Yvin spoke about my people and me utterly interchangeably. I suppose there was something ambassadorial in that. ¤ Moss over marble: you ask which thing spoils the other? You don't seem to accept whole propositions. ¤

I got up and leaned against the stubby wall of the kletch. The currents that powered across the basin carried living plants and creatures, perfectly adapted to Vould, to this deep, hot world. I wanted to see more of the planet; the flux riders, the polar attics and the factories on the harbour of the metallic sea where the whales come down to drown their young. But Yvin refused to wander more than a few minutes from the central court, where he was regularly petitioning the influential and pivotal people involved in the vrys.

It seemed more likely that he would try their patience and throw out his case entirely: though I kept that opinion to myself. His persistent behaviour as a terrible host didn't suppress the sensation that some opportunity would present itself.

Officers of exploration teams were forbidden unapproved romantic, let alone procreative, relationships. Once they were reported, they were reviewed. If there was any doubt that the couple, or group, would cause disruption, they must separate or leave the exploratory missions. I could see why. Who'd want to be stuck on a ship with Yvin?

¤ Let's just take a look at Yamriss? It's just a few minutes away, and I have to see *something* today. This may be my last few weeks of freedom, Yvin. Feng, who knows, it might even be my last few weeks of life. ¤

Yvin rolled his entire body in a Para expression of angst that was only available to a few of the more aerial forms. The vuro were particularly good in that register. It was both a sigh, a protest and a form of showing off.

¤ We will go quickly then, ¤ Yvin said, ¤ but you need to prepare for the Shifting Mountain dinner. I have promised you will be present, so we must take no more than a quick swim through the markets. I won't be embarrassed by you making a fool of yourself in front of critical officials. We've all heard about the idiotic stunt on Onis. Anything similar may reflect upon my suitability to Arbaun-Da-Felentual, so you do nothing without my say so. Are we clear? ¤

174

I had managed to rouse him into performing a small part of his duties, the minimum amount possible, without getting into trouble with his masters. The boat appeared from where it had been examining a cliff wall for tiny fossils, now configured in a remarkably compact form, no more than five times the size of my old apartment. It had assured me that the entire spaceship I had travelled in was still contained somewhere inside itself. We took up residence with Annie in a depression on the boat's roof that acted as a passenger area for short journeys and sailed up into the jet stream. Immune to the supersonic winds, the boat flew to the west for a minute or two.

Considerate as always, our transport pulled alongside a market platform in Yamriss for us to begin our exploration. It excused itself from our company with a comment that it would like to visit a nearby friend, though I may have misinterpreted the scope of 'nearby' in the boat's vocabulary.

Yvin pointed out displays of note nearby, all populated with crafted goods. His race considered the hand-production of artefacts one of their greatest cultural signifiers. Disappointing, as I really needed to steal a death ray or transporter or some other godlike technology.

Most of the stalls were without visible attendants though several other customers wandered in and out of the delicate stalls. A tall Paraunion with pendulously long limbs browsed the vuro wares. The market was invisibly protected from Vould's ravenous weather, enabling the stall owners to make delicate shop displays of their products. It was a exquisite spectacle like all the festive shop displays I'd ever seen in my life rolled into one, but without commercial crudity and strangely uninhabited. It was enough to get Annie out of her funk.

Yvin glowed with pride when he saw how moved I was by it. He quite forgot how forlorn and heartbroken he was for almost an entire hour.

We stopped at a stall made of a section of coral reef. It shone deep green and blue, cool and clear compared to the hot, deep pressure of Vould. The reef reminded me of Border and the moments when I'd been happy running along the bridges over the flat ocean. Thoughts of Border led me to think about Nian. Was she exploring alien markets? Had her Paraunion host recognised what a talented woman she was or was she as lonely as we were, with only a reluctant guide for company?

I stopped to examine articles spinning slowly in their display, each sculpted from indigo-hued scales. One appeared to me to be a necklace though that probably wasn't the intended purpose.

¤ How do I purchase an item? ¤ I asked.

This appeared to make Yvin extremely pleased.

¤ I will see what arrangements can be made. It would be my great honour to see one of our items pass into your hands. ¤

He explained to me as we walked through the stalls of Yamriss that acquiring art was not a matter of 'buying' it in the sense of a monetary deal. The buyer was a curator and a guardian of the item. During the exchange, the customer and the artist entered a relationship more like courtship than commerce.

An elderly vuro swam down the main avenue that split the market east and west. He scanned the area until he saw us. Something about his manner immediately drew me to him. Unfathomably gentle and ancient, a true sky spirit.

Yvin introduced us and explained my background to the artist, who introduced himself as Rorsk. He turned and gave a short but shockingly accurate biography of Annie's life as an artist and actor, at which she very nearly blushed.

¤ It seems that we were destined to meet early, Ambassador Evans. I am due at the Shifting Mountain dinner with all its tiresome pomp. So much nicer to encounter you here in Yamriss, a better example of our culture than this evening's affair will be, I'm afraid. ¤

I commented how refreshing it was to be in a place where no one stole anything.

¤ What a dark place it must be that you have come from, ambassador. The vuro won't accept they own anything unless they create it themselves or if they have been given safekeeping of it, all other items are *chasna.* ¤ Rorsk referred to a small weed-like plant, *chasna,* that floated about on the winds and had been eaten by the very poor despite having almost no nutritional value in previous times.

Vould's massive sun threw down bars of light, calmed and transmitted through reflecting clouds around us. The market was motionless compared to the world of hurricanes, whirlpools and eternal dust.

¤ The weather around Yamriss is carefully designed to help both acquirers and artists concentrate, ¤ Rorsk said after seeing my look at the sky.

¤ Impressive. I understand you can sell me an item here? ¤

¤ Once I'm convinced that you genuinely want it and will be a good guardian for that item, ¤ said Rorsk. His context was kind but completely serious. I realised I'd approached the matter too lightly. For both Rorsk and Yvin, this was a serious topic.

¤ And that you will make arrangements for it after your own life is over, ¤ added Yvin.

¤ Well, I see how that focuses people to choose wisely. How do you deal with gifts? I wasn't thinking of this for myself but for my colleague, Nian. ¤

After a moment, the translation got through to Annie, and she broke all the rules of being an ambassador's aide by laughing like a hyena.

¤ That depends on your relationship with this Nian creature, ¤ said Yvin.

¤ You're proposing a gesture of goodwill with one of our artworks? I can see that might be very noble, but implicitly by granting you ownership of the object, we would consent to the gesture, ¤ Rorsk said thoughtfully. ¤ We'll need to know a lot more. ¤

¤ Also, giving someone a life obligation might not be the impression you are trying to make, ¤ said Yvin.

Both Yvin and Rorsk bombarded me with questions about Nian. What type of person was she? Did she mean very much to me? Could I command her to care for the object properly? The last of these seemed to cause the most issue. Such a commonplace Paraunion thing as compelling another being to care for something is strange and offensive to human freedom. The artist and Yvin struggled to come to a conclusion. Our discussion ranged over which positions of responsibility were possible in our society until I stumbled across the obvious trump card.

¤ She's the other new ambassador to the Paraunion. That's a significant position of responsibility. I think you'd agree? ¤

Both the old salamander and my young chaperone were more than happy with this qualification. *How sweetly the gift is given.*

¤ A gift representing respect and affection from one ambassador of a fledgling race to another. I shall note it in my ledger. ¤ Rorsk purred in satisfaction.

In his enthusiasm, Yvin offered to have the item delivered to Nian immediately, but I politely refused, mentioning that I'd prefer to give it in person when we next met. *Next, meet in prison.*

¤ Of course! ¤ laughed Rorsk and bent theatrically to his younger friend's ear. ¤ He wishes to receive her gratitude in person. ¤

More laughter from my less than helpful aide.

I protested that Nian was like a sister to me, that we were close friends and no more, but I wondered if that was absolutely true. Perhaps I argued too much. What was the problem? She was a fascinating, beautiful adult. Was I scared that she wouldn't be interested in a burnt-out lyricist? Possibly. I rubbed the soles of my shoes on the dusty floor of the market.

¤ I'm afraid the truth is that neither Nian nor I can guarantee we will be free or alive to care for this gift, Rorsk. ¤ I looked fondly at the necklace one last time and handed it back like a customer who'd discovered he was short on credit.

Rorsk nodded and was genuinely moved at our plight. He looked thoughtfully at the fragile indigo pieces he held in his hands and said, ¤ I shall hold on to this for a few years, and if fate should go your way, perhaps you'll get a chance to come back and take ownership of it. ¤

I thanked him, we said goodbye and called the boat to pick us up.

Onboard the boat, I found that my attitude to Yvin had changed. True, he was young and moody, but for a moment, I'd seen the person that his masters and parents were so proud of. Though we were roughly the same age and his culture much more advanced, perhaps I could still help him. *Quid pro quo.* I watched him settle into the travelling deck on the boat, seeing the thoughts of his forbidden love with Arbaun-de-Felentual creep back over him, sullening him, bending him like an invisible weight in the corrosive red evening light.

To make Yvin less surly and help us see something more than the dusty kletches, Annie stumbled upon a plan that should have been transparent to Yvin.

'Shopping for jewellery isn't going to get us out of jail, Evans.'

'I know,' I replied, exasperated. 'Feng! I didn't know it'd be a craft fair. You *know* we're being kept away from anything interesting.'

'Yeah, but somebody,' she stared at the rapidly introspecting Yvin, 'is obsessed with someone who works somewhere very interesting.'

Just when you think Annie is the worst ambassador's aide possible, she comes up with gold. I wandered to Yvin and used my new context of respect for him to open a conversation, carrying over notes of the excitement from the market.

179

¤ The dark flow exploration programme, it's being staged nearby, isn't it? ¤ I asked.

¤ Near, Evans? It's being staged everywhere! Of course it's near. You should feel free to bore the boat with these questions and leave me out of them. ¤

¤ Oh,¤ I said, crestfallen,¤ I thought you might show me just a part of it after dinner. I mean, I won't understand what I'm looking at, but just to grasp the motives of the crew and why they are applying so much effort. Explorers and adventurers always intrigue humans. ¤

¤ You want to report on some heroes and put some pizazz in your reports home? Egotistical of you, making yourself out to be a regular Marco Polo? ¤

¤ It would be nice to discuss with all those influential figures at Shifting Mountain how impressive the teams are and how cut from the same cloth the brave crews are? What inspiring souls, say, you and Arbaun-de-Felentual are? Unrelated, of course, to your other issues? ¤

¤ Good, yes! ¤ Yvin said. ¤ Definitely discuss that with them. You don't want to see whales and cliffs. You should see what the Paraunion are really up to at the fringe of our progress. Now, this is something I can tell you about! Not just tell you: show you. As soon as you are recovered from Shifting Mountain's endless badinage, we will go straight to the research platform and show you her. ¤

The 'her' Yvin mentioned was a compound of the platform and hidden just underneath, the object of his affections. *Our motives increasingly unclear.* I hoped that I was serving both our best wishes.

*

Dinner was a twenty-course marathon during which the visitor ring manipulated my metabolism and earth-conditioned body to stop me from falling asleep. Rorsk was a tremendous help and a gallant conversationalist.

¤ Crews on the exploratory ships must be of hardier stuff than the average Paraunion, ¤ he explained. ¤ A crew will frequently be cut off from communication for unknown periods and may be forced to make decisions without the supportive umbrella of their masters. ¤

¤ Not just scientific decisions, ¤ another guest commented across the table, ¤ moral judgements that may have long-lasting connotations. ¤

¤ Like the *Meadows Gladiator*? ¤ I asked.

Answers came from all around the table. Not in a cacophony as it would be with a dozen humans speaking at once, in a rushed Movey nouwiti bar, say. It was far more orderly, musical and precise.

¤ A little like that. ¤

¤ No wrong has been done by the crew. Instead, they are the kind who would willingly bear it. ¤

¤ The Ambassador makes a good point. They are skilled, just like the *Gladiator,* beyond their opposition. Their fight is really against themselves. ¤

¤ We *hope* they are skilled beyond their opposition. ¤

¤ They aren't alone. ¤

¤ I fear we're eating too quickly. ¤

¤ Not quickly enough for the Ambassador. Do you know how hastily his world spins? ¤

¤ Hang on in there. Only ten courses to go! ¤

And so it continued for hours.

After dinner, with little time to sleep, we were frog-marched by Yvin back onto the boat to see the research platform, Arbaun-de-Felentual and the great endeavour of the Paraunion culture.

It was as if someone had smashed the space before us, and the area had ruptured like glass, fragments wavered like reeds underwater and in the centre, a twisted trunk of light reached down to the floor. *She is distant music.*

She wasn't what I'd expected to see. I suppose it was the crude description of her that I had heard: a crystal tree. She was intoxicating. *I alone of Arabia's sons.*

Her species naturally possessed that aspect of higher dimensional living that was added to the rest of the Paraunion. It allowed them to seem so unencumbered with technology while at the same time being drenched with it. I pieced as much together as a layman could of the machinery of the anamata. Humans augmented their realities and impaled machines into our flesh, but that paled into insignificance—made us look gruesome or mutilated—compared to the finessed enhancement of a Paraunion, except for the races such as Arbaun-de-Felentual where no addition was required. Just as the Kappa drive stored momentum in closet dimensions, so the minds of these people stored potentially infinite memories and interconnections. *And now mine.*

On Movampton, I'd been used to feeling roughly equal to any other person I might meet. But among the Paraunion, I was a dim child, despite their polite attempts not to point out my inferior mental powers. No one ever made me so acutely aware of that than Arbaun-Da-Felentual when she was gracefully kind to me. She was the only Paraunion I ever heard speak to Annie in human.

Yvin told me she was considered a young adult, just as he was. His beloved was maturing into a being capable of reaching into and sensing the tiny wrapped up dimensions within normal space and the broader shores of a universe beyond my senses and, I suspected, beyond Yvin.

When she moved, there was a strange sensation of stop motion. She phased through positions and seemed held in other poses. She could warp her filaments to give a variety of body shapes, each put on for the comfort of those she was conversing with. Speaking with Yvin, she would course into an abstract of serpent-like shapes, but she clearly felt I needed more assistance and would move into a humanoid outline, even with the impression of a face. When she spoke to Annie, she shrunk to a glimmering star-like point.

Did she love Yvin? I wasn't qualified to tell, but when they talked, it was with such intensity that I switched between embarrassment and confusion over the complexities of their conversation. Her dialogues with me made me question whether the relationship was more one-sided than Yvin hoped.

Arbaun's motes and slivers meshed in front of me in a shining figure, a river dryad in flashing blue-white. She spoke with such warmth that I struggled to remember if I had ever heard anyone talk to me with that kind of care. It wouldn't be hard to believe that she was a mother, a sister or even a lover.

¤ Are you well, Ambassador Evans? So far from home and your own kind, thrown into this giant machine of a society: are you all right? It must be terrible to be condemned to trial by your own people. ¤

¤ I am well. There's still hope, although I confess I don't know by what means. Yvin has taken good care of me. ¤

She laughed.

¤ Yvin has not taken good care of you. He has been a remiss host. For all his great soul, he struggles to listen to the feelings of others. He wouldn't see that you bear a terrible burden of responsibility for your people and wear the mantle uneasily. Isn't that so? You are travelling but would prefer to stand still and watch the universe pass. ¤

I nodded, dumbstruck by her candour.

183

The flowship was making ready for its exploration into unknown parts of the universe. The great slab of equipment was being prepared at the nearest flow to Vould, and the boat transported us there in just a few hours. The ship was a brutish oblong of construction. I could only guess the purpose of each section, but the primary mission was to detect and record, trying to answer mysteries even the Paraunion didn't know the answer to. It was almost as long as the New Osaka but only carried a crew of ten. Yvin told us that thousands of vessels were being sent out into the furthest reaches by the Paraunion, but he didn't give any details of what they were looking for.

Arbaun-da-felentual and Yvin had met during their training for exploration. I watched them in close conversation as they exchanged facts about the vessel's readiness. Threaded into their discussion were their feelings for one another, and subtly below, there was a hint of debate about me and what I should be taken to see. The Paraunion didn't feel any need to separate work and pleasure. *Concentrate.*

Unlike the New Osaka, the exploration platform was a dark, lifeless storage unit filled with mysterious, semi-functional equipment. Not ideal material for an exciting tour. Yvin explained the readings the ship was designed to take, but his Para became impenetrable to me.

¤ I didn't quite catch that, ¤ I said. ¤ Could you go a little slower for me? ¤

Yvin sighed and began again.

¤ The long detector array over there will look for… ¤

'The translator just gave up,' said Annie with a shrug.

I found whatever he said utterly untranslatable. Arbaun-da-felentual came to our rescue. She appeared beside us and spoke in human.

'When he talks about physics and mathematics, that's when the problem starts, isn't it? I'm afraid you may have to admit defeat for the moment. Para doesn't have any metaphors for science; it speaks them out directly.'

184

I suppose I could take consolation in being an artist of a sort. Were I a scientist, it would probably have been the most depressing conversation of my life.

¤ It's not that I can't make a metaphor about physics, ¤ Yvin said thoughtfully, ¤ it's that we'll all be able to tell that it is wildly inaccurate. Usually, that's a problem. I could say that this part of the vessel somehow measures the heat of the surrounding space: but you see, you know immediately I am unsure of myself. ¤

His words and gestures struggled to give the best approximation. There was no choice but for me to accept that this was an exploration ship and leave the details for a future, smarter ambassador to try to figure out.

Little transport scooters took us on a tour of the accessible parts of the ship, mainly in the dark, although the scooter occasionally released inspection lights to help us see. At a junction, Annie shouted out for my attention as her flock of willow-o-the-wisps traced out a giant metallic closed fist in a chamber below. When we stepped off the transports and walked along a gantry, I thought of Rolliard, now zealously loyal to Nian in his duties. I'd have loved to have told him how the grating didn't ring when you walked on it like the decks on New Osaka. Annie and I found ourselves on a promontory overlooking a dark canyon.

'You know what this reminds me of?' she asked.

'What?'

'The vertical farms we rode through the last time I saw you on Shang Lo.'

'Those were a lot sunnier. You wanted them opened up to the public, remember?'

'I meant more that it's just you and I, seeing something most people haven't been to or know about.'

'You know, I never said how sorry I was that we didn't get to try *us* out properly, and then I cut you off on the New Osaka.'

'Fuck me, Evans,' she said, 'Was it the mountain or the brain surgery that fixed you? I don't think it would have lasted long with me as your djalkitten. We're better off like this: a couple of Movey losers sneaking into the backdoors of whatever this is.'

She was right. We looked at the incomprehensible layers and strata lit by the drifting inspection lights.

'You're a good friend, Annie,' I said, feeling a cheesy grin spread across my face.

'Piss off.'

'I'll be fenged if I'm going to let Crossley screw us all so he can carry on believing he's the messiah.'

'Any ideas?'

'Just the edge of something. Sometimes, I get flashes of whatever the mountain said to me when I look at something, but I can't recall the words or sounds.'

I sat with my legs dangling through the rails of the gantry, contemplating the secret architecture of the flow ship. My chin rested on the rail's cool metal, and I wondered whether I was doing a good job of being an ambassador.

'Anything right now?' asked Annie.

'Oh yes,' I said, waving my arm at the ship's machinery. 'But what we should both keep in mind is that everything we say and have said is almost always a conversation between you, me and the boat.'

'Yeah, that's a nice thought, isn't it,' she said sweetly while screwing up her face in disgust.

I needed to rely on Annie to follow my lead without discussing details. I was reasonably sure that the dark flowship was the only alternate form of transportation we would likely see, other than the boat, which had to be critical.

¤ Will you be joining us for a meal before we return? ¤ Yvin's voice spoke from a place just in front of me, ¤ Or shall I send the boat to get you later? ¤

We returned to the explorers. I worried briefly that I might be caught in more of their flirting. After the marathon dinner at

186

Shifting Mountain, we joined them at the table to be polite rather than eat. I couldn't shake the feeling that ideas were forming in the back of my mind, almost against my will, but if you'd asked me what they were, I wouldn't have been unable to tell you.

¤ How do they expect you to carry on with your ambassador's mission when they know the danger you'll face on your return? ¤ asked Arbaun.

¤ This visit is a small mercy. The Paraunion can't grant asylum to ambassadors recalled by their host nation, but we get a little extra time this way. Who knows, maybe something will have changed for the better when we return? ¤

In the subtext of my Para, I tried to include that I'd be open to being helped, which was difficult as it demanded a mastery I had only recently attained. Spindle would have done it without thinking.

¤ Can you tell me, ambassador, why you chose to walk onto the mountain of Onis? ¤

Arbaun asked the question while demonstrating how to construct simple responses within closed contexts. She could use every register in Para but signalled her sympathy in that phrase 'walk on the mountain' in cadences perfect for a humanoid. *I would have too*, she said. Something I had never suspected was possible. Only the closest observation of every party in the conversation would reveal the subtext.

¤ I was out of options. I felt that it could help. ¤ *I see you.*

¤ And did it help? What did it say to you? ¤ *How can I help?*

¤ I can't quite recall it. I get slivers of it now and again. ¤ *Save my people.*

¤ This may be difficult for you to believe, Evans, but I sympathise. I was deeply drawn to the mountain of Onis the moment I heard about it but was forbidden to go. I think it suffers from a malady that now you share with it. ¤ *Save you two?*

¤ What's that? ¤ *Save our race.*

¤ It is unique in the universe and suffers attention because of it, and what mountains want most to be is alone, like you. ¤ *Not allowed.*

¤ Being the only human with an anamata will be rather sad if I'm also the last one. ¤ *What can you do?*

¤ That's interesting, isn't it? You have a manifold in your brain, like every Paraunion child, but outside our culture. Without exercising our arts and sciences, you'll develop independently, or perhaps not. ¤ *I can help you remember.*

Yvin was either jealous of our intimate conversation or had twigged that something extra was going on. He put aside the readiness simulation that had absorbed his attention. I gave Annie a look, and she, like the natural performer she was, started a distraction campaign. She knew the auto-translator really annoyed him.

'Yvin, when you and your crew go out into the unknown, presumably you don't really have any masters anymore? You're kind of a new little colony? You can do whatever you like?' she asked.

¤ Not at all. You're under the impression that we are all desperate to break free. We're trained so hard to cope without the support of the master system and make our best approximation of it when incommunicado. ¤

'And why are you out of contact? Can't you set up a zillion qubit factories?'

¤ The distances we are talking about here are immense, negligible or correctible effects over ordinary distances, like from here to Onis, overwhelm the signal. The number of correction copies that we have to send to counter corrupt qubits goes up exponentially… ¤

'And you'll be Captain?' Annie was rapidly running low on scientific material, so she had decided to move to gossip.

¤ Pardon? ¤

'What do you think the first order is that you'll give Arbaun?'

She had him there. And she kept him wracked over the minutia of the ship's mission as Arbaun led me discretely away to look at a visualization space, actually a rather intense white hemispherical igloo.

¤ You could think of this as the navigator's seat, ¤ she said, ¤ turning it on for a full demonstration will take a few moments. ¤ *Wait.*

¤ Any chance you can show me where we are relative to Shanglo or Earth? ¤ *Ok.*

¤ Of course, you'll have to remember that we intend to map and navigate vastly greater and much less flat distances.¤

The hemisphere started populating with celestial data of all the nearby systems, every floating rock, every spinning bleeping thing between ourselves and Shanglo.

Arbaun-de-felentual turned to me and extended a shimmering hand. My tolerance for risks was extraordinarily high. In less than a handful of days, we'd be diplomatically returned into the hands of humanity's first despot for centuries. When the Paraunion child had offered to share a memory with me to make the cafe on Onis, the adults had stepped in quickly to avoid something potentially damaging, having said that now I was a Paraunion half-breed with my own anamata. *O brave monster! Lead the way.*

I reached out to her.

I-she recalled the sight of my-her hand pressed into the blue rock keeping her-me for a moment balanced, crouched on one knee, my-her vision blurring. She-I notes how calm we've become even though her-my mind is caught in the soundless storm. As the moment of impact arrives, I-she slows the event down to a second's tiniest fragments. I-she wonders if there will be nothing, and the great thunderword was a relic of an addled mind reconstructed by the boat. Slowing more, she-I feel the gong beat of her-my eyelashes last blink, the give in the back of the neck as the ability to stay upright begins to fail, and just as the lamp of reality fails, it comes:

189

QUINCUNXCOUPAUCOEURBALESTRADJINNKWI
FLECHEBOLTMINHKOWONHBLACKCARDTEPTEPT
EPUNSINGMORTHORLEANZORNHAU

We parted, and I was sad to be back in my own lonely body with my little senses.

¤ And that's how the sensors work, ¤ Arbaun said while staring deep into my eyes. *I'll call you.*

The moth and the feather / travel together. That evening on Vould, Annie and I crossed the plains and ravines to a grand kletch set out for another reception. The vuros themselves even moaned about how frequent they were.

We arrived serenely on the boat's back with the protection of the visitor rings. I could tell Annie desperately wanted to find out what had gone on between myself and Arbaun. Why wouldn't she? Her life depended on it too, but I was forced to keep my assurances down to some intense positive looks, which I hoped she was reading correctly. All assuming that I was reading Arbaun correctly too.

Amongst forty vuros and a smaller subset of other species, I suffered lapses of recognition, except with Yvin and Rorsk. I had to wait for a note in the conversation to tell me if I had spoken to someone before, sometimes only ten minutes ago. I could only blame the fatigue of the situation and being preoccupied. As soon as I was reminded, my new brain summoned up the details of previous conversations without effort. Eating, talking and shuffling around the kletch disorientated me, but the hosts were genial and took special lengths to provide something for Annie and me in each of the meal's eighteen courses.

After five courses, a recital of sky singers was arranged in my honour, even though it was out of season for the tradition. The giant harpies arrayed themselves in tiers up into the night, their proximity to each other ionizing the sky above the roofless cathedral of the kletch. Their voices chimed out the *Vould Symphony,* and their wings passed lightning across one another, projecting sound, light and heat.

At the finish, the figures faded into the blackness of the sky as the thunder rolled away.

'Well, that's me giving up live performance,' said Annie wiping away a streaky black makeup tear that had rolled down her face.

¤ My god, ¤ I stuttered, ¤ If we're just filling time before a prison sentence, this is how I want to do it. Rorsk, can we hear it again? ¤

The old vuro craftsman shook his head, almost gleefully, ¤ Not for another season, I'm afraid. That is what makes it precious. They made this rare exception because I explained your situation and why you could not take the necklace. No one should die without hearing the *Vould Symphony*. ¤

Rorsk, along with a genteel pashanow called Ovu, whose spines made it seem like a cross between a cactus and grizzly bear, entertained us and provided welcome shelter from most of the dinner goers. Many vuros clearly found talking to a condemned ape distasteful but were too fascinated to stay away.

¤ I wanted to be a pashanow for ages and ages, so making a trip to Vould seemed like the ideal opportunity. I still have a visitor ring to assist with the environment, but it's far better than trying to see things as a Naman, ¤ Ovu said.

¤ What's difficult about being a Naman on Kosselback? ¤ I asked.

¤ It's possible, ¤ said Rorsk, ¤ but there's something about visiting ancient ruins and seaside villages that loses its magic when you're a two-kilometre tall plasma giant. You could have gone the whole way Ovu and taken up being a vuro for a cycle or two? ¤

¤ I like to remember that I am a tourist. It helps me maintain attention to detail and appreciate what's around me. Don't you find that Ambassador? That you're more open to the wonder of everyday things?¤

They both looked expectantly at me.

¤ Where I come from, there's only one species of people to look at. The planet's entire surface is covered in junk food outlets, Marketorias, and the cheapest possible housing. You wouldn't be able to tell if you were in Movampton or Critishins district unless a local told you or you looked it up. Every remarkable thing has long since been digitised and bulldozed. Honestly, Ovu, I am in constant wonder about everything I see, the space, the freedom you all have. I'm beginning to fear I've got the same affliction as Spindle, and soon it'll all be gone, locked away from us behind an iron curtain. ¤

¤ What affliction does Spindle have? ¤ Ovu asked, concerned.

¤ Let's just say that Spindle and the *Penniless Fisherman Shipwrecked* have a great deal in common. ¤

¤ My dear Ambassador, ¤ said Rorsk, ¤ you're causing a hubbub amongst the guests tonight. What with your political status and this worry that the professor cannot acclimatise to being with his own kind—it's all the hall is talking of. What's the difference between the two of you? ¤

¤ I have friends and family there. There's even an argument I'm responsible for some of our troubles. We humans suffer because we can't rise above being selfish consumers. We prey on each other. That's why I'm here, to find out how we move on to the next level. In many ways, I'm the wrong man for the job, but Spindle is one hundred per cent committed to the cause. ¤

¤ Then *he's* definitely the wrong man for the job, ¤ Ovu said with a shimmy that rustled every one of its thousand quills. ¤ Ambassadorships are a two-way experience. We want to hear about you too. ¤

Rorsk agreed, ¤ You must give yourself more credit. Now listen. Being very old and part of a superior race tells me precisely what you must do next. ¤

¤ What is that? ¤ I asked eagerly.

¤ Try this wild changecloud. It really is extraordinary. ¤ Ovu chortled until its spines needed smoothing.

By the final course, I was flagging at sustaining the necessary etiquettes of an ambassador. The tension of waiting for Arbaun to get in touch was a constant distraction. A small bowl of clear tangerine-smelling liquid was brought to me. *Now wash your hands.* My neighbours' bowls contained a far more fiery looking orange substance. The visitor ring allowed through any smells that it deemed safe for me to experience. I was about to ask about the contents when a cry from nearby stopped me.

Yvin rose backwards from his dish and coiled in anguish. He lashed out and smashed the bowl from the pedestal before him. Black liquid ran across the floor and vaporised like a dark spirit rising. The young vuro shot into the air and coursed over the kletch wall like a banished soul.

Rorsk leaned close.

¤ Bad news. Unexpectedly bad. They've decided against him and Arbaun-de-felentual being on the same crew. It's one of many possible symbols. This is how suitors were refused among the vuro; it is done so that no individual has to tell him and bear the stigma. Do you understand Ambassador Evans? It's not intended as a cruelty. ¤

I signalled my comprehension, but my heart went out to Yvin, who only hours ago I had despised as an over-privileged, feckless teen. *Sympathy / our unwelcome guest.*

*

When I found him, he was curled up tight in the corner of a kletch whose name meant *Little River Silence* on a precipice above a black ravine. Outside, dust jetted up from the gorge against a rock pillar, but there was silence in the kletch. The boat hovered out over the wall. Yvin's snout was buried in the ash settled at the base of the kletch. It dawned on me that I had nothing to say to him – what consolation could I give? I had no power with the Paraunion hierarchy. I was just a visitor. Was there – is there always hope? Or is that an excuse we invent to act inexcusably? Were we now cut off from Arbaun?

I sat close to him for a while and waited for events to unfold. It seemed all other Paraunion had decided to politely

194

ignore him and wait for things to blow over. Periodically I went to the boat, but he was still coiled with his face pressed into the dirt when I returned. It was an expression of suffering more adamant than I'd ever seen, and I have tried very hard to express suffering in my life.

The boat, at my request, sent a short message to Meletrus asking if I was acting incorrectly by staying with Yvin. Her reply was, "Any consolation you can provide is welcome". So I stayed.

¤ I'll make someone pay for this injustice, ¤ were his first words from the dust.

I thought carefully about my reply.

¤ My culture is rich in forgetfulness and most people you meet are forgiving. Our lives are short, our seasons fleeting. But maybe I can offer some advice if you'll take it from a condemned man? ¤

He didn't move, so I continued.

¤ You think you're being treated unfairly? Love comes in a hundred forms, and if you're lucky, you get to try some of them before you die. In the long run, it's better to have tried a new flavour, even if it ended in hurt and heartbreak. Later, you'll see it was worth it. The trick is to forgive life for being so cruel.¤

Annie overheard that little snippet from the hatchway of the boat. She carefully ambled away as if she hadn't been listening at all.

I expected him to pause over my thought-out answer, but it wasn't to be: he gushed on.

¤ You don't understand what it's like to live in the Paraunion! Certainty is at its core. A thousand races live side-by-side, suckling at that absolute, and it doesn't allow your grand poetic hopes, little 'man'. It doesn't allow revolutions of the soul so quick as forgiveness. You'll find out, or your kin will discover this in years to come. We are crushed by the oppression of the greater good. No Romeos survive, much less the Juliets. Soon, all too soon, you'll put a social value on love, and only the lucky will be allowed to live it out. ¤

195

He was right. *Across the street lurches / loves singing loon / barred from churches.* But I wanted to give him hope, unjustifiable hope. I wanted to prove that he was wrong, not about his situation but his defeatism. And deep down within me, a part glimmered that loved people angry and militant.

¤ I'm just a broken poet, ¤ I said, ¤ and soon, someone will put a bullet in my head, but here's what keeps me from laying down in the gutter and giving up. You can't live without a grain of hope: stupid, irrational hope. I never thought I'd make it to the Paraunion, but here I am. And the same rule applies right here in the Paraunion: change is inevitable, but you have to spot it. No one gets to dodge it.

¤ You say that the Paraunion hasn't changed for a thousand generations? I can tell you today alone, a brand new thing happened between a human and a Paraunion. What else might happen down a dark flow? Something totally different. Isn't that why we keep exploring—to generate more differences, more possibilities? You only lose when they squeeze the fight out of you. ¤

I'll admit that I was thinking more of myself than Yvin when I said those words. For years I'd kept the faith and battled the faceless system, even inspiring others to do the same, but I recalled the night on a Movampton street when I wondered if laying down to die rather than make it to the hospital might be easier.

¤ They won't permit us to be together on the mission, and I can't bear to wait for, or think of, my feelings changing. Should I resign myself to it? Or can it be overcome? ¤

His jowl was beside my face, and without thought, my demons rose up and said, ¤ *Anything can be overcome if you are prepared to succeed or cease to be.* ¤

¤ Will you help me then? ¤ he asked.

¤ I'll do what I can. ¤

Yvin pulled himself up out of the dust of the kletch. He braced himself and scanned the cloud boiling in the starless night above his head.

¤ I have the strangest feeling that I have decided something but I have no idea what it is, ¤ he said.

¤ Let's sleep on it. I used to have that same feeling a long time ago. The answer will emerge in the morning. ¤

Learn by rote / the world is spun / about this note. Yvin's new attitude concerned me, and his Para had a rabid logical edge that I struggled to read. All I had done was get a distraught boy up out of the grime and on with his life, but Yvin was a bright spark, even by Paraunion standards, unused to being told that something couldn't be done. Unaccustomed to the sound of 'no'.

I walked back to the boat to sleep, hoping all could be solved in the morning with a little more gentle guidance, hoping we'd hear from the divine Arbaun.

The night is full of tears, but the morning is beyond imagining.

Meletrus looked out of a rusted steel window frame in the ceiling-less dining hall of a modest kletch.

¤ Explain to me again the condition that you left him in? ¤

¤ He was different. ¤

¤ How? ¤

¤ He seemed to have put aside his problem. ¤

¤ I see. ¤

Our little one-to-one had been arranged by the boat, summoning a simulacrum of Meletrus out of thin air. It'd printed a copy and then allowed her to possess it. *I am not a clone / don't shred me.* This conversation was unusually taciturn for Para. Meletrus' lack of subtext showed how worried she was about her charge.

¤ I'd thought that perhaps the preparation of the Vould platform would stop this particular decision from being resolved for a lot longer. How foolish the vrys make us all look, ¤ Meletrus remarked.

¤ Why did they reject them? ¤ I asked.

¤ Lots of reasons; mental compatibility, perceived lack of life experience, doubts over the conjunction of natural dimensional and enhanced dimensional individuals. The list goes on and on. ¤

¤ But it doesn't stop them from being together? ¤

¤ Not at all. Just from being on the same dark flow crew where their relationship might impair their performance. Admittedly both have trained their whole life to be on that crew and once the mission begins, who knows how long they will be apart? It is effectively an order to separate for the foreseeable future. ¤

Meletrus rubbed a finger along the corroded frame, her additional limbs clasped behind her back. Simplified, her Para tonality said: "we're not in the business of arranged marriages". She turned to face me and brushed the dust from the front of her splendid cobalt and gold tunic.

¤ We're getting diverted from your ambassadorial duties. If you wish, I can find another host or habitation for you to visit for the remainder of your time? I'm aware of how precious it must be. ¤

I pictured Yvin in the marketplace when he had helped me barter for Nian's gift. It didn't feel right to abandon him.

¤ I'd rather stay with him. There's still a lot of Vould that I haven't seen, and it would be a shame to leave just as I'm getting to grips with the vuro arrangement of Para. After all, they've only just stopped looking at me as if a chair spontaneously started talking to them. ¤

¤ You're right, ¤ Meletrus laughed at the wooden imagery I added to the phrase, ¤ you should finish what you've started here. Remember, your notes and impressions will be an important historical artefact, no matter the outcome of your own government's power struggle. They will be preserved here in the Paraunion for posterity. ¤

Meletrus returned the wooden chair imagery that I'd used as an echo in the context of an archive that might be useful for future historians. Her sympathy for me was plain as day in her Para, as was her distress at being forbidden to intervene. To demonstrate her empathy, she began her following comment with a tilt of the head and a smile, an entirely human gesture with no basis in Para. She must have researched it.

¤ If you don't mind, can I shed a little light on why you're so unnerving to us? ¤

¤ Please do, ¤ I said.

¤ Back in the early history of your race, a bizarre mental process formed in just a few individuals that allowed those people to think about thinking. I'm radically simplifying for explanation, but they used that first building block to strategize about the world around them, to plan and overcome nature. Eventually, they capped that achievement by finding an outward expression of those processes in verbal form—giving you what you think of as language today.

¤ You see, that process is the same for humans and Paraunion species, but it continues through and beyond the digital ages of civilisations, most profoundly in parallelism. You haven't arrived at this evolutionary tipping point yet. It should be impossible for a human to learn Para without unnatural assistance. Do you see the contradiction? ¤

¤ You're saying I shouldn't be able to speak Para? ¤

¤ Exactly, you've been through the training, and you know what a state change is required. Ask yourself: weren't you surprised that you managed to master it at all? ¤

I cast my mind back to the lesson when Spindle took us fully into Para for the first time. *I love the spoon.* Truthfully I hadn't just been surprised to make progress. It was a miracle. Meletrus signalled her recognition of my inner thoughts. Her perceptiveness was troublingly close to telepathy. With Spindle, Lutsk and Nian: yes, they could be the cutting edge of human evolution, but me: no.

¤ In the test centre in Movampton,¤ I asked, ¤ the operator and the administrators had no idea what they were looking for. They couldn't tell that I was getting close to passing. What was the machine trying to find? ¤

¤ The spark of the faculty that emerged in an ancient generation of our ancestors, but we only needed human candidates where the primitive process was broken or evolved through a sheer chance of birth, mental trauma or extreme environment. Even then, it must be broken in just the right way to make Para possible. So, all the potential candidates are brought into direct contact with a Para speaker, where the vast majority will inevitably fail. Hence, Spindle and Border. ¤

¤ The Crush broke, or changed, my ability to think? ¤ *A broken toy / still holds the door open / as children play.*

She nodded. Saffron clouds of dust billowed past the window of the kletch. Even here, Meletrus was helping me join the dots, trying to get me to understand.

¤ I hope you find this helpful, Ambassador Evans. If you understand why and how you got here, I think it will aid your experience of the Paraunion. ¤

I used an outcrop from the wall as a makeshift seat. Was I so surprised? That graphomanic frenzy resulted from some broken plumbing in my brain pouring out language. This is why my hosts couldn't hide their disbelief that I had gained a super-human ability by a billions-to-one chance. It was like someone getting out of a car crash and gaining a hundred IQ points.

¤ This is just supposition on my part, ¤ Meletrus continued, ¤ but I suspect that you may have had a strange relationship to language before you suffered your collapse. Parts of *The Pollutant Speaks* have a distinctly Para flavour. ¤

¤ I'm flattered that you've taken the time to read it. ¤

¤ There is some additional information I have for you, passed to me from Border. ¤

Her body language told me to prepare for bad news and that it wasn't an accident that she had read *The Pollutant*.

She continued.

¤ The CannotBeGrouped developed a breakaway faction, smaller but more militant than the original. They take *The Pollutant Speaks* as holy scripture. They want to capture the city ships to make flight between worlds free to people they deem worthy or deny it to anyone they consider unclean. ¤

Meletrus paused before putting a hand on my shoulder.

¤ A kappa ship delivering passengers to *New Osaka* was tampered with. It struck the vessel like a missile and caused enormous damage. The majority lost their lives within the first moments. All communication with the ship was lost, and it is feared that the remaining crew and passengers have little or no chance of survival. The Cannot faction claimed responsibility for the attack and said that if they were denied access to living space, the rich and influential shouldn't have it either. The *New Osaka* was bound for Border. ¤

I held my head in my hands and stared into the red dust on the floor. I'd never felt so far from home. The affairs of my

201

people had been like an embarrassing family feud, a grief observed from a distance, but now I realised how finely balanced it all was. One hundred and fifty thousand people were on the *New Osaka*. People who struggled, worked, wrote songs and had children. Rolliard and I had used their spare rooms, eaten their food and shared in their ceremonies. But they were gone because someone thought they needed to kill them as a demonstration. *Fragrant myrtle / shining limes / just ash and coal.*

Meletrus waited in respect. It was clear she had been terse during our early conversation as she built up the courage to break the news to me.

¤ Can you help them? ¤ I asked.

¤ Not officially. We can find the remains of the New Osaka and get that information through to someone, but there's likely no one to rescue. If the government wishes, we can bring the ship to a standstill so that recoveries can be made. If our intervention in these matters became public, it might worsen the situation. Can I ask why you think they did it? ¤

¤ The captains are a different breed, less easily steamrolled than the polilawyers in the assembly. I imagine they wouldn't bend, couldn't be bought or brainwashed. Crossley probably hates them. ¤

Meletrus acknowledged my point with a sad gesture and walked slowly among the abandoned trestles and pedestals of the kletch.

¤ I know you find this upsetting, but I think you should know. They claim they are following revolutionary principles laid down in your book. After the attack, they published sections over and over again. ¤

I'd suspected that they would. It was unbearable to hear people had used *The Pollutant* to justify their own violent ends. A mix of anger and grief boiled in my stomach, leaving a bilious taste in my mouth. How would they twist what I had said into a call for destruction? Anger got the better of grief, and I shouted at the innocent Meletrus.

202

¤ Which parts? ¤ I ranted. ¤ No, don't tell me. Let's see if I can play their evil fucking game, shall I? How about "*I will make no more!*" or "*We deck the Appian street with cadavers?*" Shall I go again? Why not? "*Now I speak in nightmares made real!*" ¤

¤ All of those and more. The philosophical fit doesn't seem to worry them. It's the rebellion in the tone that mesmerises them. Their methods are unrelated to the inspiration. I considered not telling you these details, but the anti-CBG cohorts suggest you aren't as detached from the Cannots as you claim. They are demanding that you be called back from this mission to be interrogated or possibly used as a tool to suppress the CBG. The opposition parties are lobbying for population control, capital punishment and instantiation of military law, anything to counter the swing towards populism. ¤

Even during the attack on Border, I'd never felt so broken and lost. The cataclysm of the meteor strike numbed my feelings and made me mourn the loss of my friend. But here, deep in a strange world, being told that thousands of the people I cared for had been cruelly stripped from the world, I was desolated. Memories of *Osaka* flicked on and off like a movie in my head, but I held myself together for another sentence.

¤ I'd like to be alone. ¤

¤ I understand. The boat is, as ever, at your disposal. Take time to think. ¤

She brought her hands together in a respectful bow and then stood at pure neutral. Whatever field held the simulacrum together was removed, and the body dissolved into a glitter of dust, crushed by the atmosphere of Vould.

I sat alone for an hour, revolving through thoughts of revenge, despair, disgust and prayers for the lost. If only I could have talked to Lutsk for a moment or two—it might have set my mind straight. As it was, I drowned in a sea of confusion. Was I responsible in some way? Could anything I say to the Cannots and the polilawyers do more good than getting the

Paraunion to engage with humanity? *Pallas Athena come forth / your servant is lost.*

I walked back to the promontory to be picked up by the boat, still as stunned as I had been when Meletrus told me about the New Osaka, worse perhaps. The need to make sense of it and do something definitive ate away inside me.

Something about Meletrus dissolving into nothing before my eyes haunted me, and I asked the boat to take me out and orbit Vould on its dark side. I sat on the deck watching the pale fire around the planet's horizon and brooding while the boat kept its opinion and counsel considerately to itself.

And still no news from Arbaun.

The crescent of the harbour faced out across the metal sea, grey ripples reflecting the pre-dawn's faint purple and orange colours. A wet ozone smell hung in the air.

My thoughts were lost in the destruction of the New Osaka, and I was thankful for the quiet around me. Tourists and locals alike waited for a special moment on Vould. We stood respectfully distanced; a few vuro, Ovu the porcupine, and a handful of tourist species looked across the seascape below a granite sky. *What metal tides see / belts of mercury.*

A lone *crewyat* tumbled out of the cloud cover, singing and rolling in the air until it turned and shot back up out of sight. A distant band brightened where the sea met the sky, and the ocean and sky churned together. A thunder peal boomed from the horizon, and the metallic sea boiled while the lip of the monstrous sun filled the eastern quarter of our view.

Waves leapt up into the clouds, cutting them apart with crackling streamers of antimony vapour which formed new glittering clouds. I felt the concussions in my chest and stomach, the heat of the flares on my face. Every natural part of me told me to run away, that Vould had finally decided to tear me apart, but through the sorcery of the visitor ring, I had a box seat to see day and night tear each other apart. The phrase for dawn was mixed with the word for fear by the primitive vuro long before their ascent to technological power.

The sweltering face of Vould's star grinned orange-red and victorious over the steaming remains of the seabed as I stood on the harbour enjoying the post-cataclysm silence. It made me forget my anger about the New Osaka for the briefest moment until I was disturbed by a familiar voice behind me.

¤ Finally getting some sightseeing done, Evans? ¤ said Yvin.

¤ Just this, before I'm shipped back. ¤

¤ That's it then, no more Ambassador Evans? ¤

¤ Exactly. ¤

I walked away from the edge of the harbour. The last thing I wanted was to speak to the self-involved Yvin while I was still reeling from the news from home. He inevitably tagged along behind me, clearly full of his own schemes. I strode along as if I had something important to attend to nearby, but all of my subtlety was wasted on the dogged mind of Yvin.

¤ Maybe we can petition for a little more time? I've thought of several cultural hot spots for you now. You've still not been to the flux riders yet, have you? I can make arrangements for you to get in the leading peloton. ¤

My frustration levels peaked.

¤ I'm afraid we've missed that opportunity now. I will not be staying to advise you on the details of your love life. Thousands, millions, of my people are dying, and there's a bunch of lunatics claiming that it's all in my name. Soon they'll disappear me just as they did Jones and Green. So please, Yvin, leave me alone. ¤

¤ I'm afraid I can't. ¤

¤ Why? ¤

¤ Arbaun wants to say goodbye to you both. She's decided to leave the research department so I can stay on the mission,¤ Yvin sounded guilty. ¤ She insisted I come and collect you in person. She said it was the least I could do after being such a poor host. ¤

Arbaun. I didn't dare hope that she'd found a way to help, but when you've had nothing but bad news for so long, you jump immediately on any trace of something going your way. As a bonus, Yvin genuinely sounded repentant.

The research platform wasn't dark anymore: it sparkled like an ornament in the dark. It was as if Arbaun were running every last system she had laboured to produce. Fields cast rainbows over the length of the vessel, dishes and antennae

206

crackled with life, each measuring and probing as if the craft were deep in the unknown frontier of the universe and not within sight of its own construction. There was something a little sad about the spectacle, as if the owner just once wanted to turn on all the lights before leaving it to lesser minds to take into action.

The boat entered a cavernous bay and unloaded us as close to the command centre as it could park itself. Annie and I followed our vuro host as he guided us through an airlock and up to the nerve centre of the platform.

Arbaun had split into three different figures on the flight deck, each linked by blue-white tracery. She ran checks and analysed the performance of the systems. One of the figures coalesced into something humanoid as Annie and I approached. It rushed towards me and reached out its hands to clasp either side of my head.

¤ Oh, ambassador! Forgive me. Time is of the essence. ¤

Instantly, the bridge between our consciousnesses was reformed in a gut-wrenching psychic flip-flop. Yvin was stunned by the sight of his beloved communing with a savage such as myself. As we shared thoughts, I knew that the collaboration was unevenly biased. For Arbaun, this was merely a whisper in the ear, but I felt a total co-opting of my consciousness.

I-she had broken the code that the mountain thundered, her mind so much more spacious could unfold the compressed concepts, five stages that could save humanity had blithely occurred to the mountain of the universe at the moment we contacted. I-she wondered if the giant mind saw all the ways the universe could be healed but was doomed to exist purely as an observer. The great oracle had foreseen the cost to anyone who chose to execute the plan, its premise based on doing the unthinkable and the least expected: breaking the law. She-I needed to know if the price was too high for me-her. A citizen like her-me could serve a long sentence, shared with as many masters who showed leniency to make up for our transgression, but a masterless creature such as myself-herself would suffer the full weight, unshared, for the crime. A sin undissolved was always death in the Paraunion.

It was not too late to undo and hide all her-my preparation. Other plans might still be made.

I-she felt the thought stolen from the mountain pointed us to throw all our effort into a single chance to stop the madness of my-our kind, then that's what I-she would pay.

She-I was willing.

I-she would happily die trying.

She moved back from me, separating our connection. The last glimpse I felt from her mind was a great welling of pride and sorrow, but it was cut off from me almost the moment it appeared.

Yvin looked outraged at the pair of us. His pressure scales hackled at the sense that something was deathly wrong.

¤ What is happening here? Arbaun, explain yourself! ¤

Arbaun moved one of her bodies towards him in a gesture of pacification, nearly surrounding him in lights and curves.

¤ I'm afraid, dearest, that there was no easy way to separate you from our friends. I'm confident, however, that no one will confuse this with collusion on your part. The blame will fall entirely on myself and the ambassador. ¤

¤ Blame for what? Tell me what is going on! ¤

¤ We will enact a plan which the mountain of Onis felt profoundly was the morally correct thing to do, but that involves disobeying the decree not to interfere in human affairs. You see? Morally right but legally wrong. Every good thing that cannot be executed within the realms of a justice system must be tested, or the system itself is corrupt. Even if we succeed, which is questionable, it will cost our friend his life to see the right thing done. ¤

Yvin was dumbfounded. No ordinary Paraunion could conceive of the route of civil disobedience; that wasn't how matters were solved. They were debated and argued in the tussles of the vrys, philosophy and reason were brought to bear, but never, ever was the will of society overthrown by an individual. That was why the mountain's plan was so inconceivable to the average citizen; Arbaun had at least had several days to think the matter over.

A calming thought dawned on the young vuro, and his hackles smoothed.

¤ The boat simply won't allow it, ¤ he said. ¤ I'm afraid all this insurgence has been for nothing. ¤

From nowhere, the voice of the boat sounded out of the air.

¤ That is correct. I cannot allow this to continue. ¤

'It's just outside in the cargo bay,' Annie growled, 'there's no way to get away from it now, especially now that the two of you have made your plan public.'

¤ Your aide is correct, Ambassador Evans. Please return to the bay now. All this talk of treason will really do nothing to help your position. ¤

¤ I'm afraid that won't be possible, loyal boat, ¤ said Arbaun.

¤ And why is that? ¤ it asked.

¤ Because I ejected that cargo bay quite some time ago. ¤

*

In a remarkable achievement of deceit, Arbaun had rigged all the hum and whirr of the vast platform as a sensory distraction, a hazy backdrop painstakingly recreated by the scientific instruments on the research vessel. This allowed the remainder of the craft to disappear into the dark night and evade pursuit.

Yvin watched as his lover guided the ship into dark flow after dark flow, randomizing and truncating each course to throw off the immense tracking powers of the boat. I knew he was conflicted. His loyalty to her was unswerving, but so was his life-long dedication to the principles of his upbringing. He remained in speechless deadlock between the two, neither halting our escape nor stepping in to join our cause. We had unwittingly taken a hostage.

'Is he going to be trouble?' asked Annie, looking at a creature more than a physical match for us all.

'If he was going to do anything, I think we would have already seen it,' I replied.

One of the embodiments of Arbaun gestured for us all to gather around. She reached out to include Yvin in the conversation, which, after some hesitation, he did. The other mirrors of Arbaun continued to move silently about, playing their dark game of hide and seek against the boat.

¤ The plan laid out by the mountain is folded into five highly abstract concepts which we must find ways to realise: choose the vital target, escape our pursuers, strike quickly, cause or commit a crime and remove our enemy's weapon. First is the target; where must we attack our enemy to defeat them? I'm convinced we must save the gestalt collective, the G-russ, from the control of Crossley. If turned against him, the marketeers can break the political movement's power, the weapon, over the human culture, and your people will be free to choose whichever future they truly want. One of the five of the G-russ is the weakness that allows them to be controlled. We must determine which it is. ¤

'That's a good choice,' agreed Annie, 'the G-russ aren't what you'd call moral crusaders but being controlled under duress for a year or more will have really built up a thirst for revenge. If they feel safe to strike back, they could undermine everything Crossley has done.'

Yvin passed no comment but raised a hunch as if the logic was undeniable.

¤ We stand amid the second phase now, ¤ Arbaun continued. ¤ From the first moment Evans shared the experience with me, I knew that I would be called upon to do what must be done. What is our culture if it is too self-interested to preserve lives? Who are we if we don't see that our existence sets the groundwork for the radicals that Crossley is exploiting? Who are we if, when asked for help, we refuse? ¤

She looked at me in a strange mixture of shame and love. A participant can try on or tune into an emotional position in the fugue of a Para conversation. Arbaun invited her partner to do so, to feel what it was like to stand in my place and see in us what she saw. Yvin relented and took part. His grace in defeat was a credit to him.

¤ For all its rumination, the mountain thinks of everything at a greater distance than us, ¤ he mused. ¤ It sees "good" as what might finally develop from circumstances after centuries or more. If it offers you a plan—or perhaps if you even steal a concept it was mulling over—then there is no guarantee it is "good" in the way we conceive it. ¤

¤ Then I shall do what I feel to be defensibly right, ¤ replied Arbaun.

¤ Ah well, I suppose there is at least one bright side, ¤ Yvin sighed.

¤ And what is that? ¤ she asked.

¤ We will get to crew our ship together at least once before they throw us into the dingiest part of the Paraunion. ¤

We'd corrupted two young Paraunion, and they worked frantically to fly us where we needed to go with our jailor in hot pursuit. There was little Annie or I could do but watch them guide us discretely through weeks of side alleys and underworlds, the dead spaces and disused passages of the universe back to our own doorstep and Shang Lo's chaos.

'Break into the Marketoria?'

'That's where they'll be.'

Annie worried that the later stages of our mission would be less easy to realise than the first two. Discussing them on the dimmed flight deck while our pilots concentrated, quite a few details seemed sketchy.

'The g-Russ are incredibly skittish,' she pointed out. 'Remember, anything that threatens the mental stability of one of them threatens them all, making the gestalts incredibly paranoid, even superstitious. They don't know that we're coming to help them, and even if they did, they might suspect that when we can't help them. We might fall back on trying to eliminate them to slow down Crossley. I'm saying that we can't rely on them welcoming us with open arms.'

'Fair point,' I said. 'It doesn't seem very inconspicuous to land a city-sized spaceship. We need to get in there quietly and take care of business.'

¤ You forget we have two advantages that the rest of your kind do not. ¤ Yvin turned and pointed at the ring on my finger.

It had bugged me for a long time when D-t-arr sneered at how primitive we were and pointed out we couldn't properly utilise the visitor rings. His point had been clear: you use it to float about or protect yourself from being hit or crushed when its true purpose is miracles. We were going to need lessons. *You shall possess the origin of all poems.*

'Maybe we can get a message to the g-Russ telling them our plan? Maybe just parlay with them?' said Annie.

'How do we know they won't be forced to relay that message to Crossley? No, let's catch them off guard. One of them has a weakness for Crossley's meme, and we need to stop that one. Arbaun, can you wipe something from a human mind?'

¤ This exploration platform, focused through me, can superimpose new patterns on a human brain, much as the boat did to save your life. But the subject must focus on it. We must know what to remove. ¤

'And what happens if it's more than one of them?' I asked.

'Then we'll try and cure them all,' Annie said with conviction, 'but the g-Russ lost control in the first place because it's just one: the original dominant, Lawrence.'

¤ What makes you so sure? ¤ Yvin asked.

'One of the g-Russ had loaded Alone early on in their life before they joined the gestalt, whether they used it much or not. It must have been before joining. Once in the gestalt, it wouldn't be allowed.'

'Ok, that's the only way I can imagine Crossley getting the upper hand on them. But how can you be sure it's Lawrence?' I asked.

'Well, picture the evolution of the g-Russ. As each new member joins, they are thoroughly vetted for instabilities: red flags like loading the Alone program.'

'That leaves only the first two as suspects, the original gestalts.' Arbaun sparkled with delight as she followed the logic.

'Lawrence and Manuel. I can tell you for an absolute certainty that it isn't Manuel because I knew Manuel exceptionally well before Lawrence fell deeply and madly in love with him. You can't see it now, but Manuel is the stable, carefree sunshine of their crazy milkshake. Lawrence is the volatile, depressive genius.'

'Bugatti, you're a genius!' I cried.

'I knew casual sex would one day save my life.'

There was little for us to do except worry about all the other possibilities as we crept closer to our old home. Having one of the largest populations of Cannots, it had fallen into a state of martial law, rich areas being shut off and patrolled by expensive private peace keepers. Other districts like

Movampton fell into chaos, with basic amenities being cut off and the rule of law failing completely.

We descended from the sky into the centre of the Marketoria, Bugatti and I dropping unnaturally under the protection of the rings, Arbaun and Yvin levitated by the power of the research platform or perhaps exercising their powers independently. The hot drear of uncontrolled weather cast a pall among the shifting columns of dirty atmosphere. The spectacle alarmed passers-by, and those there to see it ran in fear as if we were some new branch of torment for them.

The glass offices with their huge sculpted logos and peek-a-boo architecture still moved, but without the money men, the entrepreneurs and the consultants who'd fled to safer districts, perhaps even different worlds. Empty meeting tables and desolate break rooms drifted around in the glass boxes of the Marketoria.

'It's not often I feel sorry for ad-men,' Annie said.

'Don't start now,' I answered.

From high up on one of the shuttleways, usually packed with droves of commuters, a neverrider, near-naked and covered from head to toe in long whip marks, shook an illegally printed rifle over his head.

'*Who clogged and killed Old Movey? Who jammed the system built to sustain? I. The pollutant who learnt to speak!*' he raged and remorselessly fired the rifle at us until every round had been spent from its clip. Frustrated that not a single bullet seemed to affect us, he flung the weapon itself down at us, turned and ran back into the darkness of the station.

Almost as soon as he had disappeared, figures appeared on the side roads and entryways of the plaza.

Neverriders, glitterbeasts, lowpunks and megabetties, more Cannots than I had ever seen, rushed past each other, all looking for the target they had so nearly missed nine years earlier, the lying author of their holy book. It was hard to remember that they were innocent, that they were the victims.

On sight of me, they threw and fired anything they could lay their hands on. They screamed as if words themselves might spear me down. The four of us ran to the lobby of the Marketoria, but this time there was no security guard to greet us. Yvin waved his hand with a gesture of mild frustration, seizing control of the building's computer systems and then sealing all the doors and entrances. The Cannots threw themselves against the gates with howls of anger.

'We need to get down to the lowest level,' yelled Annie.

I led Arbaun to the elevator we'd used on our last visit to see the g-Russ. It seemed as easy as thinking for her to make the doors open.

I hesitated at the elevator. What if the G-russ were dead already? Killed by Crossley through paranoia or spite? Annie pulled me into the cubicle.

'Now that we're so close, this whole plan seems like it could easily go wrong.'

'You're the lightning rod that sent us here, Evans. No time to worry about the fine details now,' said Bugatti.

¤ We have minimal time. Every use of Paraunion technology will be like a beacon to the boat, and when it arrives, it will end anything we might be doing,¤ Arbaun warned.

She willed the elevator to send us all to the deepest circle of the Marketoria. I was glad to see the doors close on the faces of those chanting Cannots.

The sanctum of the g-Russ was untouched by the collapse of the world above. The stark, brilliant foyer still contained the two sweeping marble counters, behind which sat pristine, androgynous holographic assistants, apparently blind to our existence. Down in the walled glass circle, the five gestalts continued their labours, oblivious to the descent of their race into a new dark age of the will.

Their clothes accentuated their similarities, the haute couture so pressed, as if they were manikins in an advertisement, not real market makers. On close inspection, though none was identical, not one a perfect clone of the others, each was unique with reflections of four others dressed over them.

But now, in the corner of each eye, about the turn of each set of lips, was an unspoken worry that all was not well in paradise, a worry none of them dared mention. Gestalts fear disruption.

Bugatti threw open the double door to the atrium office, the circle of glass and screens, and pointed with an accusing finger.

'That fucker is Lawrence.'

Whatever Lawrence was about to say was cut short as he fell unconscious at a gesture from Yvin, who darted gracefully through the doors, incongruous with the surroundings of human bureaucracy. The vuro simulated the buoyancy of his homeworld and caught the patient in his arms before Lawrence could hit the ground.

¤ Don't be alarmed, ¤ he said.

The other four stood dumbfounded at their workstations, some with tools still in hand, gawking at the otherworldy salamander that held their soul brother so gently. Moments later, they noticed the stunning humanoid arrangement of arcane starlight that was Arbaun. I suppose that sometimes it doesn't matter how smart you are. You're just upstaged.

'I'm here to chat about some bad advice I received,' I said.

By whatever means Yvin had rendered Lawrence unconscious, it didn't appear to be doing any immediate harm to either Manuel, Christopher, Johan or Kio. They stared at the Paraunion, unsure if he was shielding or about to eat their twin. I should have predicted their reaction to meeting with a Paraunion, a truly "other" thing. Without training, instincts kick in at sights evolution had not prepared them for. Alien form and motion grasped the irrational part of their psyche and created fear.

Yvin brought Lawrence's ragdoll body over to a desk, holding his head carefully with his hands but levitating the rest of his mass with unseen force, an ability he used without effort. I thought it best to get the remaining gestalts to focus on me.

'I'm sorry, gentlemen, but we're pushed for time. We need you to confirm that Lawrence here is forcing you to work for Crossley?'

Eventually, all four nodded.

'And that none of you is at risk from this virus or meme?'

All four looked at each other questioningly until Kio addressed me.

'No. We didn't know for sure until we were free of Lawrence, but now we are certain that no one else is infected. Whatever it is, it doesn't spread by empathy,' he said.

'Let me introduce my two friends from the Paraunion who have risked their necks to be here, Yvin of Vould and Arbaun-de-felentual, both breaking laws to be here and cure Lawrence. I can't explain all the details to you as time is limited. Very, very soon, their equivalent of the police will be here.'

¤ Genuinely, at any moment, Evans, ¤ said Yvin, ¤ we must make an attempt now. ¤

'I'll take care of them,' said Annie and ushered the four to one side, where they stood like nervous relatives watching their own bypass surgery.

Arbaun leant over Lawrence, formed a halo around his head and looked deep into the hidden realms of his mind.

'What have you done to each other?' she said in horror directly to the quartet of watchers.

'What we,' said Johan.

'Had,' said Christopher.

'To do,' said Manuel.

'To live,' said Kio.

I caught the brief Para context between Arbaun and Yvin. It seemed to them that they had entered a horror show where the freaks mutilated themselves.

¤ Can you isolate Lawrence and wake him up? ¤ I asked.

¤ I believe so, but we must be quick. The bridge between these creatures is fragile, ¤ said Arbaun.

With that, I saw Lawrence open his eyes. Fear and horror passed across his face. It was the first time he'd been alone in decades, and clearly not a pleasant experience.

'Lawrence, don't be afraid,' I said gently, 'we're here to help you. Is something forcing you to help Crossley? Can you focus on that for us?'

The patient's fear became a sneer as he struggled against unseen bonds.

'Nothing controls me except the need to do the right thing for once!' Lawrence raged.

'That's not true, Lawrence,' said Kio.

'You're unbalancing us,' said Johan.

'We're afraid of you, Lorry,' said Christopher.

'There's something unhinged in you,' said Kio.

The concerned relatives became an intervention. They wagged their heads and looked down miserably at the furious victim. I felt sure that whatever spell was enslaving Lawrence must be active in him now, but Arbaun's expression said no. How could there be nothing to find? Had we wildly misjudged

Crossley, and he was genuinely converting people all this time? But then the other gestalts seemed to prove it was an infection.

Lawrence turned his attention away from his brothers and to me.

'How have you done this to me, Evans? You've turned my loved ones against me. You with your disgusting, inhuman puppets! Release me! Or are you *deaf from the sound of chains?*'

Arbaun couldn't pinpoint the source of Crossley's madness, but as Lawrence spat my own words at me, she found a trace of something unnatural within him. Doubt bounced between her and Yvin. This was not how the g-Russ acted. Every moment, I was more convinced that we were right, yet the concrete evidence and a cure remained invisible to Arbaun. She could only remove the means of control if she could see it.

'Did you hear that last part, Bugatti?' I said. 'That's my kind of roro. That's the *Pollutant* flavour of crazy just mixed up a bit.'

'Like the Cannots,' she said.

¤ Everyone who Crossley controls had Alone and later became obsessed with a corrupt form of the *Pollutant*. So we know the entry method and part of the mechanism: nothing more. We don't know what Crossley's contagion is: a meme, a virus or a drug? It could be something else entirely. ¤

My Paraunion colleagues had followed my train of thought, but the g-Russ looked mystified by my Para comments. Annie slowly caught up through the translator in the visitor ring but still seemed confused.

¤ If we eliminate *The Pollutant Speaks* from Lawrence's memory, then without the hypnotic trigger, Crossley may not have control of him.¤ I looked at the victim held rigid by an invisible field, ¤ But Lawrence must not suspect.¤

¤ That would leave the control mechanism with no means to rationalise itself to the victim,¤ Yvin ruminated. ¤ No way for it to convince the sufferer or those around them to do what Crossley wants. ¤ He moved towards the curved glass doors of the g-Russ's office as if he could smell or hear something wrong.

I looked at Lawrence's face. Disgust and anger emanated from him like a furnace, but I had to be sure that he was under control, not that he had simply gone mad. *People you know have.*

Green had drilled into me repeatedly that each mind, human or not, has a unique landscape to be explored—explored—not reasoned out or judged, not to be entered into with an agenda of change. I desperately could have used his advice about Lawrence. As a Paraunion and human criminal about to be charged and sentenced to death, time was not on my side. I followed my gut instinct. *Unsing the song.*

¤ Something is wrong, ¤ said Yvin, ¤ our protection around the building has collapsed. ¤

'Are the Cannots back?' Bugatti asked, alarming the g-Russ, who only got half of the conversation.

'You won't stop us, Evans!' screamed Lawrence.

¤ They shouldn't be able to break that barrier down, ¤ said Yvin as he worried around the perimeter, looking upward at the ceiling.

¤ Is it the boat already? ¤ I asked.

¤ If the boat were close enough to meddle with the building, it would have disabled and arrested all of us immediately. ¤

¤ Whatever is happening, we need to complete what we came for now, ¤ said Arbaun. ¤ Let's cure Lawrence and then get out of this place. Evans, I think it's time for a rendition. ¤

Believe it or not, it had been some years since I had recited the *Pollutant*. Like many things, it's always the first word that is the hardest. For just a single moment, I thought that maybe I'd lost it when the boat rebuilt me, that perhaps it had made another me without the *Pollutant*. That would be what it would be like for Lawrence forever.

When it came to me, I sounded it out slowly. Recalling each line just as I spoke the previous one.

'*Wait until I have made no sense,*

*Wait until I tell you of Wingate, the dashboards, Johnny Po-lotti and
Susie Mayday, Dr Boda and Lovedreary: masters of sex, dreams and
escape;*

*Wait until I tell you about the billions gone, clouded out of sanity,
besotted with life and crushed like dots on spheres that collide,*

Wait until that last lost syllable.

Wait. Let the pollutant speak.'

The further I got, the more it flowed, the more the next
word was the only word. As the stanzas passed, Arbaun
removed its pattern from Lawrence's memory. I made it to
about halfway through.

'In the chapel of black air,

I am every lost tree and extinct creature,

Metamorphed to every surgical glitterbeast and androchild,

Filled with every choking ambition,

Changed, saturated, I am....'

'That's quite enough,' said Crossley.

He stood at the opened doors of the elevator.

More troubling was the great, dark figure of D-t-arr
standing behind him, shaking his head and tutting as if he had
discovered children misbehaving. Yvin placed himself between
them and us.

'Everywhere you go, Evans, you corrupt individuals. Look
at these two children you've made criminals of. What is it that
compels you to such terrible acts of sedition? Even now, you
are brainwashing a fellow human! If the Paraunion don't
execute you,'

'Which we will,' said D-t-arr.

'Then we humans surely will,' Crossley finished with a grin.

'Feng you, Crossley!' Bugatti shouted and immediately
picked up a projection bar as a cudgel.

I looked at Arbaun. Would removing half of the *Pollutant* be
enough? She seemed to be struggling with the same question,
but it didn't seem we would be allowed the chance to complete
the erasure of the rest. Perhaps stimulating the *Pollutant* in

221

Lawrence's mind was linked to the whole and not just the lines I had recited, so Arbaun may have eradicated it.

She released Lawrence back to his gestalt siblings. It was a calculated risk. If removing half of the Pollutant had done nothing, they would be back under Crossley's control. If not, then we had the confirmation we needed.

Lawrence rushed into the waiting arms of his beautifully suited brethren, weeping and gushing like a child after a nightmare. It wasn't long until they turned their attention to their former captor. *Quincunx.*

'We will erase every scrap of influence you have,' said Johan.

'We will turn you and your movement into a half-remembered circus,' said Kio.

'We will purge every Cannot,' said Manuel.

'We will see you destroyed,' said Christopher, holding the distraught Lawrence in his arms.

In all my life, I'd never heard such a cold threat. Not a threat. That wouldn't have been so penetrating. They were *promising* Crossley what would happen to him next as if they were rapt in a vision of the future, and Crossley wasn't immune to the primal force of their menace.

'No, I think it's time to cut my losses. Evans and Lawrence, you've both been useful, but you were scaffolding, never intended to be viewed by the public in my final masterpiece. The end of your act has come, and another scene must begin. D-t-arr, you've seen the crimes that all these people are guilty of. What good citizen would not deputize himself to see that no more horrors are committed? You must handle this.'

D-t-arr resonated with conflict, his black limbs shook, and his faceplates ground together in dissonance.

'The boat will be here soon,' he muttered weakly.

'Soon? Soon? Should justice wait? Am I not the voice of reason and freedom not just for the human race but the universe? When I speak of the law, do you think I mean just the Paraunion law that can be enforced by an idiotic robot, or do I mean a divine law which every being must be the enforcer of?'

Visibly, the mechanism cracked D-t-arr's spirit as Crossley spoke, each syllable somehow getting into the crevices of his free will and pulling the poor creature apart. It didn't really matter what Crossley said, whether it was his messianic drivel or repeating the order over and over. The posturing and teasing were part of the fun for Crossley, all for his own ego and self-justification.

When the control programme broke him, D-t-arr lurched forward with murderous intent, flashing out his black tendrils and throwing furniture out of his way. He made a straight line towards me and the g-Russ.

Yvin stood his ground.

I remembered all the silly little things that I had held against Yvin, his selfishness and his petty comments. They all felt shameful judgements when set against the honest courage I saw then. D-t-arr was an ancient Paraunion in comparison to him. He had centuries longer to craft the energies and forces at his disposal. There wasn't even the pretence of a fair fight.

Each projected a shield, and as D-t-arr rushed on, they compressed against each other, burning white-hot in the air between them. The closer they got, the more layers of tortured flux boiled between them. Too late, it occurred to Yvin that in a simple matter of energy control, he was going to lose to his elder, and too late, he began construction of a physical mesh. D-t-arr reached like a nightmare directly through the remains of the shield and mesh alike, taking Yvin by the throat in a vicious grip.

Arbaun started forward to engage with the rogue Paraunion, but her instincts for conflict were unrefined. Why should they be? She lived in a society that hadn't seen individuals at war for generations. Even sports in the Paraunion had sublimated from veiled combat into the development of the mind. Power was measured by influence, not military reach.

She moved towards the struggling vuro clasped by the immense form of D-t-arr, too late to stop him from raising another glimmering hand and piercing it deep into the thorax of Yvin as if the limb were a sword. D-t-arr spread his arms apart in a single gesture, one hand throwing the body off to his left and the other, rapier-like, slicing through the victim's chest and organs, opening up Yvin like a gutted fish. Bile and gut, blood and intestine cascaded onto the floor.

Yvin struck the far glass wall and fell to the floor. He struggled to clutch at himself, covered as he was in parts of his own viscera, until his grip faded, his beautiful face turned dim, and his head bowed.

Arbaun screamed and flickered into several versions of herself. Each broke apart, becoming less distinct but moving too fast for me to register. All converged on the fallen body of her lover, surrounding him. Perhaps sustaining him.

'I shall exert no such efforts on you, Evans,' said D-t-arr, seeing me watch the tragic lovers.

An object flew across the room from the corner of my eye, spinning end over end until it stopped inches from D-t-arr's faceplates, crushed into a pea-like ball of metal.

It was the projection bar hurled by Bugatti.

'Why don't you fucking come and get some *djal* sucker?' she said, giving him the Critishins gang sign.

D-t-arr sighed and considered what to do with the difficult female, troubled by something deep within that disagreed with his actions, but the control programme won him over. It twisted his moral fugue and turned frustration into anger. He flung out a tentacle, smashing her over a desk and into a display unit where he paid no more attention to her and steadily advanced upon me. The g-Russ cowered behind me, Lawrence lying prone in Kio's arms.

¤ Aren't you forgetting something? ¤ I asked.

¤ I'm a superior being Evans, you little freak. I don't forget things, ¤ D-t-arr replied.

224

I held up my hand, giving him a good look at the visitor ring.

¤ Virtually immortal, that's what Meletrus said. ¤

¤ True, true, ¤ D-t-arr rasped. ¤ If only you knew how to use it properly, we might have an interesting scenario. ¤

Always swing for the big guy. I customised the thought that let me do the one thing I knew with the visitor ring: to air walk really quickly. I thought of just one step, but as if I was travelling a long distance, a long distance with my fist held out.

Did I really hit him? Did I make contact with his actual face? I don't know, but his mantle reeled away from the blow. I had crossed the distance between us in the blink of an eye and was caught close to the roiling body of slick black tendrils. He saw his opportunity and wrapped his curtain limbs around me.

¤ What good is holding me if you can't hit me, D-t-arr? Let's stop and wait for the boat. Crossley's using you! ¤

Close up, glittering black planes moved around his callous, hooded eyes. Eyes with the same madness that every Cannot had. Eyes that couldn't resolve their inner conflict and in which paradoxes squirmed like maggots in the brain. A tendril of darkness spiralled up my arm.

¤ Tell me, what good is a visitor ring if you aren't wearing it? ¤

The heavy limbs around me crackled and squealed as they crushed the field projected by the ring. The black, starry tendril reached my hand and gripped the ring's circumference, rolling it around and edging it millimetre by millimetre off my straining fingers, held straight and open by threads and bars of black sinew, glistening and extending from D-t-arr.

The ring was at the last knuckle. The next moment, it would be off. I felt the tentacles begin to exert themselves. In his fury, the alien would crush me like a bag of meat. The moment I thought I was drawing my last breath, he stopped. It took me a few moments to realise that neither he nor I nor anything in the room was moving.

A voice filled the circle of carnage.

¤ Stop. You are under arrest. ¤

The shouts of the crowd surprised me.

A Ramaton cloud loudly disagreed with an Ut-eey seed mat somewhere up on the third tier of the forum while a glass prowler acted as a neutral referee, repeating and reflecting the arguments out to the massed audience.

Arbaun remained defiant in the centre of the debate, her guilt and sentence already decided, the punishment being the only one a Paraunion court ever passed: death. Now all that remained was to see how large a portion of that sentence her masters and the layers above her masters would commute away by taking a part of the guilt upon themselves.

Her stance was implacable, indomitable. She had done what she felt was right and was more than willing to pay the price for it. Her lover remained in intensive care, being treated for the immense mental trauma of his dismemberment and the reconstruction of his physical form. She had managed to shield his mind from dying along with his broken body until the boat arrived. That act and the revelation that Crossley had control of D-t-arr were why her sentence was rapidly dwindling to an irrelevancy, as thousands of masters took fragments of responsibility for her actions, paying a tiny portion of her sentence themselves.

By convention, the Paraunion agreed that the division of an infinitely final sentence, death, became a tangible and finite sentence through division, similar to how our own courts would decide that a life sentence might become twenty years or less.

Many jurors appeared in their primary form, but others whose location was more distant or inconvenient were present as simulacrums. These copies did not have to reflect the current body of the user, formats more appropriate to the atmosphere of the Gun Wharf could be chosen. Most Paraunion kept a utility species available and familiar to them on hand. I had no way of telling which was which.

A sense of distance came over me, knowing that soon they would be done with the matter of Arbaun's punishment and move on to my own case. I twisted the visitor ring around my finger and looked up to take in the sky above the Wharf, filled with stars as if it were night even though gentle daylight shone around us without a sun in sight. *It is not enough to survive / I must remain.*

Meletrus patted my arm, bringing my attention to the odd combination of a forum and a court. In the centre, a camera fish, a rusted log with a greasy eyeball on one end, registered the incoming final decisions from the assembled members and made the concluding pronouncement: Arbaun would serve two years of penitential work with compulsory mental assessment, the allocation of a dependent charge would be delayed and reviewed after a few more decades. This was a fleeting inconvenience to an entity as long-lived as the Paraunion. The leniency showed the court had considered the benefits of revealing a potential threat to the culture. D-t-arr would not be tried as he was demonstrably an unwilling participant; the creature had perhaps already paid enough in the shame of his position.

When asked if she understood the sentence, Arbaun threw a defiant expression at her assembled peers and turned her gaze towards me. It was as if she was challenging them to be as brave and principled as she was when they came to my consideration. After all, they would not be able to enforce the letter of the law while still sympathizing. They could not agree with her and still prosecute me. It must be one or the other. She challenged them to take the higher path.

Arbaun was led away.

Meletrus walked into the centre of the tiered forum, regal in her posture though humble in her speech. *That which you are, my thoughts cannot transpose.* It was clear to every Para watching that

228

she blamed herself for what had happened. She had already accepted a share of the punishment for Arbaun's breach of the law.

¤ Fellow citizens, we move on to the next and most distressing matter, which I ask you to consider carefully before coming to a conclusion. We have invited into our midst Ambassadors to see for themselves the wisdom and peace of Paraunion society, and by walking among us, they are subject to the laws and principles of our community, exempt from claiming asylum. The Graph and Paraunion remain absolute for everyone inside our borders without exception. These are the principles which our state is founded upon. Not a single exception has ever been made. ¤

From the steps of the forum, the crowd sent confirmations of support. Meletrus's context clarified that she was open to being replaced as a facilitator, but she received only approval despite that. Some in the crowd were sure that she would do the right thing for the Paraunion, and some encouraged her to fight for mercy on the poor creature that found itself accused of sedition in a world it could hardly understand. *Don't kill it / or throw it in the garden.*

Meletrus adapted her stance to confirm what was expected of her. She took a moment to correct a seam on her tunic as a captain preparing for battle or marshalling a firing squad.

¤ The charge against Ambassador Evans is sedition. He should only be convicted of this charge if you, representatives of our culture, decide that he was a direct contributor to the misconduct we have just adjudicated on. According to the letter of the law, we may not concern ourselves with the potential diplomatic or emotional consequences of the outcome. This discussion is open to all to observe, including any that wish to from the Ambassador's own culture. Nor is there any time limitation on how long we take to come to a just answer. ¤

I struggled to follow the complex dialogue coming from the massed Paraunion, managing to follow just a few threads at a time but unable to grasp the whole state of the argument. There

229

were too many of them, and the interplay was too complex. I stood and absorbed the noise of their discussion, a child under the dinner table, and realised in a moment how out of my control the whole situation had become. Despair, a familiar enemy, threatened to swallow me, but something gritty inside me refused to be crushed. It refused to be defeated by those that chopped up my work, to be paralysed by the countless innocent dead, to be thrown by the confusion of the courtroom and wouldn't be foxed now by cruel circumstances.

I'd be called to speak in my defence. My palms felt dry as I rubbed them with my fingertips. Should I ask for the Paraunion to make me an exception to the backbone of their law? Here disobedience meant death, a philosophy they had spent untold generations refining and making as humane as possible? Could I lead them to believe that I didn't encourage my hosts' criminal behaviour? Fear squeezed my skull as I tried to follow the web of parallel discussions across the forum. Should I manipulate the story?

¤ Is he really responsible if he's a primitive? ¤

¤ All law is protection against primitive nature. ¤

¤ To be an ambassador is to accept responsibility. ¤

¤ There must be an intention to undermine to constitute sedition.¤

¤ Can he undermine what he doesn't understand? ¤

¤ You can destroy a bridge without being able to build new one. ¤

I concentrated on the debate and sensed the undercurrent in the group, the downward movement in the symphony. They were mindful of how terrified of a civilized execution I was. Behind all the formality of the court proceedings, I saw via the penetrating, near-perfect communication of the Para language that they couldn't forget that this wasn't just a legal or abstract philosophical point. *Let them see inside.*

Immersed in the details of the court, I saw the reasons bounce between the jurors in the amphitheatre, and I was caught off-guard by a tap on my shoulder.

Nian.

She dressed in what appeared to be glittering, dusty rags from the culture she had left to come and see me. Her expression was creased with worry. The planes of her face looked tougher than before. Something out there far along a dark river had ground the facets of our young diamond.

¤ What's going on? Are you ok? ¤ she asked.

¤ It'll be fine. We'll sort it all out. They won't let a mission of mercy cause someone to die. What are you dressed up as? ¤

Bravery begins / for the eyes of others / and creeps within.

¤ It's complicated. I spoke to the boat on the way here, and it's not very happy. It thinks that the outlook is bad. It didn't say that directly, but I could tell. It's worried that its own testimony hasn't benefited your case, and now it's gone off for a sort of retreat. ¤

¤ Well, if you believe what they are saying, that may be my fault too. It's good to see you, though. When the boat stepped up to war footing to deal with us, it had to change its psyche. It's a failsafe that they use to ensure that violence is never willingly entered into. From what I've been told, it always goes away to agonize over what it's done. I had a gift for you, but I think the boat will have left with it. ¤

¤ No, I have it. It may be upset, but it never forgets a chore. Only you, Evans, can buy a gift that comes with a lifelong obligation. I want to be angry with you for being irresponsible, but you've probably saved us all. ¤

And there it was. That little spark of brother/sister that we had had on Border. I think it was all I really needed to face the coming ordeal. *We were not alone.* Annie looked knowingly at me from the sideline, nodded sidelong at Nian and gave me the dirtiest wink. Thank god Nian didn't see it. Bugatti was exempt from facing charges as she didn't speak Para and hadn't actively done anything to enable our escape from the boat. She could be seen as an unwitting accomplice. That was how the court chose to view the evidence: they didn't want any more difficult executions on their hands than necessary.

Ordu, all rustling spines and fur, came across the open ground of the amphitheatre. She made a polite gesture for permission to interrupt us.

¤ You should speak, Ambassador. The assembly has reviewed all the evidence from the visitor ring and the boat's recollections. We have transmitted the details to your people so they can see them, but it will not be as complete when translated. You should try to give us your perspective on the matter. ¤

The idea that everything I'd said and done was being transmitted to the remaining extremists of my home audience annoyed me.

Not everyone had returned to perfect citizens once the *Pollutant* was expunged from existence. Many still maintained extreme isolationist manifestos. Without their puppet master, they were simply back to being a few billion Crush victims, and you wouldn't get a coherent answer out of any two of them. They were trying to use my trial as a stick to beat the hated alien culture.

Nian looked shocked at me. She had read the undertone in Ordu's phrasing. If I didn't change their perspective on the facts, the judgment would go against me. The argument needed to be moved onto a subjective footing. The Paraunion were by no means immune to ideas from different points of view.

I thanked Ordu. She had only my best interests at heart, but she might vote to have me executed if it preserved the sanctity of the Paraunion way of life, she'd feel terrible, but there was no question about them putting their principles to one side.

I walked to the centre of the forum. *Deep breath.*

¤ At this moment, there are pieces of a vessel floating in the dark, filled with the bodies of families and crewmen who will never return to the ground, travellers who will never send messages back from their voyage, dockers who will never land their goods, technicians who will never make the engines hum again and reporters whose deadlines will pass without a word.

232

All because some people say I wrote something that told them to do it.

¤ Those who know me will understand this is the opposite of everything I stand for. Imagine how you would feel if you knew that people were destroying the only worthwhile creation you'd made and stitched it back together to spell out the thing you most hate. Your best thoughts corrupted into violence: how would you react? ¤

The crowd on the tiers looked on patiently, listening but not silent. No one is ever truly silent in a Para conversation. That could be turned to my advantage like an actor gauging an audience. I could emphasise, even steal, points they found compelling from their reflections on my defence. I stalked about the dusty floor and harangued them. I engaged individuals in a personal dialogue, talked at the Ramaton cloud, at Meletrus, projected high above to the sympathetic partner of a glass prowler, to the camera fish that had deferentially moved to the edge of the stage.

¤ It's true I'm ignorant, and I grant you that I certainly am relative to the sheer knowledge you've accumulated. It's staggering that I'm talking to you, and let's examine that. How am I able to stand here and speak to you? Not through intellectual endeavour but through incredible chance. *You see the freak, but are you afraid the freak sees you?*

¤ A bizarre accident allows me to speak Para. Was it the Crush or outlandish genetics? Who knows? By accident, I'm an ambassador and here to be implicated in the crimes I am forced to do to save my race. That's a cruel trap, isn't it? You set up this system and wait for sufferers of this disorder to come along and then put them to death. That's how it seems by one way of thinking, but then I'm too stupid to understand the details of what I'm suffering from. ¤

¤ Maybe there is no free will, and this is the trap I was destined to walk into? When I think of it, everything truly good I've ever done has come out of thin air—not through hard work or hours of research. The *Pollutant* was a report more than a creation because someone had to say what was happening and not let the injustices or tragedies escape our notice. Was I destined to write it? Was it always going to threaten a population? Had I any choice than to do what we did to stop Crossley? ¤

On the second tier up, an old vuro that I'd seen at one of the grand dinners sympathized and reflected a recalled piece of the *Pollutant* to me. *We barred roads on Tivolli / and held up cars that could not kill us / and remembered dreams of zarjaz moments / published on walls until the police and life arrested us.*

¤ I have suffered from gossip and viral slander that cannot be extinguished. As soon as you think you've ended it, it rises again. I have to start all over, pointing out the same old arguments, and every time the discussion ends, I am somehow a slightly darker character in the eyes of the public. No one likes being told that what they'd thought they'd discovered isn't true.

¤ You would think that the authorities, the polilawyers, the marketrists, and the cultural surveyors, would appreciate me saying I'm not a fomenter of violence. You'd think, wouldn't you? But no. For them, you'd have to come out and read the words they give you, to say you believe the things they believe—which I don't—and then, perhaps, you could rise to the lofty status of 'not suspect' in their eyes.

¤ So my history, or what my own people might tell you about my reputation, isn't a fair representation of my character. If you are thinking, 'Ah! Here is another case of Evans undermining authority.' You're mistaken. As you're mistaken in this prosecution, I have never instigated anyone to harm or limit the freedoms of another. ¤

I paused to take a look back at Nian. Her expression told me that more was needed to swing the argument. So, I gambled and brought out anything that I thought might help.

¤ No doubt you think that this might be a case of the *Proud Teacher*? Will this jury listen patiently to my protests before you demonstrate that I am wrong? Let's ask what the *Proud Teacher* might say? Do you utterly control the classroom with your wisdom? If that was so, then how did this situation ever occur? How did it get so entirely out of hand? With your great minds, you should have seen this eventuality coming. Is it that, like the *Proud Teacher,* you seem all-knowing to the student, but actually, you're only one step ahead on an indefinitely long road? ¤

Now the Paraunion really got involved with the arguments. Not only had I brought it to a more personal level, but I'd used an archetype that allowed them to be far more aggressive in their debate.

¤ Even the *Proud Teacher* doesn't deny his students' free will to do good or wrong. ¤

¤ This isn't teaching. There's no pride in condemning animals. ¤

¤ There's no claim to be all-knowing. ¤

¤ Let the evidence speak. ¤

¤ I don't see any arguments for the *Teacher* here! Use the *Widowed Clockmaker.* ¤

That had stirred things up. There was an underlying current of opinion among the gathered Paraunion in the comments flying back and forth. It split the jury into two camps: those who believed my presence directly affected their citizens' misdeed and those who thought I was a dumb player—my actions and comments a distracting sideshow irrelevant to the crime itself.

¤ Let's address the question of motivation. Did I intend to become an ambassador? Not initially, I followed the advice to escape. Did I intend to break the law when I walked on the mountain of Onis? No, I was desperate to save myself and my people. I was compelled to do what I did by other people and circumstances. ¤

¤ As I said at the start, thousands of people were floating dead in space, and all I wanted was to be left alone. ¤

Meletrus, who had remained tight-lipped throughout my address, tensed and looked about the congregation to see if others had reacted. Some had. The camera fish directed its long tubular body at me.

¤ When Yvin took you back to see Arbaun, ¤ it chimed, ¤ you had already shared thoughts with her once, and although we know there can be no transcript of the event, her testimony has told us you both relived the few steps you took on the mountain.

¤ I also recall that when you spoke to Yvin, you told him, "anything can be overcome if you are prepared to succeed or cease to be". A desperate philosophy. When you returned and Arbaun divulged what she had discovered, did she ask you what to do next? ¤

Silence.

Even in thinking about how I might present the honest answer in a less incriminating way, I realised that I could not withhold the truth from emerging. The gritty core within me didn't want to. I remembered Arbaun had said it could cost me my life. Who was I to back out now? When, against all odds, we had succeeded.

¤ I told her I would pay any price. She was prepared to back down and forget the plan because the mountain had foreseen it would cost a life. It could have meant an abstract form of life or freedom, but we were making the mountain's thought a reality. We suspected what might happen. ¤ I answered.

I could tell things had taken a fatal turn for me in the jurors' minds. My arguments sounded more and more like a final summary.

¤ You knew she was going to do something criminal, something expressly against the wishes of her masters, and you told her to proceed with it. Though you didn't care about the action's details, you still pushed Arbaun to commit a criminal act? Isn't that true, Ambassador Evans? ¤

¤ There was nothing else to be done. It was that or return to an execution in a dark back room. ¤

¤ Your Para suggests you know your own guilt. ¤

236

Paraunion courts don't require representation for the prosecution or the defence because there is no pretence, no layers of deceit that will stand up to rigorous interrogation. Dale had the opportunity to pretend that he couldn't master the language and fake misunderstandings when hiding details that might incriminate him with memetics, and even his teachers were Para novices. On the other hand, I paraded the truth in front of my inquisitors every time I spoke.

There are moments when a fighter decides to stop dodging and simply trades punches to see who is prepared to accept the most pain. We would see how bloody the Paraunion were prepared to get.

¤ I knew. I told her to begin the escape. I knew it was a crime. ¤

The crowd heaved in an uproar.

The trial was over.

The surrounding jurors were openly revolted by the gaunt, mad figure who reached out, almost affectionately, towards them. Behind their disgust at his savagery and irrationality was the disturbing thought that he had created a weapon they didn't understand, even now that he was in their custody.

Before I was sentenced, Crossley's case had to be heard. The Paraunion didn't harbour much hope that its facts would change my own.

¤ As you aren't a citizen of the Paraunion, there are two possibilities. We either consider you a political activist, in which case we would endeavour to send you back to your own culture, or consider your attack on one of our citizens as an act of war and hold you until that threat is resolved. ¤

Crossley listened carefully to the translation, smiling and nodding as the camera fish's words came to him.

'He who declares war on me declares war against nature and the universe.'

¤ You remain a threat to the union's safety while refusing to discuss the nature of the coercion you inflicted on D-t-arr. The state of war between yourself and our state could be unresolved indefinitely. We shall confine you to a safe and isolated world where any harm you might cause can be contained, and wiser minds than those present here may eventually turn their attention to you. ¤

Crossley had clearly thought he would be returned to his own people, where he might have a chance to retake control. At the news that the Paraunion would hold him prisoner, he lost his false demeanour of calm. Spittle flew from his mouth as he threw himself against an unseen force preventing him from harming himself or others.

'You'll throw me in your dungeon? You maggots! You unholy scum!'

The camera fish glided away from him, but Meletrus stepped forward to take up the cause.

¤ Not at all. You will have anything you wish constructed, but you will not come directly into contact with another being until this matter is resolved. ¤

'A gilded cage held without sentencing!'

¤ When normal relations are established with your own culture, they will be included in any decision on your treatment. They may ultimately decide how you will pay for your crimes among your own kind. ¤

'Indeed, my legions will seek my release. What right do you have to hold their greatest leader? Simply because he masters a technology you don't understand? Do you force your will on every nation that has something you don't?'

Crossley scowled at Meletrus and pointed at me.

'Trust me, *trust me*, that when the details of this trial and my pursuit of these criminals are shown in the true light—not this mockery—you will have no choice but to bow to humanity and release me back to my people.'

Meletrus was unshaken.

¤ That's possible, but I feel you're labouring under the impression that your followers are crying out for your return? Once the gestalt entity was saved by our own fugitives, we knew how to disrupt your method, even if we didn't know its details. The gestalts were keen to deliver that cure to as broad a cross-section of the innocent public as possible. ¤

'What have you done? You vultures! Is nothing sacred!'

¤ As you surmise, we have assisted them in providing treatment. The entire human population will forget that *The Pollutant Speaks* existed, excluding those present. A tiny proportion remains militant but cannot agree on what they want; order has been returned to your planets. By large scale agreement, we have sent *humanitarian* aid to the worst recovering areas. ¤

239

Annie looked horrified and outraged at the notion of the *Pollutant* being wiped from our collective consciousness. Nian, on the other hand, all in dusty sackcloth from head to toe, nodded at the wisdom of the action. Whatever incredible place she had been to had drawn her further into the Paraunion character than I could have believed. She was further gone than Spindle, if I had to judge. Was the Para language itself something like Crossley's belief madness? I tried to stop thinking about that as soon as it occurred to me.

The camera fish moved to take the floor from Meletrus, who gave way with good grace. Crossley spat at it. His rage became incandescent.

'You disgust me! All of you! You aren't natural. You'll destroy everything. You're devils! Devils, all of you!'

The camera fish sighed and escorted the prisoner from the court with invisible hands.

'If I suffer you to incarcerate me, it is because I allow it. Even now, I serve a higher purpose. Rejoice! For you serve the divine cause,' bellowed Crossley.

In that last moment, as he was dragged bodily away, it occurred to me that Crossley might be so far gone that he had forgotten how he controlled people in the first place. Had the Crush destroyed the memory of the invention? Maybe once Green had been found, he could discover what happened inside the broken man's head. Assuming he hadn't been executed by that lunatic.

Crossley would live in a genuine version of his own Alone program.

There was a recess before sentencing. Nian and I walked into the nearby jungle to gather our thoughts. The sun had set on the Gun Wharf, but a halo of light bathed the landscape, a glow emitted from stardust being swallowed by the black hole of the binary system.

¤ Interesting word: 'sentencing'. ¤

¤ Stop trying to distract me, ¤ said Nian.

¤ Excuse me, but if this is really going to be the end, I'd like to live the right way, saying what I think. I messed it up most of my life. Annie said it—all I needed was to regrow a backbone. I spent a long time not trusting what came out of my brain. Green knew it. Annie knows it. ¤

Nian's eyes looked larger when she worried. We stood among the radiant vines with zilling linnets flying about as hot fog clung to the buildings. My fear turned to resignation.

¤ If it makes any difference, I always thought you were pretty good as you were, ¤ she said.

¤ It's lucky you only met me after the hospital. Border was a good place for me. I've lost a dozen years of life to the Crush, to tell the truth. The jury was never really going to return any verdict other than guilty. They needed to struggle with their consciences for a bit, just as they agonised over the sentence because they're fundamentally good people unable to escape their own promises. ¤

¤ Meletrus is decent. She won't let this happen, and her opinion carries weight. ¤

¤ She's compromised, don't you see? They do. She allowed a master to try to cure a bolshie teenager by getting him to babysit an Ambassador. That was Meletrus, and if this were an ordinary Para trial, she'd be falling on her sword immediately. ¤

¤ But Spindle will be here soon. ¤

She said it as if the impish professor's presence would improve the situation. Nian had survived outlandish civilisations and mental hardship, yet she retained an odd faith in seniority. I had the utmost respect for Spindle, but he was only flesh and blood like the rest of us.

We didn't have to wait long. On the short walk back to the centre of the forum, the boat set down, and Spindle himself disembarked. He trod down the gangway with his head bowed in thought. For the first time, he appeared genuinely frail. The jury returned to their places in the amphitheatre, their spaces lit by cones of light pinned in the air.

We hurried to meet him while the boat darted vertically up, almost in a Para phrase, 'I am too upset to speak to you,' which saddened me more than my impending judgment. The thought I might die before making peace with a friend disturbed me.

Spindle ran his fingers through his grey hair as we greeted him. It looked as if he hadn't slept in a decade, although he still summoned up one of his knowing smiles for us.

¤ I wish I could be in several places at one time like those Para avatars, don't you? There are far too many things that demand our physical presence lately. It almost makes me miss the net. ¤

That Spindle would virtually attend my execution, might just phone it in, made me chuckle. Nian was in no mood for gallows humour.

¤ Get whoever has the most diplomatic sway with the Paraunion here now. This process needs to be stopped immediately before things go too far, ¤ she said.

¤ The people you see here are the most influential diplomats, lawyers and thinkers of the Paraunion. That Ramaton, for instance, Dies Vien, is the greatest proponent of new cultures joining the Paraunion. The gentleperson who prefers to use a camera fish as their mouthpiece is Kay-anora-kay-anara, one of the celestials of legal philosophy. Any chance of finding a loophole or play in the founding principles of the Paraunion relies solely upon him. I'm saying that the authorities to make or break the law and move jurisprudence sit in this court. The preeminent experts across two thousand races of Paraunion are here in the hope of saving you from execution. That glass prowler is an ice ring dweller who runs the entire dark river exploration programme. ¤

Nian looked dejected that the cavalry wasn't going to ride in and put a stop to the whole proceeding. Just how I had felt when I realised our government knew about the horrors of life-basic, but they just didn't care. That was just before I started writing *The Pollutant*.

The camera fish's rusted cylinder moved to the court's centre and inspected the congregation. Spindle, Nian and I stood to one side. Rolliard and Annie were relegated to the first tier.

¤ We heard that the defendant knew what he was saying and that it would cause a criminal act. I think we all agree that under normal circumstances, there would be a great deal of clemency at this point. After all, wasn't this just moments after being informed of a disaster among his people? A disaster caused by a group claiming that he was the author who inspired their actions. Those are difficult circumstances to cope with in a strange environment, but our law does not allow for knowing transgressions.

¤ We are in a dilemma. Our system, founded on mercy, finds no sympathy for a criminal without masters. The fundamental tenet is that breaking a law of your own volition will cost you your life without exception. This is what drives our culture and the structure of our lives. We know that eroding this resolution causes wars and suffering. We know we must not create loopholes or backdoors in the basic tenets of our society. We know all this, but we feel that we must save this person's life if there is any other way. ¤

Spindle left us with a hurried signal that he would return as soon as possible. He scurried to Meletrus' side, and even though they were performing the Para version of a huddled whisper, gestures leaked out that implied the diplomat was researching something for Spindle. I admired their industry, and somewhere in the back of my mind, I allowed a little hope that they might come up with something, but the realist in me told me to accept I was going to die and make sure I did it my own way.

Kay-anora-kay-anara may as well have already announced it. His subtext and the micro-gestures of every juror around the auditorium converged on a single thought, an orchestra dropping to a single note. What I needed was not the rude indestructibility of my youth. That vandal wouldn't have been able to understand. I reached deep for material only a battle-scarred, Crush-recovered, Para-speaking me could dredge up.

After all, weren't the remaining extremists watching? Wouldn't my family sooner or later bring themselves to see this? Wouldn't Annie? Nian was right beside me, and she, more than anyone else, needed something positive to lean on. *Step aside, let the pollutant speak.*

Spindle sent Meletrus out on yet another fact-finding mission amongst the jurors, presumably because he was disappointed at the last result. Kay-anora-kay-anara drifted back to the centre of the arena. After a period of gathering context from anyone who wanted to express an opinion, the beings arrayed on the amphitheatre steps grew still as the whole assembly set itself at neutral.

¤ After reflection and consulting with every community member who might have a vested interest in this case, it is with great sadness that, following a guilty verdict, we sentence Ambassador Evans to a death sentence without mitigation, ¤ it said.

Every member of the jury shrank back. What was about to happen was so unheard of and distasteful that they couldn't bear to be present. I convinced myself that there couldn't be another verdict. I had a laser-clear premonition of my own death, so I didn't crumble. Still, it would be a lie to say that I didn't shake as I stared at the dejected forms of the Ramaton, the glass prowler, the seed mats and the panoply of species, each ashamed to do the right thing. Ordu moved to support Nian, who turned her back on the scene. *Voices in the wind sing. Let the Pollutant speak.*

Kay-anora-kay-anara invited me to comment, and I stepped to the centre.

¤ How ghoulish it is when good people come together and value something invisible, like society, over a life. It's difficult to explain to strangers why those hidden things are so important that someone else has to die.

244

¤ Don't think of me as a stranger, though. I've come to the same judgement. *I serve a double purpose.* The Cannots, those misled enough to take the lives of everyone aboard the *New Osaka,* had to be stopped and, even now, even after their scripture, the *Pollutant,* is gone, this event must not be used by them to hold the human race back. It's fear of people unlike ourselves, with different customs and morals, that made Crossley and the Cannots mix up every other thing: poverty, sickness, pride, into a confused excuse not to be brave. Not to come out here and offer our hand in friendship. ¤

¤ Soon, no one will remember the *Pollutant.* It has been excised from humanity and quarantined among the Paraunion. Maybe instead of a poet, I can be a good ambassador who paid the price for peace. ¤

The crowd remained introverted and shocked. Spindle had his arm around Nian's shoulder. On the third tier, I saw Arbaun-de-Felentual, and she alone responded to my statement. She was the only creature present with such incredible empathy that she understood and accepted my position as I meant it. I continued, now directly addressing her.

¤ A human once wrote: "Men who dream unequally fear the dreamer in the day, who dreamt with hot open eyes of dangerous men, who built the palace of unnational thoughts". We all feel when we read that we are the 'dreamer in the day'. I did when I was young and first heard it. At the time, maybe I was. But now, and most of the time, we are the little men who dream unequally, and the scope of our vision for the future isn't deep at all. The Cannots want more space to live. That isn't a dream; it's survival. They want their problems cured, as do we all, as do you who have sentenced me to die. And I'm going to make you do it. I tell you, be careful, you future builders of a new civilisation. You're the ones who are dreaming unequally.¤

Arbaun shimmered into the shape of an electrified man, perhaps myself, projecting my words and sentiment to the whole assembly in perfect, beautiful Para. My hands shook with

245

fear as I listened to my thoughts reflect back, and I fought to finish my speech with dignity.

¤ Somehow, the Cannots, or their leaders, suggested that I was corrupt, that I'd been bought out, and that I was trying to change the message of *The Pollutant Speaks*. At least this forum, this moment gives me a chance to show that there is no way I can be lying: the *Pollutant* is a call to end suffering, not to foment violence. It's a demand to move to a better state of being, not throwing down everyone else to save yourself.

¤ Make no more is the key. The Pollutant asks you to stop now, not slow down or just try harder. Make no more. No more atrocities of the stained bunkhouse cots. No third floor, life-basic accidents. No more automatic paper victims on the tracks at Tivoli, and no more news, news and more news that screw the view. ¤

As Arbaun finished relaying my words, she melted back into the tree-like structure she usually took, but the human shape continued to stand in the heart of the form.

I had no idea how the Paraunion might execute me. Something painless and instant, like a kappa accident, I guessed. Looking at Nian next to Ordu and Spindle, it occurred to me I didn't want her to see me crumble to dust like Meletrus's simulacrum had.

Nian cried. Ordu comforted her, but the little professor had a strange look on his face.

He set out to join me in the middle.

35   The molossus unwound

Spindle glanced at me and gave me a wholly human glare not transferrable in Para, which I think I'd only really seen on the faces of school teachers and parents. He turned and guided me by the elbow to stand just behind him. *They fuck you up, your mum and dad.*

'Play along,' he whispered through ventriloquist lips.

I was shocked that Spindle interrupted my last words, but his attitude stopped me from replying.

¤ I beg the indulgence of this court to hear a potential alternative to the execution of this young human. ¤

The jurors were all too willing to hear anything that might stop or delay them from witnessing my execution, so it didn't take long for general consent to be given for Spindle to continue.

¤ The system of masters isn't reflected in human law, but there is a close parallel in our educational system. I taught Ambassador Evans how to speak Para. I guided him on living in the Paraunion community. I briefed him on the nature of Paraunion law. The basis of your law is that guilt is transferred to another, preferably many others, to reflect the actual fault in a matter. This profound value makes society reflect on the causes of a crime, not just in the criminal but in ourselves. ¤ He engaged the court with a sweeping gesture, suggesting implicitly that *ourselves* was everyone who understood that point. The Ramaton rumbled agreement. *I see the dreamer in the day.*

¤ This principle of transference is central to my proposal. If Evans had been trained adequately on Border by me, he would never have committed the infringement that we are here today to punish. In short, if this Ambassador is flawed, then the responsibility is mine because it was my duty to teach this student to live as a Paraunion, to be a master to him. If I had executed that job correctly, Evans would not have erred. ¤

The assembly broke out in a cacophony of discussion.

¤ Training does not carry with it a moral imperative. ¤

¤ What is being a master if not training another to conduct oneself as a citizen? ¤ asked Ordu.

¤Are we saying that the Ambassador was improperly equipped? How can we find any fault in him then? ¤

¤ Only the master of a criminal can accept some of the punishment. This is a legal matter and only reaches as far as the law recognises, ¤ the Ramaton bellowed. ¤ This human is not a legal master of Evans. ¤

¤ I object, that is not what he is saying! ¤ Etrew, the prowler noted. ¤ He says that he *is* the criminal, not Evans. Evans is the innocent in our midst. Consider the tragic circumstances the ambassador was under during the moment of fault? Who was responsible for that? Here is a wise master confessing his guilt to the court—we cannot disrespect that— we must prosecute the cause, not the symptom. ¤

¤ Agreed. Spindle tells us that he should have known better, ¤ Ordu responded. ¤ Evans, on the other hand, believes that he is courageously being martyred; isn't that proof enough that one understands that they are guilty and the other does not? Let the sentence be transferred. ¤

Spindle turned his back to the crowd as they debated where the true origin of the crime lay, but he knew that they wanted to accept his argument and would eventually find reasons to justify it.

'This is not what I wanted,' I said quietly.

'I know, and I apologise. Old age may have made me rash.'

'Getting you killed would round off my accidental destruction of hope for humanity.'

'Yes, wouldn't it,' his eyes widened in mock horror, 'but I have no intention of getting myself killed without a final gambit. Now, if you could adopt the attitude of a chastised student while I try and pull our fat from the fire, that would be very helpful.'

As he turned, the glass prowler finished his survey of the jurors and addressed Spindle.

¤ Your proposal is accepted. We take no pleasure in your execution but grant that you may wholly transfer the sentence if you accept responsibility. You should be willing to execute the sentence upon yourself to signify your acceptance. ¤

¤ I accept, ¤ he said without hesitation. ¤ If the court is willing to grant me a moment of indulgence before carrying out the sentence, I may also have a solution to the distaste we all feel for terminating a civilised being because there has been an infraction of the rules. ¤

His last comment shocked the Ramaton and the camera fish. Arbaun, with Annie by her side on a high tier, sparkled with laughter and applauded. Clearly, they were both forewarned of what might happen. Meletrus stepped forward and joined us at the centre of the amphitheatre. From the murmurs nearby, I gleaned from astute jurors what was afoot.

¤ Spindle's going to attempt to become a citizen, ¤ I said to Nian. She had read the undercurrent from the crowd and nodded with disbelief.

¤ And if he's rejected... ¤ she continued the thought.

¤ Then he'll have to commit suicide, ¤ I answered.

The act of joining the Paraunion was an individual matter, even though whole civilisations had converted in its history. It was closer to a religious confirmation than a citizenship test. Critically, command of written Para was required. Without it, a candidate couldn't be integrated into the network that joined every master and student, every adult and child in the whole culture. In this way, it was less a contract and more a compatibility test. There was no point in committing to a civilisation you weren't equipped to cohabit with.

I remembered seeing Spindle labouring over the basics of written Para in his office, struggling to sign his own name. Was it possible that he had seen this moment coming from all that time ago?

Meletrus bowed to her peers and turned to Spindle.

¤ Are you ready, my friend? ¤

¤ I'll do my best. ¤

Dies Vien, the Ramaton cloud, and a scattering of others were not quieted so easily. With the participation of Meletrus, they felt that a conspiracy was stirring. They suggested intentional manipulation of power through vrys might be at play. Ordu and Gingana, a formidable metal being who appreciated the turnaround of events, intervened.

¤ Clearly state your objection or let matters proceed,¤ the Gingana said, the lights from the Ramaton reflecting off its sleek body.

¤ This court is stepping far outside the normal boundaries of legal practice; we need to consider the ramifications of setting this precedent. ¤

The sheer violence of the lightning concussions within the body of Dies Vien underlined how seriously he took the argument.

¤ How long would you have these humans wait and suffer until we determine if we will heartlessly execute them? ¤ Ordu asked.

¤ The law must be considered slowly, ¤ muttered Dies Vien.

¤ I remind you that the law itself does not permit undue suffering,¤ noted the Gingana.

Ordu drew in close to the seething cloud.

¤ Tell me, Dies, would you become the executioner if you succeed in throwing out this course of action? Or perhaps you feel the ambassador killing himself would make you less responsible? ¤

The Ramaton knew it was beaten, and through its demeanour, all support for the counteraction declined.

A chair and table were summoned into being in the middle of the court. It may have been the changeable climate of the

Gun Wharf, but gravity seemed to decline, the twilight air became harder to breathe, and lazy dust, possibly spores from the jungle, drifted past us. *Bad exam.*

I caught Meletrus's attention as she spoke with the Gingana.

¤ Can he do it? ¤ I asked.

¤ He has improved immensely under the boat's tutelage. ¤

¤ He asked the boat to tutor him? ¤

¤ I can't tell you who suggested it; they have become very close.¤

Spindle seated himself. *Forbidden words he'll trace / he writes the time and the place.*

He looked up at Nian. The expression he gave her puzzled me. It seemed to say, "You and I know what this is about". She nodded to him and stood rock-still in her stardust rags. Whatever far-flung place they had taken her to had tempered her, clearly not a place as gentle and picturesque as the deep comfort of Vould. They judged rightly that she was tougher and more flexible than I. *Whom God loveth he chasteneth.*

The creatures filed away from the tiers of the amphitheatre; some disappeared into thin air. Ordu guided Nian to walk away with her. Meletrus indicated that I should follow them.

¤ You should give him all the privacy he needs, like the *Searching Courtesan.* Kay-anora-kay-anara will remain vigilant to provide for our friend's needs, ¤ she said.

So we walked and tried to encourage each other. Around us, the Gun Wharf burst into life, perhaps the final phase of the artist's millennium-long evolving work. The vines gave birth to flying seeds that flocked in the demi-magical night. The creepers transformed into great winding trees. *The woods are lovely dark and deep.* By the time we returned to the amphitheatre, new forest groves thickened around us.

Spindle remained in the centre of the arc. The giant eye of the camera fish was bent close to listen to his words. His final few gestures caused the invigilator to turn and swim away into the returning crowd.

Nian pushed out her chin and braced herself for bad news, and I found I couldn't bring myself to walk up to a man who'd taken my place on the executioner's block and ask if he would have to kill himself. I hung in limbo, watching Annie, Rolliard, and Arbaun rush down the tiers and run to Spindle, whose head was bowed. But I wasn't the only one who couldn't bear to hear the news.

Meletrus was there. Locked in place, riddled with despair. *Gods and men alike.*

Then, between the camera fish and Annie, I saw the little professor's grin. His whole body seemed broken with exhaustion and relief, but like an athlete setting a record, he couldn't stop smiling. Annie smothered him in kisses, the giant Rolliard wept so much that Spindle had to comfort him, and Arbaun became a shimmering wall among and around them all.

Nian waved for us to come and join in.

Meletrus and I looked at each other. We exchanged expressions of relief and support with one another in a moment, both of us assuring the other that everything was alright. This was not a dream.

36   He sings the song twice over

They hid me away in a place where they thought I'd be happy, which was also the easiest place to keep me secure.

Knee deep in the warm sea, the water rose around my legs in slow breaths. *I am old, I am old, I shall wear my trousers rolled.* I waited to see the back of a basking shark. I didn't like to leave until I saw one, and, after all, I had all the time in the world to waste. So I stared out across the sea, where a lonely cloud wandered amongst the new islands dotted out on the horizon. *Between two waves of the sea.*

In the afternoon, I was due to talk to Jones and the academic board about increasing the number of candidates, but the thought of speaking out of Para for so long turned my stomach.

I was the machine that the primitives didn't know how to use. *I am the nuclear jukebox.* Behind me, the taproot trees rustled in the breeze, and the wind crinkled the surface of the sea like a ghostly shiver.

Nian was there.

¤ I'd rather not get my feet wet to come out and speak to you. ¤

¤ Build a path. You can do that now, can't you? ¤

¤ You make it seem petty. ¤

The sea drew out as if the tides had suddenly changed, and I did feel small-minded asking for a demonstration of her new powers, so I turned and walked up the beach. Behind her, the boat drifted over the palms and the little roof of my quarters.

¤ Maybe you should be teaching the new intake of candidates? ¤ I asked.

¤ I think we both know that people need stepping stones. ¤

¤ Then what brings you back among the savages? ¤

She cringed at my phrase, but her context didn't deny she felt that way about most humans. Nian was as pained by returning to non-Para people as Spindle had been. *First-generation woes / come and go.*

¤ How many talkers have you got so far? ¤

¤ Two. ¤

¤ Ha. That's less than Spindle! He'll be delighted to hear he's not so easy to replace. ¤

¤ I wouldn't dream of trying to replace him. ¤

¤ Wanna hear something interesting? ¤

¤ Always interested in what you have to say, Nian, even more now you're the only person I have to listen to, ¤ I made a sweeping gesture at the empty sea.

¤ Oh yes, so totally alone, except for Rolliard, Jones and the others who sneak over to play cards and drink every other night? Don't mope. ¤

¤ No man is an island, ¤ I said, pointedly ignoring my island.

¤ Why don't you get the next few ambassadors together and cross over? You know you want to. ¤

She made a good point. If there were a handful of good Para speakers on Border, I could just switch citizenship. I had an advantage as I was half-converted already. But I couldn't bring myself to do it. It felt like a betrayal, but of what, I couldn't tell you.

¤ You know what Green's up to? ¤ I asked.

¤ He's on Earth, the last I heard. ¤

¤ He took the concentration camp they found him in and turned it into a hospital. He's treating ex-Cannots. There are no fees inside the hospital, there's no culcap, the patients are never forced to leave, and each mentors three others. ¤

¤ The man's a revolutionary. They'll burn him at the stake, ¤ Nian said with a smirk. We both stared at the broad, shallow sea for a while. *Zzz, says the doctor.* What else can one do in the face of true sainthood?

¤ Is it still not talking to me? ¤ I asked.

Behind her, the brooding profile of the boat faced over the roof as if something out of sight on the other side of the island interested it. Reticently, the vessel gravitated in our direction, folding inner spaces of itself as it went until it quartered and quartered its volume. Finally, it loomed behind Nian.

¤ It is talking to you again, ¤ it said.

¤ And you both just popped in to see an old friend? ¤

Only in Para can a geometric shape tilt and shift in an expression of *why wouldn't I come and see an old friend.*

¤ Not entirely. We're here to make planets as well, ¤ it said

¤ Shang Lo is getting three more twins, so there'll be space for everyone, and we're putting nature reserves on each, ¤ said Nian.

They sounded like architects after a wartime bombing, a time to start with a blank slate. I struggled to imagine Movampton with woodland and seaside walks. What gave me pleasure was hearing Nian talk like the excited student I'd first met on Border. She'd been so grave since her visit to the fringe of the Paraunion. Maybe we were a fringe civilisation as far as she and the boat were concerned?

¤ How long is that going to take? ¤ I asked.

¤ I'll be finished with the first two in a month, ¤ said the boat, ¤ the third will be left as a project for the student. ¤

¤ Nian's world? ¤

She laughed at that.

¤ You've no idea how big the committee of polilawyers and activists is to decide the names. Same for Xin later on, then there's the whole argument about whether Earth should stay as it is. ¤

She saw a basking shark's lazy fin and tail over my shoulder as it wallowed and scooped plankton from the warm shallows. I turned to watch.

¤ Things should change, ¤ I said. ¤ I guess there's been discussion about whether to let the last human who remembers the *Pollutant* keep it?¤

255

¤ There has, ¤ the boat tilted sympathetically, ¤ and if anything could have been extracted from the demented brain of Crossley, if there was another way, we wouldn't ask you to part with it. Someday when the mystery of his technique has been resolved, we'll release the text back to you. ¤

¤ I won't even remember writing it? ¤

¤ Not the exact words. You'll remember that you spent that time writing, how you felt and all of your life around that time but not the actual words. You'll know they've been wiped, but there'll be no confusion about where that time went. ¤

I'd thought about it too. The wrench of losing *The Pollutant*, like putting a child into a distant school, weighed heavily on me. My new, tougher mind told me that the sooner I pushed through it, the more I would adapt, but the old brain, the one that had dreamed on the streets of Movampton and shuffled penniless through its kamicafes and made silent notes on the lost and the dying—that soul felt a watery grief rising at the thought of it. *We, the centrifugal gang, fling and are flung, leaving orders for our affairs.*

¤ How do we do it? ¤ I asked.

¤ If you let me, I'll take care of it, ¤ she said.

¤ Am I a project for the student? ¤

¤ Let's say that I did the first few billion, ¤ said the boat, ¤ and if I'm honest, erasing peoples' minds, no matter how surgically, goes against the grain. I don't think I have it in me to do the last one, ¤ said the boat.

I could have refused. I could have made a fuss.

¤ I notice you waited until Annie's away sorting out her exhibition. ¤

¤ A happy coincidence. ¤

¤ Let's get on with it then. ¤

Nian hesitated.

¤ There's no gun to your head, Evans. You're not like the rest of humanity. You've got a paraunion brain, and we can't do this without your consent. ¤

She knew this was a grey action, mostly good but with some bad. It was cruel of me not to take responsibility for that little sin away from her. It's what Green, Rolliard or Annie would have done, and before I knew it, I had. Had they made me a better person? Or had they seen this version of me all along?

¤ Since I've had this wonderful new brain, I feel much more myself. I remember everything that happened and why it happened since the mountain, all in rich detail, but before my recollection, my history of myself is grainy, degenerate.

¤ Long ago, someone with my name wrote *The Pollutant*. I know how and where, but apart from tiny flashes of memory, that person is a distant cousin. I'm not the same man in many ways. Every day, we see the world through new eyes. *We stand in a different river.* It really isn't that different from what you're suggesting, Nian. ¤

She nodded, relieved by my comments.

¤ Take a seat for a moment, ¤ she gestured at the sand.

I lowered myself onto the warm grains of the beach, and she stood behind me. Soon, there would be parks and beaches for everyone to see, bees and grass for the tin shifter and the viddy girl, bunkhouse sprogs would look for whales and run along the shore rather than wander the underpasses. *Turned out on the street: Wingates, Henries, Johnny Po-Lotti and Mayday Susie of the hundred tricks, west gong, Lovedreary: masters of sex, dreams and escape.*

A smile spread across my face at the recollection of the words, and then, a moment later, I could not recall quite why I was smiling.

o

Our thanks to you for reading. If you've enjoyed this book, please leave a review.

Many thanks to Emily Cochran for copy editing with such tremendous attention, Eyal Soffer for his feedback on the early drafts of *The Pollutant* and Abi Cochran for being generally wonderful.

Printed in Great Britain
by Amazon

39575327R00148